VISCOUNT OF VILLAINY

SINS AND SCOUNDRELS

BOOK SEVEN

SCARLETT SCOTT

Happily Ever After Books

Viscount of Villainy

Sins and Scoundrels Book Seven

In memory of Violetta Rand, who originally edited the first six books in the Sins and Scoundrels series.

CHAPTER 1

$\mathscr{T}$he rear door at the Earl of Worthing's town house, which connected the stables to the main house, had been left unlatched, just as Eugenia had promised it would be. Torrie slipped inside through the familiar halls, a customary routine whenever Worthing was otherwise occupied, leaving his significantly younger wife alone. Fortunately for Torrie, Eugenia's loneliness could be assuaged in any number of ways—all of them infinitely pleasurable—and he was more than eager to accommodate.

Anything to distract him from the demons inhabiting his skull.

Which was why he had come to her tonight at this late hour, dressed in black, bearing the accoutrements for a kidnapping. All in the name of indulging her most unusual whims for the evening.

But then, what better way to celebrate being risen from the dead than drowning oneself in vice? With the fragments of Torrie's lost memory gradually returning two years after the phaeton accident that had nearly killed him, he was all the more in need of distraction. In desperate need to escape everyone who had known him before.

Because he was different now, and even with the pieces of his old life filtering into his mind like sunlight through attic slats, he would never again be the Torrie he once had been. But those who knew the old Torrie were having a damned difficult time accepting that. His sister, for instance, and his mother, too. His old friend Monty, the Duke of Montrose. Every chum and passing acquaintance he'd been forced to face without knowing their mutual history, what he might have said and done in the past, and what terms they had last parted on.

Being with Eugenia was easy in comparison. Comforting, in a sense. She hadn't known him then, the man he had apparently been. A man who was a stranger, even to himself. Quite naturally, it helped that she had an insatiable appetite in bed. A lusty nature was the one part of himself, aside from his physical appearance, which he hadn't lost.

No servants were about on account of the late hour, and he made his way through the quiet halls with ease, finding the staircase which led to the first floor where he knew the library dwelled. Halfway down the hall, he located his quarry. Beneath a partially closed door, the light of a lone taper flickered, calling to him like a lighthouse beacon.

Torrie paused at the threshold and reached into his sack to extract the rope he'd brought to bind Eugenia at her request. She wanted to feel the fear of being swept away from her lavish town house and carried off to her captor's carriage. Wanted to be ravished as they traveled through Mayfair.

He'd never kidnapped a woman before. At least, he didn't think he had. The past aside, he was ready. The notion of kidnapping her didn't titillate him the same way it did Eugenia. Rather, it was the result when they were safely ensconced in his carriage that did.

He heard the creak of a floorboard within, heralding a footstep. Movement. Knowing Eugenia, she was likely growing impatient as she awaited him. He took another moment to sort out the mechanics of what he was about to do. And then he remembered the cravat he'd brought to gag her. A quite ingenious stroke, he'd thought. Feeling about in the sack, he retrieved the cravat as well.

And then, he pushed into the room just as the occupant blew out the candle, cloaking the chamber in darkness.

"Is someone there?" whispered Eugenia, a convincing tremble in her voice.

She sounded oddly vulnerable and unlike herself. Perhaps she was taking this little kidnapping notion of hers seriously.

Should he say something? No, he decided hastily. That would ruin the illusion for her. Instead, he strode toward the sound of the voice. Moonlight shone through the bank of windows, illuminating her silhouette. Showing him where to find her. She truly had thought about every last detail.

He swooped into action, moving behind her and swiftly wrapping his cravat around her mouth, stifling the sound of startlement she made, and tying it in a stern knot. Another low, unintelligible sound of outrage rumbled from her, the cravat doing its work. She tried to spin toward him, but it was futile. He was far stronger, and he caught her with ease, wrapping his rope around her wrists behind her back.

"*Unnnhnnnd mrrrrr*," she protested, her words comically muffled as she tugged at her bound wrists, attempting to free herself, to no avail.

Next came the sack, which he draped over her head.

The action appeared to have a quelling effect on her fight. She went still for a moment, and he wondered if he'd gone

3

too far with his preparations. Well, he'd only been aiming to please.

"You can breathe properly, can you not?" he asked softly.

"*Mrrrr nrrrr rarjera*," she said, her voice now going high-pitched, as if she were truly terrified.

If she was speaking, one could reasonably assume she could also breathe, despite the cravat and sack.

"Another moment," he said, for he had to admit that now that he'd begun this business, it had significantly lessened his ardor.

His cock, hard for the duration of the ride to Worthing's town house in anticipation of another night with Eugenia, had gone distinctly limp. But he reckoned she could restore it to its former glory when they were ensconced in his carriage and the "kidnapping" was at an end.

She launched herself at him suddenly, taking him by surprise. But with the sack over her head, she was effectively blinded. She stormed to his left, and Torrie simply bent, catching her over his shoulder. Much to his aggravation, she continued her struggles.

Eugenia ought to have recalled the injuries he'd suffered in the accident, which had left him with a back that chose to remind him of his follies with alarming frequency and any change of the weather. He swatted her rump for good measure.

"Damn it, Eugenia," he said, taking care to keep his voice low to avoid any lingering servants overhearing and raising the alarm. "Cease wriggling, if you please."

His warning seemed to only heighten her frenzy. More muffled sounds of protest emerged.

"*Mmmmmrrrr, mrrrrrrrrrrr, mrrrrrrrrrrr!*"

This was growing tedious. On the next occasion Eugenia sent a note to him telling him her husband would be away for the evening, he was going to bloody well suggest they simply fuck in her bed in the ordinary fashion. He was growing too old for such nonsense.

Or perhaps he'd always been too old for it.

Either way, he didn't care to revisit this particular worm which had somehow found its way into Eugenia's mind. Holding her struggling form to keep her from toppling from his shoulder, he carried her through the darkness. Down the staircase. Through the hall.

By the time Torrie reached the door and ventured through the mews to his carriage, he had nearly dropped her thrice, his back ached, and he was struggling to catch his breath. But he managed to gently deposit his prize within before climbing inside himself and slamming the door closed. Two solid raps on the roof, and they were in motion, the coach rattling over the road.

It was done.

He heaved a sigh of relief, allowing his head to relax against the Morocco leather.

"*Mmmmm, meeeeee, mrrrrr,*" Eugenia squealed, shifting wildly on the squabs in an effort to get her hands free.

Her discontent hadn't subsided as he had expected it would when they were ensconced in the carriage. If anything, her panic had appeared to increase.

"Calm down, Eugenia," he cautioned. "You'll do yourself harm."

"*Raaaaaaaaa!*" was her only response.

Not quite what he'd imagined either.

Frowning, he straightened. And that was when he took note, in the flickering glow of the carriage lamp, of what Eugenia was wearing. Which was decidedly unlike anything he'd ever previously seen her don.

Her full breasts were covered. Entirely. Larger, too.

Her gown was not just demure, but subdued. And prim. *Proper.* The color of it was gray, like the sky before it

5

unleashed rain. Her arms were covered. Her figure, beneath that chaste gown, was not at all the same. He could see it despite the way the garment hung on her frame, as if it had originally been sewn for someone with a much sturdier build.

"Eugenia?" he asked weakly.

"*Mrrrr!*" she said, sounding frantic.

He swallowed hard against a knot of dread threatening to rise in his throat and plucked the sack from her head. The wide-eyed woman facing him was not Eugenia at all. No, indeed. She was dark-haired instead of blonde, twin patches of scarlet fury painted on her cheeks.

"Oh God," he muttered. "Blazing hellfire."

He'd kidnapped the wrong woman.

"*Unnhiiiiii neeeee,*" she said, struggling with the wrists tied behind her back.

"If I remove the gag, do you promise not to scream?" he asked her, wondering just who the devil he *had* absconded with, if not Eugenia.

A servant?

An errant parlor maid?

Sweet Christ, he thought.

"*Mmmmfffff,*" she said.

Which Torrie took to mean *yes*, she agreed not to scream.

"I haven't any intention of hurting you," he told her, aiming to sound reassuring. No easy feat when he was too aware of how he must look to her, a stranger who had swept into a darkened room, bound, gagged, and spirited her away.

She nodded, telling him something with her eyes, which were brown and quite unlike Eugenia's blue. Or were Eugenia's green? He couldn't recall, and it hardly signified at the moment.

Torrie leaned forward, closing the space between them across the carriage, and made a show of slowly reaching behind her, fingers working on the knot he'd tied with far too much confidence. The blasted cravat was pulled tight. It took him longer than he would have liked for it to loosen, before he was able to slip the gag from her mouth and over her head.

She screamed. A shrill, loud, soul-curdling, ear-destroying shriek.

"Damn it." He cupped his hand over her mouth. "I said no screaming. You promised."

But then, had she? Incoherent sounds likely didn't signal acquiescence. By God, Eugenia would hear from him after this colossal monstrosity.

Suddenly, Torrie felt the sharp nip of teeth sinking into his fingers.

He removed his hand, shaking it, scowling at the mystery woman he had mistakenly spirited away. "Why the devil did you do that? I've told you I won't do you any harm."

"Untie me!" she cried, ignoring his question.

Torrie watched her struggling with her bindings in an impressive show of temper and bravado. He suspected he would be dodging flailing fists if he surrendered to her demand. There was something oddly rousing about her pique.

He shook his head. "I'm afraid that wouldn't be wise. You seem to be in rather a state, my dear. Would you care to tell me who you are?"

"Miss Brooke," declared the woman he'd carried from Worthing's town house. "I'm a respectable governess in the employ of Lord and Lady Worthing, and I demand you return me to his lordship's residence at once."

He stared at her, aghast, a sinking weight of dread lodging heavy as a stone somewhere in the vicinity of his conscience.

Good God, he had stolen a *governess*.

And a furious one, at that.

7

He opened his mouth, intending to say something intelligent. An explanation. Perhaps, even some nonsense with which he might placate her.

Instead, all that emerged was two words, low and growled. "Damn it."

There went his evening.

Her nostrils flared. "Sirrah, your language."

It was, he thought, a castigation only a governess would make in such a moment. He would have laughed, were their circumstances not so perilous. Perilous for her virtue. A gentleman didn't kidnap a governess, an innocent, and cart her away into the night without ramifications. And here she was, still bound in his carriage, protesting his epithet. Hadn't she any notion of how dire the mistake he'd made this night was?

"You're fretting over my language?" he asked her calmly.

Torrie had an ability to stay unruffled in the face of others' unwieldy emotions. Perhaps because from the moment he had awoken, a broken, painful stranger to himself, mind wiped free of memories, he had felt nothing inside but a great, gaping hollowness. A complete lack of emotion. It was easy to remain composed when one felt nothing. When one *knew* nothing.

Unfortunately, he knew enough of his present predicament to understand he was about to find himself mired in rather a lot of trouble.

"You might untie me," she said coldly.

"Yes, but at present, I wish very much not to have my eyes clawed out by an angry governess," he pointed out dryly.

"Why have you taken me?" she demanded.

He noted she hadn't argued that she had no intention of doing him bodily harm.

Yes, best to keep her bound for now.

Also, he wasn't inclined to admit that he'd been

attempting to kidnap the wife of her employer and had taken her in error.

"Perhaps we would be wise to begin in a more proper vein," he suggested wryly, attempting to distract her from her query. "I am Viscount Torrington. At your service, Miss…"

Blast, he'd already forgotten her name.

The lady didn't appear to be impressed by his lapse.

She scowled. "Miss Brooke."

"At your service, Miss Brooke," he amended, offering her his most charming grin.

"What do you intend to do with me?" she asked next, clearly undeterred from her course by his attempt at distraction. "And why have you taken me, my lord?"

There was an edge to her voice that he sincerely hoped wasn't fear. Guilt lanced him at the notion. Perhaps he should untie her after all, potential danger to his eyes aside.

He winced. "It wasn't you I was meant to take."

"If not me, then whom?"

He cleared his throat, his cravat too tight and stealing all the air in the cramped confines of the carriage. "I would prefer not to elaborate."

Although it was quite obvious, was it not? A gentleman would not steal into a fellow lord's town house to take one of his servants.

Confirming his thoughts, Miss Brooke gasped softly, the color leaching from her cheeks and leaving her pale, a study in contrast with her dark hair. "Lady Worthing."

"Your discretion would be most appreciated," he offered grimly, as way of confirmation.

But his inquisitive companion was not finished.

"Is this the sort of thing you do often, then?" she asked with a tart tone "Kidnapping your mistresses?"

Ah, damnation.

He eyed her dourly, thinking she shouldn't be nearly so

9

appealing, given all the trouble she'd thus far caused him. Also, that he didn't have an answer to her sharp query.

"I've only one mistress currently," he said. "Not more than one."

"That wasn't what I asked."

His mystery governess was dashed good at stinging reprimands. She rather made him feel like a recalcitrant lad who'd been caught thieving sweets from the kitchens.

"Not in recent memory, I haven't," he offered with an indolent shrug. "Before that, I couldn't say."

Pretending as if his lack of memory didn't affect him had become commonplace. If he feigned contentedness in his wretched state, no one looked at him with pity. He could not abide being looked at as if he were a stray mongrel who'd just been kicked.

Her brow furrowed. "What do you mean you couldn't say?"

Ah, fortunately for him, he had kidnapped the one person in London who apparently had yet to hear the salacious tale of Lord Torrington's disastrous phaeton accident and ensuing amnesia. It wasn't a tale he particularly enjoyed retelling. Nor one he cared to elaborate upon now.

"It doesn't matter," he told her, his mind whirling with the implications of what he had done, and what it would mean for not just him but for Miss Brooke as well. "What *does* matter is returning you to where you belong without anyone else being the wiser."

A largely impossible feat, he was beginning to fear. One from which, it was almost certain, neither of them would manage to escape unscathed, reputations intact.

CHAPTER 2

The carriage swayed over the Mayfair road, lumbering slowly through the darkness of the night to take Elizabeth back where she belonged. Her wrists chafed where the rope he had used to bind her mercilessly rubbed against her sensitive skin. Her pride was in tatters. Her reputation was in shreds. And her situation as governess —won in desperation when Lady Andromeda had finally told her she must find a different set of circumstances for herself—was in dreadful danger.

"How do you propose to return me to Worthing House without anyone discovering?" she asked coldly.

His long fingers drummed on his thigh idly. She told herself she would not take notice of the figure he cut in his evening clothes. Nor would she be affected by the strong slash of his jaw.

"I shall think of something," he told her with a hopeful air that made her long to box his ears for his lack of care.

Elizabeth needed her position.

Without it, she had no roof over her head. No hope. No future.

"How reassuring," she snapped, tugging ineffectually at her wrists yet again. "Untie me now, if you please."

He had instructed his coachman to return them to the earl's town house. With each moment, every clop of the horses' hooves beyond the carriage, she was one step closer to imminent doom. But at least she might face her complete and utter ruination without a rope binding her wrists behind her back.

"You're quite angry," he said, as if she were the unreasonable one amongst them.

Of all the reprobates and rakes in London, why did it have to be *him* who had happened upon her in the library on the lone occasion she had stolen from her chamber in search of a book to read? Why did it have to be *him* who had kidnapped her in the midst of the night?

Viscount Torrington.

The tormentor of her failed Seasons. The unspeakably handsome, debonair rogue for whom she had once held a foolish *tendre*. A silly, girlish infatuation. He was the gentleman whose notice she had tried with unrelenting determination to earn, the one on whom she had pinned all her fragile hopes. Until she had unintentionally eavesdropped on his crushing words at a ball, and she had been forced to admit that he would never return her feelings.

But although she had eventually tamped down her inconvenient and pathetic longing where he was concerned, watching him flirting his way shamelessly through the *ton* hadn't been any easier.

"I am indeed angry, my lord," she managed, banishing all thoughts of the past. "You have spirited me away in scandalous fashion, at great peril to my reputation and my situation. If Lord and Lady Worthing discover what has happened, I will be dismissed from my position. To say nothing of the fright you have given me."

Her mouth was still dry from all the terror he had visited upon her during the abduction.

He winced. "Forgive me, Miss Brooke. It wasn't my intention to frighten you, as you know."

Did he suppose such a reminder would ameliorate the sting? He had mistaken her for his mistress, the undeniably beautiful, diamond of the first water, Countess of Worthing. Lady Worthing was golden-haired and ethereal, her skin pale, her eyes blue, her face perfect in every way. She didn't possess a pointed nose, dark hair, brown eyes, a mouth too large for her face, and a cumbersome figure that was more plump than willowy. Lady Worthing was not a woman who had ever been referred to as *plain*.

"Nonetheless, Lord Torrington, you did, indeed, frighten me."

He had also smacked her quite firmly on the bottom. Her cheeks filled with unwanted heat at the thought, and that portion of her anatomy which had been so rudely abused tingled with remembrance. She had not liked it. Except, now that she knew it was the viscount who had taken her from Worthing House...

No, she stopped that dreadful, traitorous thought before it could be completed. He hadn't been swatting *her* rump in his mind. He had been doing it to Lady Worthing, who was apparently cuckolding the earl with the only man Elizabeth had ever foolishly carried romantic inclinations toward. But that was years ago now, and Lord Torrington himself had disabused her of all such youthful folderol in cutting fashion.

"I am very sorry," he apologized, sounding sincere, pressing his fingers to his temples as if to assuage some manner of ache lodged in his head. "You must know that this is most extraordinary for me. I would never have spirited you away if I had realized you were not Eugenia."

Eugenia.

Elizabeth couldn't say why, but his use of Lady Worthing's given name nettled her. It certainly wasn't jealousy; she had long ago abandoned her silly infatuation. Perhaps it was merely the acknowledgment, so plain and unrepentant, that he was engaging in an affair with a married woman. That the marriage between the earl and the countess was yet another cold society match founded on the need for heirs rather than true love. And that the viscount was happily bedding another man's wife. But then, Elizabeth had abandoned all hopes of true love for herself long ago. She should not be disappointed by this discovery.

"I am greatly relieved to know that you only kidnap the wives of other lords and not their governesses," she forced out.

Her fingers were falling asleep, going numb. Just how tightly had he tied the dratted knot on the rope?

"If it be of any solace to you, Miss Brooke, I don't ordinarily kidnap anyone," he said.

She glared at him. Was he an imbecile? She didn't think he had always possessed such a feeble intellect. But then, he had never deigned to speak directly to her, only *about* her, and Elizabeth would eternally regret ever unintentionally eavesdropping on those cutting words. How could she know his intelligence? And what manner of goose imagined herself in love with a man she knew so little about? It was humiliating, this situation notwithstanding.

"Solace would be found in the removal of the rope you've knotted around my wrists," she hissed, struggling against them again.

The action only served to tighten the binding further.

"Do sit still, Miss Brooke," he said with irritating calm. "I'll never be able to untie you if you continue squirming."

Outrage bubbled inside her. A governess wasn't allowed the luxury of emotions. But then, neither was a poor relative.

Her lot was to serve. To smile. To pretend. To bear every indignity foisted upon her and act as if each one was her due. But to the devil with that. She had been kidnapped! She was going to lose everything. And all because the handsome scoundrel she'd once pined for in her girlish ignorance had decided to spirit away his mistress. As what? A lark?

More emotion boiled to the surface, and she embarrassed herself by emitting a high-pitched noise that was half incredulous laugh, half hiccup. Hot tears of shame were burning her eyes, and something tickled her throat.

"I cannot tell if you are laughing or crying."

Nor could she.

"Both," she cried, and then allowed her head to fall back against the carriage squabs so that she could consult the ceiling of the conveyance, as if divine intervention might miraculously appear on her behalf.

It did not.

All that happened was a large, warm, masculine hand.

On her knee.

His hand.

The temerity of the man! How dare he? She jerked away from him, sidling along the bench, and inadvertently struck her head on the wall of the carriage. The collision hurt, but not nearly as much as the blow to her pride in knowing not only had he mistaken her for another, but he hadn't even known who she was.

"My dear Miss Brooke," he began, using a tone she imagined he might use upon a Bedlamite who had been graceless enough to wander into his path, dirtied and mad.

"I am not your dear anything," she interrupted coldly. "You are too familiar, and pray do not touch me again!"

Not ever.

Because she liked it too much, and he was insufferable. He was an arrogant, handsome lord who was bedding another man's wife. Oh, the horror of it all. To have reached the undignified point in her life of finding herself firmly on the shelf, cast off by every relative of means, made to become a governess, and then for the man she had once yearned for to be the source of her destruction.

Surely, *surely*, the gods were laughing in fickle amusement somewhere at her expense.

"Of course." He had retracted his hand, and he was frowning now, looking so grim, so thoroughly lacking in joy that for a moment, Elizabeth found herself pitying him. "You must believe that I never wished for this to happen, and that your distress pains me greatly. Does your head ache? You struck it on the carriage wall."

"Yes, my head aches. My head aches because I am about to lose my situation and the roof over my head, and every modicum of respectability I yet possess!"

Oh dear.

She was shouting by the time she had finished. And shouting was most unlike her. She hadn't raised her voice in years, aside from her terrified screams during Lord Torrington's kidnapping. But that couldn't have been helped. She had been persuaded, until they had been in the carriage, and she had at last seen his face, that a villain intent on murdering her or worse had absconded with her.

"I fear if you don't lower your voice, you will only make this unfortunate mistake even worse for the both of us," the viscount said with an unflappable composure that made her yearn to yell again.

"This *unfortunate mistake*, as you call it, will make me forfeit what little I have, Lord Torrington," she reminded him.

A man of his station could do anything, commit any sin, and be forgiven. But a woman such as herself, relying on the goodwill of her employers, with nothing but her reputation and Lady Andromeda's letter to recommend her, would suffer greatly. Dread was heavier than a brick in her stomach.

He leaned across the small, enclosed space of the carriage, resting his elbows on his knees. "You'll not lose anything, my —*madam*. This, I promise you. I own the responsibility for what has transpired this night, and I will make certain that any damages done are rectified by me."

She hardly believed he would or could. Easy enough for him to offer such platitudes as a means of mollifying her. But what could he truly do, if Lord and Lady Worthing discovered that she had transgressed enough to enter their library in the late hours of the night, and then had further been alone with a known rake in his carriage, without chaperone? What would he do? Nothing, and they both knew it.

"If I lose my situation, what do you propose, my lord?" she dared to ask, wiggling her fingers behind her back in an effort to restore some of the sensation in them. "Are you in need of a governess?"

"I…" He paused, frowning, and it was clear he had not thought beyond his calming words of reassurance. "No."

"And do you know of anyone in need of one?" she pressed.

His brow furrowed even deeper. "I'm afraid I do not."

Just as she had thought. The urge to swing a wild kick toward his shins rose, tempting indeed.

"Then how do you propose to rectify the damages?" she demanded. "What if Lord and Lady Worthing dismiss me because of your carelessness?"

Elizabeth was being unwise, and she knew it. There was no benefit in arguing with the viscount.

"Eugenia would never dismiss you over such an unintentional error," he said, surprising her by swiftly moving across the carriage and sitting on the squabs at her side.

Eugenia again. Oh, how that telling intimacy rankled, and she could not deny it.

Her earlier slide on the bench left Elizabeth pressed to the carriage wall with nowhere else to go. No means of escape. And Torrington was crowding her with his large, masculine form.

"What are you doing?" she demanded, her ire rising to a crescendo, along with her panic.

Was it not terrible enough that he had kidnapped her? Why must he also seat himself on the same side of the carriage, nearly pressed against her, so close that his scent teased her senses? Leather, bay, a hint of citrus and something else she could not quite define—perhaps a floral note. Naturally, Viscount Torrington would smell as divine as he looked.

"I intend to untie you," he said, raising a dark brow. "If you will allow it."

It would seem that he no longer believed her capable of *clawing* his eyes out, as he had so indelicately phrased it. Well, he was decidedly wrong. She most certainly ought to retaliate against him, to make him suffer for his reckless philandering and where it had inadvertently led the both of them. If only she had feeling in her fingers so that she might.

"Yes," she agreed, nettled with herself for the breathless quality to her own voice. "Please do."

He reached behind her, the movement forcing her shoulder to graze his broad chest. He was studying her with an expression of such intensity that it quite flustered Elizabeth. Heat stung her cheeks, and she averted her gaze, pinning a glare at the empty squab opposite her, which seemed to mock.

"Have we met before, Miss Brooke?" he asked, his voice a low, decadent rumble that played with old emotions long left dormant.

"I dare say not," she forced out firmly.

And that was not an untruth. They had never been formally introduced. The extent of their interactions had been her naïve adoration as she watched his handsome form from across various ballrooms.

"Hmm," he said, a noncommittal hum, and she couldn't be certain what it meant.

Perhaps nothing.

But then, his bare fingertips grazed the sensitive skin of her inner wrist as he attempted to work the knot free, and her ability to contemplate anything other than his touch vanished.

He was not wearing gloves. Apparently, kidnappings did not require the trappings of gentility. And nor was she, for neither did surreptitious jaunts to one's employer's library. Her one lapse in judgment and look at what had come of it.

His fingertips brushed over her again, this time her palms, and she discovered that she was not entirely incapable of feeling there. Her heart beat fast and hard, and she could not suppress a quick inhalation of breath, nor the sudden shower of sparks burning up her arm. Elizabeth didn't want these feelings. She didn't want this man's proximity, nor the reminders of her past foolishness he was unwittingly dredging up within her.

"Please, my lord, make haste," she urged, surrounded by his scent and undone by his touch.

How pathetic she was.

"I'm trying, madam. However, the knot has tightened. Perhaps you would not mind shifting on the seat so that I may have better access?"

Yes, perhaps if he were at her back, ignoring him would be easier.

She moved as he had asked, trying to ignore the manner in which her bottom brushed against his thigh. "Better?"

"One hopes," he quipped, apparently seeking to find the levity in their disastrous predicament.

When there was none.

She was all too aware of everything—his presence at her back, his fingers working on her bonds, his steady, even breaths falling hotly on her nape.

"Blast," he muttered. "The dratted thing does not wish to be opened."

The carriage slowed, and Elizabeth wondered if they had reached Lord Worthing's town house. Panic rose, mingling with the detested effects of his nearness on her.

"I must get back inside at once." She made the mistake of glancing over her shoulder, which proved just how truly close Lord Torrington was.

As close as she had once dreamed he would be. Her heart thudded faster, and to her chagrin, it didn't have anything to do with the impending dread of being discovered by Lord or Lady Worthing. Rather, it had everything to do with the viscount. He was frowning down at the knot, looking terribly handsome, the sensual curve of his lips drawing her attention. His gaze flicked up to hers, his eyes a rich shade of green that seemed far more vibrant now than it had in the shadows from across the carriage.

For a moment, it was as if years of disappointment and rejection had not intervened since she'd first spied him from across a ballroom. Her breath caught, and a queer sensation tightened within her. Was it her imagination, or was there a flare of awareness between them?

"You'll have to wait until I can untie this knot," he said, dashing the stupid thought at once.

Of course, there was no awareness. She was the plain wallflower he had never noticed for five Seasons, unless it had been to disparage her in passing. The mistake he had unintentionally kidnapped instead of his beautiful mistress. Did her foolishness know no bounds?

She jerked her head forward so that he would not see the heat rising in her cheeks, the humiliated expression on her face. "Naturally, I didn't intend to race into the town house with my hands tied behind my back."

Elizabeth was doing her utmost to affect a cool, disinterested tone. But she was swimming in misery. In old memories. In longing. In fear of what she was about to lose.

Because if she lost her situation as governess to the earl's young children, she doubted she could find another. And Lady Andromeda had been clear that her dwindling funds and ill health meant that she could no longer afford to be the sponsor of Elizabeth's increasingly impossible dreams of becoming a wife and mother. Elizabeth was doomed to a life of taking care of the children of others, of never having her own. But it was preferable to becoming some wealthy man's mistress, or worse.

At last, the knot loosened and her hands came free. Elizabeth moved them to her lap, relief washing over her, along with sensation—the prickle of thousands of tiny, invisible needles in her flesh.

"Oh," she gasped softly, flexing her fingers, working the blood that had been denied them back into flowing.

"Are you hurt?" Torrington asked, taking up her hands in his.

Why had he not removed himself to the opposite squabs?

She attempted to tug herself free of his grasp, but he held firm. "My hands have fallen asleep, my lord. In a few moments, they shall be fine."

"I am sorry," he apologized again. "Christ, what a muddle." His fingers traced over her wrist, sending not just awareness but the sting of pain along with it. "Good God, the rope cut into your skin. You're bleeding."

She glanced down to their entwined hands, feeling as if she were in a daze. How could he be so unaffected by this intimacy? Belatedly, she realized that she was, indeed, chafed and bleeding from the binding.

"I shall heal." Another tug, and she removed her hands from his possession, severing the connection.

"I never intended to do you any harm."

There was genuine contrition in his voice. She might have felt sympathy for him, were the circumstances less severe.

"The carriage has stopped," she pointed out needlessly. "I must go inside."

He dropped the rope to the floor. "I will accompany you."

More time in his presence, the chance they'd be caught together? She thought not.

"That won't be necessary, Lord Torrington. I will endeavor to go inside as quickly and quietly as possible."

"I'll not allow you to go alone." His jaw flexed, as if he were determined.

"You've caused me more than enough trouble this evening," she countered crisply, reaching for the latch on the carriage door.

She opened it and made to rush outside, but a lashing rain had begun to fall, and she was wearing only her worn satin slippers. They had been quite dear, and she had been saving them for years now. She could never afford another pair now.

"It is raining and you are hardly dressed for the weather," Lord Torrington said, gently moving her out of the way to exit the carriage himself.

When he had alighted, he reached for her, his arms open, and she realized he meant to carry her. "Come, Miss Brooke."

She stared at him, thinking there was no earthly way she could allow herself to willingly be transported in his strong arms again. It was not just scandalous. The temptation was far too much for her to bear.

"It would be unseemly, my lord," she denied primly.

Rain slashed at his broad shoulders, pelted his handsome face, dashed on the cobblestones below. "I insist. It is the least I can do."

If he stood there much longer, he would be soaked. His expression was stubborn, telling her he wouldn't accept her refusal.

"Very well," she allowed reluctantly, and met him halfway.

He held her tightly to his chest and carried her through the mews. She was newly aware of a stiffness in his gait that she'd failed to take notice of during their earlier departure. But then, she'd been terrified out of her wits. Now she was merely drenched by the rain.

They had nearly reached their destination, and relief was beginning to chase the dread, when a familiar, angry figure raced toward them through the stables, the pique on her lovely face undeniable.

"What is the meaning of this?" the countess seethed.

And that quickly, the dread turned into the knowledge that Elizabeth was imminently going to lose her position as governess.

CHAPTER 3

"*I* am so sorry for everything that occurred this evening. Pray believe that if I could begin the night anew and change what happened, I would."

"With the governess," Eugenia hissed, ignoring his heartfelt apology. "That plump little mouse? I cannot credit it, Torrie. How can she have possibly attracted your attention? And when?"

He winced, the shrillness of her voice making the steadily growing ache in his head increase exponentially. They were alone in the private confines of a small anteroom where he supposed the countess ordinarily welcomed guests. Fortunately, he had persuaded her to cool her ire in the stables and avoid making any more of a scandal than they already had. The governess he'd kidnapped had been dismissed to her chamber, with the irate promise from Eugenia that she would face her reckoning on the morrow.

And here he stood, dripping on the earl's Axminster, attempting to soothe the anger of the woman he'd been meant to kidnap and thoroughly ravish in his carriage.

"I can explain, Eugenia," he said calmly, raising his palms to her in a placating gesture.

"I fail to see how you can," she snapped, stalking past him to pace the length of the chamber in a swirl of pale, dampened muslin skirts.

As always, she was magnificent. In her anger, in her passion—hell, even in polite discourse at the dinner table—Lady Worthing was ethereally lovely. Pity that her personality was not nearly as beautiful.

"You told me to meet you in the library," he began.

"Do not tell me you couldn't find the library."

"I could," he continued. "However, your governess was within. I kidnapped her, mistaking her for you."

"What was that jade doing in the library?" Eugenia's eyes narrowed. "I should have known better than to take on a new governess with no experience to recommend her. Only a letter from her distant relative, Lady Andromeda Harting, who everyone knows lost all her funds gambling. And why would Miss Brooke not tell you who she was, that you were mistaken? None of this makes sense, Torrie."

Eugenia paused at the end of the chamber and whipped around to face him in an agitated swirl of skirts.

"None of this is the fault of your governess," he felt compelled to offer. After all, it was Eugenia's nonsensical scheme to be kidnapped, coupled with his own failure, that had led to him absconding with the wrong woman. "And she did not tell me who she was because I gagged her with my cravat."

The last, he added rather weakly.

Her face was frozen into a cold mask of fury. "You might have made certain you were spiriting away the *right* woman. The mere thought of you mistaking me for that dreadful-looking girl..."

She allowed her words to trail off and shuddered, as if the

prospect engendered such disgust, she no longer had the capacity for speech.

There was nothing dreadful looking about Miss...Miss... by God, he had forgotten her name again. But her face, by the flickering light of the carriage lamp, had been lovely in its own way. There was something compelling about her, as if there were secrets and mysteries lurking beneath her prim façade. For no reason at all, the thought occurred to him of what it would be like to see beneath all her layers. To have such a woman naked in his bed.

He struck the notion away, for it was unworthy. He had already caused the poor girl enough distress without lusting after her.

"I take full responsibility for what has happened," he told his irate mistress, wondering why he had ever agreed to her addlepated idea. "I've already spoken with the lads in the stables. They are all pleased to accept my explanation that tonight was nothing more than a drunken mishap in which I entered the wrong house. I've paid them handsomely to keep your name and the governess's out of everything that transpired."

"You ought not to have paid them a ha'penny on her account," Eugenia said coldly, in high dudgeon. "I've half a mind to throw her out on her ear this very night."

He couldn't blame Eugenia for her reaction; he had bungled this affair badly. But he couldn't, in good conscience, allow the governess to bear the brunt of the shame for his own mistake.

He crossed the chamber, taking Eugenia's cool, smooth hand in his and bringing it to his lips. "Please, Eugenia. You mustn't dismiss her. It isn't fair for her to pay the price for my misdeeds."

She snatched her hand away, unplacated. "Do you have any idea how it felt to see you carrying her in your arms? To know that you spirited her away and were *alone* in your carriage with her? And my God, such a pathetic creature as she. Five Seasons and couldn't make a match. Little wonder, such a drab thing."

Her anger with him was understood. Acceptable, even. He had been careless. He had made mistakes. Not the first of those he could remember, and nor would they be the last, he knew. But he could not allow the continued aspersions being heaped upon the governess.

"You needn't pay her insult, Eugenia. It's unkind."

Her eyes widened until she almost resembled a bug in her rage.

"Unkind?" she spat. "You dare to defend that wretch?"

"Your rancor toward the governess is unnecessary," he said calmly, having endured some of Eugenia's tantrums in the past. "It ought to be aimed solely at me."

"Did you fuck her?" Eugenia demanded. "That despicable whore! Of course, you did. You're a libertine. You would bed a petticoat if it moved."

"Of course I did not," he snapped, growing rather irritated with her refusal to at least relent and see a bit of reason. To say nothing of the insults she paid the governess and himself. "A mistake was made. One I took haste in rectifying."

Bed a petticoat if it moved? That was rather a low blow, even by Eugenia's standards. God. Was that what she thought of him? Torrie shuffled that question from his mind to revisit later, because he was certain he wouldn't like the outcome.

Eugenia's eyes narrowed, and it was then that he realized their color—a cold, calculating blue. "By seducing her in your carriage and then carrying her through the rain in your arms. Well, my lord, if you truly believe I will endure your faithlessness, you are wrong. I'll not stand for it. The girl must go by morning. I'll destroy her myself and enjoy every moment of it. All London will know what she has done before I've finished."

Torrie didn't doubt the veracity of her words. The Countess of Worthing was cunning and coldhearted when she felt as if she had been betrayed. It was one of the reasons why she took such great delight in cuckolding her husband. The earl had apparently kept a mistress for years. Still kept one, a woman with whom he had fathered illegitimate children whom he had settled unentailed estates upon. Eugenia reviled him for it.

He followed Eugenia, who had resumed her furious pacing, catching her elbow in a light grasp and spinning her to face him. "Eugenia, I beg you, do not ruin the poor girl. She is an innocent in all this."

Lady Worthing's lip curled into an unbecoming sneer. "She didn't look innocent, the manner in which she was gazing up at you whilst you carried her in your arms. Do you know, Torrie, that you have never once carried me in such fashion?"

"She was going to ruin her slippers in the rain."

Eugenia wrenched her arm free and whirled away again. "I'll pitch her slippers into the fire myself!"

This was going deuced poorly. Torrie ran a hand over his jaw, wishing his head wasn't thumping with such ferocity. Wishing he had never agreed to this madcap scheme of kidnapping Eugenia, so that he might have avoided this entire, dreadful mess altogether.

"There's no need for cruelty," he chided, although he knew he should hold his tongue.

But enduring Eugenia's virulence was putting him in quite the vile mood himself. A man could only listen to so much nonsense before the threads of his patience wore thin. Yes, he had done something foolish. But he had also done everything in his power to make it right. He had ensured the silence of the grooms who had witnessed their disastrous confrontation in the mews. He had apologized, damn it. And yet, she continued to heap insults and accusations. Unfounded ones.

He had done nothing untoward to Miss...to the governess. His head was aching, his brain more muddled than it customarily was, his back ached, and the pain in his bones which always renewed its vigor when it rained had returned.

But Eugenia, it seemed, was not finished.

She stalked toward him in a rage, and before he realized her intent, he knew the sting of her palm slapping his cheek. "How dare you defend her after all you have done? How dare you choose her over me?"

He sighed heavily. "All I ask is that you not dismiss the girl in the morning."

"And have to face her every day after this humiliation?" the countess scoffed. "Never. There is nothing you can do or say to change my mind, Torrie."

He reckoned there *was* one thing he could do. One thing he *had* to do, regardless of the horror it struck in his soul.

He didn't *want* to do it.

God, if there were any other means of extricating himself from this bloody contretemps in one piece, he would. However, after cheating fate for far too long, it would appear that Torrie was finally being forced to pay for his many, many sins. Both remembered and forgotten.

He rubbed his smarting cheek, pinning his former mistress with a stern glare of his own. "Actually, Eugenia, there *is* one thing I can do."

"Oh?" She laughed, as if he had just told her the greatest sally. "Do tell, darling. Whatever shall you do?"

He held the countess's stare, unflinching. "I'll marry her."

And for the first time in their acquaintance, he'd stunned the Countess of Worthing into complete and utter silence.

ELIZABETH'S greatest fears had come to fruition.

Only, worse.

Because Lady Worthing did not possess enough compassion to wait until the morning to dismiss her from her post. Instead, she had forced a housemaid from her bed, demanding that Elizabeth be informed that she was to pack her belongings at once and leave.

And so, once again, she was without a roof over her head, without hope, and not even a letter to recommend her for a future situation. Clutching her valise and holding her head as high as she could manage given the circumstances and her fervent efforts to avoid weeping, Elizabeth stepped into the mews. On her back, she wore a serviceable redingote, which had been one of Lady Andromeda's castoffs, a parting gift. The only bonnet she owned had been tied firmly beneath her chin with trembling fingers. Every possession she possessed and wasn't presently wearing—two gowns, her satin slippers, a book, some hair pins, a brush, a cap, some gloves, and one spare petticoat and chemise—had been stuffed into her valise.

Cold, unforgiving night air greeted her as she stepped into the darkened mews where Lord Torrington's carriage remained. At least the rain of earlier had ceased. But although it was the height of foolishness to feel a pang of disappointment that he was off in Lady Worthing's arms, Elizabeth couldn't seem to tamp it down. The mews was quiet as she passed through, head tucked down, wondering where she might next go. Lady Andromeda was no longer in London. Elizabeth had scarcely enough funds remaining from what little she had managed to save of her wages, sewn into the lining of her valise.

Perhaps she might find rooms that would accept a respectable lady. But how to do so in the depths of the night?

The wind blew, cutting through her redingote and making her shiver as the door to Lord Torrington's carriage swung open. She was astounded to find the viscount descending in the low glimmer of the carriage lamplight. His handsome face was somber and pale as his greatcoat whipped around him and he offered her his arm.

"Come, if you please."

His politely worded command, issued in his velvet-smooth voice, gave Elizabeth pause. Her well-worn boots stopped on the cobblestones and she stared at him, misgiving blossoming inside her like a hothouse rose.

"What are you doing here, my lord?" she asked, eying his extended arm.

"Awaiting you, my dear." He sighed. "Hoping Eugenia would see reason, it's true. But it would seem I'm destined for disappointment this evening."

"That makes two of us," she blurted out before thinking better of it, for she was nearly hysterical.

First, she had been spirited away in the night, given the fright of her life before she'd discovered who her captor was, and then she had lost the fragile hope of a future. She had lost the roof over her head, the bed in which she slept, the position promising her the modest funds she desperately needed, and the last chance for respectability she'd had.

"Not well said of me, was it?" he asked grimly, reaching for her valise. "Allow me to take this. Come into the carriage where it is warmer, won't you? The night has grown quite wretched with cold, and I'll not have you taking a chill."

Elizabeth couldn't help herself. She laughed. The high, shrill laugh of a woman who had nothing left.

"I fear that of all the fates I'll be facing, Lord Torrington, taking a chill shall be the very least of them," she managed at last, holding fast to her valise.

But he was stronger than she; he plucked it free of her grasp with ease. "I shall endeavor not to consider that an insult, but I'm afraid you may be correct on that count, my dear."

Had she not told him she was not his dear? Why did he insist on such careless, frivolous endearments? She hated that he called her that. And she hated how very much some insipid, loathsome part of herself loved it.

But then, that was not all he had said, was it? He'd said something about trying not to consider her words an insult. What in heaven's name did he mean? She was too wearied and shocked over her sudden dismissal that she couldn't comprehend.

"I'm afraid I don't understand what insult I've paid you, my lord," she said, her mind still preoccupied with ways she might extricate herself from this disaster. "Please return my valise. It's all I have left."

Her voice broke on the last word, the sting of tears rising to prick her eyes. How humiliating it was to stand before him, her circumstances entirely reduced to nothing more than the valise he held and the pathetic shreds of her reputation. And yet, he dared to toy with her. Hadn't he done enough damage?

But he did not do as she asked. When she made to snatch her valise from his grip, he held it easily from her reach, undeterred.

"Come with me," he repeated. "Into the carriage."

She shook her head, adamant. "Going into that carriage with you against my will is what cost me my situation. I'll not ruin whatever remains of my good name by entering it again."

A particularly vicious wind picked up, tearing through the thin layers of her gown and redingote, for she hadn't been given sufficient time to properly dress for the elements.

The viscount winced, having the grace to look shame-faced at the reminder of his misdeeds. But what good did a bit of shame on his part do Elizabeth? For so many Seasons, she had watched him from across countless ballrooms, thinking him handsome and elegant and so dashing. And now here she was, staring at a man who was nothing more than a scoundrel who had shattered her world with one care-less act.

"I understand your anger, my dear," he said then, his tone firm and brusque as the wind. "However, I am determined to make amends for my sins."

"I'm not in need of charity or pity," she snapped, lunging for her valise, having done with ladylike attempts to thwart him.

But she misjudged.

He shifted quickly, and she landed firmly against his chest. His firm, broad, *strong* chest.

The scent of him was quick to infiltrate her senses before it was banished by another gust of wind. His free hand settled on her lower back, anchoring her to him in most improper fashion.

The familiarity of his touch, the way he brought her body into his as if she were meant to be there, in the half circle of his arm, stole her breath for a heartbeat before her wits returned. This man had cost her not just her position, but her respectability this evening. He was an unrepentant rake.

A viscount of villainy.

She cuffed him on the perfect, handsome slash of his jaw, fury and weariness and desperation overwhelming her.

"Damn it, woman," he ground out, releasing her to pass a

hand over the place where she had struck him. "Why did you do that?"

Elizabeth would not feel a bit of contrition for her action. Not one modicum. Truly, she ought to have hit him harder.

"Because you deserved it," she snapped tartly. "I reasoned it was preferable to clawing out your eyes, as that seems a rather messy prospect."

He laughed, and to her vexation, the sound sent heat swirling though her, chasing the cold. "You have spirit. I like it."

He liked her spirit? More unwanted warmth unfurled. How desperately foolish was she? The hour was likely approaching midnight, she had lost her governess situation, and she had nowhere to sleep, nor food to eat. Why should this man have any effect on her at all, with her future looming before her, damning and ominous?

Best to concentrate on what she needed to do, and that was finding suitable lodging for the evening, not tarrying with the handsome lord for whom she'd once held a *tendre*.

"I'm gratified, Lord Torrington." She held out her hand expectantly. "Now, if you please, my valise."

"We can stand here in the wind, arguing over your valise, or you can get inside the warmth of the carriage," he said.

"Surely you realize the impropriety of such an act," she said firmly. "I am attempting to keep the tattered remnants of my good name intact, so that I may hopefully secure another situation. I'll never be hired as a governess if I am being squired about by rogues at midnight."

"You'll not be needing another situation as a governess," he said easily. "My actions this evening were inexcusable, and I intend to take the necessary steps to ensure you don't suffer further harm. To that end, I have a proposition to make."

It struck her then, Torrington's insistence that she go into his carriage with him. His refusal to relinquish her valise.

Surely he didn't intend to make her his mistress. He had the beautiful Lady Worthing already, and a handsome rake like the viscount wouldn't look twice at a wallflower such as herself. What did he want with her? Was it guilt that spurred him?

"Whatever your proposition is, I cannot help but think it ruinous." She shook her head. "No, my lord. I'll not be accepting any offers you make."

He raised a brow, looking down at her with an inscrutable expression. "Perhaps you speak with too much haste, my dear."

"I am *not* your dear," she reminded him icily as the wind whipped at the both of them again.

He frowned, determination settling over his handsome features. "The carriage. Now. You're shivering."

So she was. It was going to be a dreadfully cold night. If she failed to find somewhere respectable to sleep, she shuddered to think what would become of her.

Elizabeth intended to offer further protest, but somehow, the viscount's arm had swept around her waist, and he was guiding her to the carriage. The conveyance beckoned, blessedly free of unforgiving wind. And she was suddenly weary, as if the weight that had threatened her all night had finally fallen on her shoulders.

Perhaps she could sacrifice her pride, if only to warm herself and find a ride to wherever she would be spending the night. She allowed the viscount to help her back into the carriage she had vacated what now seemed a lifetime ago. Primly, she settled herself on the seat with far more grace than the previous occasion had allowed. He joined her and seated himself opposite, making the confines of the carriage feel far more cramped than it had before. So much more intimate now that her initial fear of earlier, coupled with anger, had dissipated.

He settled her valise on the floor at his feet. "What direction shall I give my coachman?"

She swallowed hard against a rising knot of dread. "I haven't decided yet, my lord."

He frowned, looking stern and serious quite unlike the devil-may-care rakehell who had spirited her away earlier. "Where were you intending to go?"

"I don't know."

The frown deepened. "Have you anywhere that you can spend the night this evening, madam?"

"No," she admitted quietly, cheeks burning with shame. "I haven't."

"Christ." His jaw tightened, and he scrubbed a hand over the slashing edge in a weary gesture. "Eugenia dismissed you from your post and sent you into the night without a thought for what might become of you?"

Yes, indeed she had. And that was the manner of viper with whom he had shared his bed. But Elizabeth would not say so aloud. She was terribly cognizant that she was adrift in the vast sea of London, neither funds, nor family, nor situation to mire her.

"I expect Lady Worthing did not deem my welfare her concern any longer, given the nature of her ire," she answered carefully instead.

"And once again, I am at fault for that." He sighed heavily. "Good God, this is worse than I thought. Where did you live before you became governess?"

"My mother's distant cousin, Lady Andromeda Harting, but her reduced circumstances and ill health left her without ability to provide for me some time ago. She has gone to Bath, and her house has been let."

He grumbled an epithet that made her cheeks burn and then was silent, stroking his jaw. Elizabeth found herself fascinated by his long fingers, wondering what they would feel like, tangled in hers. Touching her bare skin. And then her cheeks stung even more furiously, for she had long ago been cured of her inconvenient *tendre* for this man. A man who didn't even remember her and likely hadn't ever noticed her. What folly was this?

"I'll take you to my sister," the viscount said suddenly.

"Your sister?" Elizabeth was not so far removed from Society that she wasn't aware of who his sister was—the Duchess of Montrose. "I wouldn't dare impose on Her Grace."

"I'll explain everything to her. It won't be an imposition for long."

"My lord, it's the midst of the night," she protested, her stomach tightening with dread at the prospect of appearing at the duke and duchess's town house at this late hour, having been dismissed of her post for reasons that did not bear repeating in polite society. "I don't suppose their Graces would welcome a stranger into their home."

"They will," Torrington countered before calling up to his coachman with their destination.

The carriage lumbered into motion.

"My lord, I cannot think this wise," she fretted, although the prospect of wandering London alone in search of a roof over her head for the night loomed, utterly terrifying.

"No more protestations," the viscount told her calmly. "I'll explain everything to them."

The carriage lumbered into motion, and it seemed that at least for the night, Elizabeth's fate was sealed.

CHAPTER 4

"*J*'m afraid I don't understand, Torrie. How in the good Lord's chemise did you manage to *steal* a governess?"

Torrie grimaced as he paced the length of the Duke of Montrose's study. The hour was exceedingly late, and he had successfully delivered the woman he was going to have to marry to his sister's efficient care. Harriet, who was kind-hearted to a fault, had taken the governess to a guest chamber, showing nary a hint of shock, surprise, or dismay at being woken from her bed to answer her brother's foibles. It was not the first time he had been grateful for his sister's remarkable self-possession since his injuries.

Nor, he feared, would it be the last.

What was he going to do with a wife? Torrie hadn't the slightest notion. The obvious answer was to send her away somewhere. To his country estate, where he might forget her existence and carry on as he was.

He turned to face the duke, who had been Torrie's closest friend before the phaeton accident. And who afterward had married his sister. Much of the years of their association remained enshrouded in mystery and shadows in his imperfect mind, but from what he had gleaned since his amnesia, Monty had been no saint himself in their wilder years. Still, how to explain the prurient nature of this evening's epic series of mishaps?

He sighed. "I was meant to kidnap the Countess of Worthing. The governess in question was in the wrong place at the wrong time, and I wasn't able to realize my error until after I had her in my carriage, bound and gagged."

"God's fichu. Bound and gagged, you say?"

Well, yes. It did sound particularly dreadful when one repeated it, but the entire affair had been Eugenia's idea, and he'd never intended to hurt anyone. Let alone to take the wrong woman, giving her the fright of her life and leaving her penniless and prospectless. Most especially not to find himself forced into marriage with a woman he'd only just met.

But still, Monty's habit of elaborate cursing grew wearisome, and whether it was the lateness of the hour, the frustration over his own foolish actions this evening, or his fury over Eugenia's treatment of the poor governess he'd inadvertently kidnapped, he couldn't say. But Torrie was vexed beyond measure, and there was something as nettlesome as a burr beneath a saddle about the duke's silly oaths.

He raked his fingers through his hair and pinned his brother-in-law with a glare, feeling distinctly ugly, as if he might tear everything in sight apart. It wasn't an unfamiliar inclination. Since he'd woken in agony on that cursed day without a memory, not even his own goddamned name, he'd been in a state that varied in degrees of terribleness.

"Have you always used these appalling epithets?" he asked the duke. "I cannot think I would have befriended you if you had. It's quite irritating."

Monty's countenance turned wry. "I've committed far

39

greater sins than inventive oaths. I would be grateful you don't recall them, but considering I'm the source of your lack of memory, an apology seems more the thing. I'm damned sorry for what happened. I know I've said it before, but with every reminder comes a waterfall of guilt."

The duke had apologized profusely for the part he had played in the phaeton accident that had grievously injured Torrie and robbed him of his memory, but Torrie didn't like being reminded of that night or its consequences. Indeed, he strove to forget it had ever happened.

Not so different from the rest of his life, only he'd forgotten that bit against his will.

"I'm here and well, am I not?" he asked.

Monty regarded him solemnly. Regretfully. And, worst of all, *kindly*. "I don't know how well you are. You've been in many scrapes—most of which we've been in together—but you've never kidnapped an innocent before."

Ah, Christ.

Yes, he had indeed committed the very worst crime this night. He had taken a respectable governess, swatted her on the rump, and cost her everything.

"I intend to pay for my sins," he said, straightening his shoulders against the rush of dread that accompanied his declaration.

For he didn't want to marry. He was in no condition to marry. He didn't even know who he was, aside from a flurry of hazy shadows of the past which had slowly and indistinctly returned. How could he promise himself to another?

It didn't matter. Not now that he'd ruined the poor woman. He had no other option.

"How do you intend to pay for your sins?" Monty asked, frowning at him and looking upon him with an expression Torrie imagined the duke might reserve for suspected footpads.

"I'm going to marry the chit, of course," he said, then huffed out a sigh and paced toward the opposite end of the unfamiliar study.

He had been within these walls before many times in his former life, he knew. But only because others had told him. The scents, the colors on the wall, the fireplace and its ormolu mantel clock—all of it was still relatively new to him, his visits to Hamilton House intentionally sparse. With so much of his past life a gaping hole, the feeling that he was hopelessly lost was never far. He'd done his best to drown it with women and whisky, but look at where that had left him.

Now, he had no choice but to wed.

"You're going to marry her?" Monty repeated, sounding stunned at the prospect. "*You?*"

Was that an insult? Was that suspicion he heard in his supposed friend's voice? Torrie spun on his heel.

"Yes, I'm going to marry her," he snarled, furious and he didn't know why. "You've married, have you not? It is the thing one does eventually. I hadn't expected to do so now, but I've snapped the parson's mousetrap upon myself with my own stupidity."

Monty sank into an overstuffed chair, looking dazed. "Hell."

"Hell? That's all you have to offer?" Torrie stalked toward his host, anger clenching his jaw. "No Beelzebub's earbobs or other such nonsense?"

His irate strides slowed as a sensation of familiarity hit him, along with a memory of laughing with the duke as they rode on Rotten Row. Of Monty tipping back his head and declaring, *"Beelzebub's earbobs, I'd give my left ballock for some whisky right now."*

But Monty didn't touch spirits these days. He knew because Harriet had been firm on the matter, that he not

41

offer the duke port following dinner, nor any other form of alcohol.

"Torrie?" Monty's voice cut through the thoughts crowding his mind, bearing an intensity which had been previously absent. "Where did you hear that phrase before?"

He rubbed at his temples, his head feeling as if it belonged to another. "From you."

"You remember." There was hope in his friend's voice.

Hope he didn't like hearing, for it would inevitably be dashed. It was the same hope in the eyes of his sister and mother, the same incorrect belief that these small pieces of the past would instantly assemble themselves in his mind, like a shattered vase miraculously repaired. He couldn't be fixed, and he knew it. He was irreparably broken.

"A vague, indistinct recollection, nothing more," he said dismissively. "I don't have my memory back. All I have are tiny shards that occasionally enter my mind, like a dream I've just recalled."

Monty's expression turned guilty. "I wish to God I'd never challenged you to a phaeton race that night. If I hadn't, you'd still be yourself."

"I *am* myself," he countered, for that was another misconception amongst those surrounding him. They missed the man he had been, but he didn't know that man. He couldn't mourn someone he couldn't recall. "And I'd prefer not to think about that night. I've far more pressing concerns facing me than the past."

"Of course," Monty agreed, gesturing to the chair adjacent to his, arranged by the fireplace. "Sit, won't you? I dislike you scowling over me like a wraith. Tell me everything from the beginning. I want to help you."

No one could help him.

And it was the devil of a thing, because everyone thought

they could. From Harriet to Mother, to Monty, and everyone in between.

But Torrie sat anyway, because his back ached, the injuries he'd suffered in the phaeton accident always eager to cause him pain anew. "All I want is for you to keep the governess here until I'm able to procure a special license and marry her. I've caused her enough harm today. Unintentionally, but the damage has been done. She's alone in the world, with nowhere to go and no family to speak of, and she's lost her situation as governess for Worthing after Eugenia dismissed her tonight."

He was responsible for all that. And he had to make amends.

"Presumably the governess has a name?" Monty suggested, inducing another wave of guilt to wash over him.

"I can't recall it," he admitted. "Her surname begins with a *B*, I believe."

Or had it been a *D*?

Never mind. It would change soon enough.

"Did you...ruin her?" Monty asked, his voice sounding stilted and awkward.

"Not truly. What must you think of me?" He shook his head, wishing it would clear the fog remaining within. "Don't answer that. I understand how all this must appear, me bringing a governess to you in the midst of the night and begging you to keep her. The kidnapping. Christ. It was all meant to be an assignation Lady Worthing planned. She wanted me to carry her away and ravish her in my carriage, and I fully intended to do so. Except, I took the wrong woman from the library. In my own defense, it was dark."

"But you *didn't* ravish the governess." An ominous pause. "Did you?"

He glared at his friend, appalled. "Of course, I didn't. I'm not a complete villain. Would I have done so, before?"

"No, never," Monty hastened to say, filling Torrie with some small measure of relief. "I'm merely asking you the difficult questions so that later, when my wife demands answers, I have them to give. Regardless of whether you've truly ruined the governess, considering the circumstances, you can expect gossip."

He smiled thinly. "I doubt any more scandal where I'm concerned could be a hardship. And if Harriet has questions, she might ask them of me. I am her brother, am I not?"

Not that he felt as if he were. He'd been told who everyone in his life was. His family, his friends, his own name. Feeling connected to those people had required a great deal of concerted effort, and in some instances, he had failed dismally. His relationship with his mother remained cool and stilted at best. She was desperate for him to return to his former self, and her determination sparked an answering resentment deep within him.

"She prefers Hattie," Monty reminded him gently.

Yet another piece of the past he had forgotten, and for some reason, his mind refused to think of his sister as her preferred sobriquet instead of her given name of Harriet.

"Hattie," he repeated, newly frustrated over his mind's refusal to completely restore itself. "All she needs to know is that I'll be marrying the governess as soon as I'm able. I'll return in the morning to speak with the both of them about it. At the moment,I think it best if I leave my future wife in peace."

"If there is any peace to be had for her after this night," the duke drawled wryly. "You needn't fear. Hattie will see to our unexpected guest's comfort. You'll be leaving her in excellent hands."

For now, he thought grimly.

Because soon enough, the only hands in which his

governess would be placed were his own. Literally and figuratively.

But he didn't give voice to any of his misgivings. Instead, he nodded. "Thank you, Monty. I owe you a debt of gratitude for allowing me to call at this late hour, bearing a stranger for you to give shelter."

Monty gave him a strange, sad smile. "You've been like a brother to me, and nothing shall change that. Not time, not an accident, and certainly not this evening's antics."

Torrie wished he could return the sentiments, but the duke's words—far from providing the sense of comfort he had no doubt intended—left his chest tight and his gut heavy with dread. The expectations of others, he'd discovered, could eat a man alive.

"Thank you," he forced out, rising from his chair abruptly. "The hour is late, and I should let your household settle. I'll return tomorrow for an interview with the governess, if that is acceptable to you."

"Of course," Monty said, rising as well, still frowning. "You know you're always welcome here at Hamilton House, Torrie."

Perhaps he had been once, but he didn't know that any longer.

Grimly, Torrie took his leave.

"THERE YOU ARE, my dear Miss Brooke," the Duchess of Montrose said, smiling brightly until her gaze traveled over Elizabeth and the serene expression faded to a frown. "Why are you dressed as if you are taking your leave?"

The Duchess of Montrose was as beautiful as she was kind.

Elizabeth found herself newly grateful for the duchess's

hospitality by the gray light of yet another rainy morning. It was difficult to believe that the lovely, soft-spoken woman who was often accompanied by a fat white cat named Sir Toby bore any relation to the handsome scoundrel who had ruined her life the night before.

"Thank you for your hospitality, Your Grace," she said earnestly, her valise held in a tight grip and Lady Andromeda's redingote once again firmly tucked around herself. "I am dressed as if I am taking my leave because I have imposed on you for long enough. I do not know how I shall ever repay you for your generosity."

Particularly since she had scarcely any funds at all, and the meager amount she had would need to be put toward affordable and respectable lodgings for the foreseeable future.

Following a hearty breakfast with the duke and duchess, she had excused herself and retreated to her guest chamber to pack her meager belongings. She'd swallowed her pride enough to accept the bath her hostess had sent to her room that morning, and to partake of the meal since she knew not when or where she might find the next. But she didn't dare linger and take advantage of the duke and duchess for another moment more.

"But you are staying here with us," the duchess protested.

"I don't dare," she countered firmly. "I'll need to find another situation, and the sooner I am able to do so, the better."

"Another situation? Has my brother not told you?"

The mentioning of Lord Torrington made unwanted, traitorous heat creep over her slowly. Her recklessness where he was concerned knew no end, it would seem.

"Has his lordship not told me what, Your Grace?" she asked, confused.

After he had delivered her to the duke and duchess's town

house, Lord Torrington had entrusted her to his sister's care and with an elegant bow, he had promptly disappeared.

The Duchess of Montrose tilted her head, then rolled her lips inward as if she were contemplating her response with care. "Precisely what did Torrie tell you yesterday before he brought you here, Miss Brooke?"

Torrie.

The familiar name, an abbreviation of his title presumably used by those closest to the viscount, suited him. She found herself wondering what Lady Worthing had called him. But a question had been asked in regard to Lord Torrington, and she must attend the conversation of her generous hostess instead of dwelling within her own whirling thoughts.

She pinned a polite smile to her lips. "His lordship told me that he would take me to you for the evening, that he would explain the...unfortunate incident which occurred, and that I wasn't to impose on you for long."

That *was* what he had said, wasn't it? Elizabeth could admit to herself that she had been in an odd state quite removed from her ordinary impenetrable composure. Ever since she had been left orphaned and penniless as a girl when her parents had died in a carriage accident, she had been living at the mercy of others. She wasn't meant to offer a difference of opinion. She was meant to make herself useful, and if she could not be pretty to look upon, and if she could not land herself a match, then she had to seek employment. And as a governess, she was meant to be useful in an entirely different manner. She was meant, rather like a child, to be seen and not heard. She had failed abysmally at that post, thanks to the viscount.

"Did he say nothing of what he intended to do to make amends for what happened?" the duchess was asking of her.

They were stopped near the entry hall, with Elizabeth just

having descended from an elegant bedchamber the likes of which she had never seen, after a night in a bed that had been so deliciously comfortable. A far cry from the cramped quarters afforded her by the Earl and Countess of Worthing. Hardly befitting her station as impromptu, thoroughly uninvited guest.

"I assumed a roof over my head for the evening was what he intended," Elizabeth responded, careful to keep any hint of censure from her voice. "And I am greatly thankful to his lordship and to Your Grace and His Grace for paying me the honor."

It had occurred to her that she might beg the duchess for a letter of recommendation to aid in her quest to find another situation. But she wasn't certain how to broach the subject.

"Paying you the honor?" The Duchess of Montrose laughed incredulously, the sound making the large white cat in her arms stir in protest and offer an indolent meow. Elizabeth thought suddenly of the cat of her youth, her beloved Mince Pie, and her heart gave a pang. "Good heavens, my dear," the duchess added. "You cannot think that after everything that transpired, Torrie would leave you here and do nothing to come to your aid."

"I don't require his lordship's aid," she said simply.

The viscount had done quite enough as it was. And none of it good.

"My brother is an honorable man, Miss Brooke." The duchess shook her head, heaving a small sigh as she scratched the cat's head and the loud sound of purring ensued. "Perhaps, in the haste of the night, he neglected to inform you of everything as he ought to have done. Fortunately, however, he has arrived to pay you a call. He is awaiting you in my salon. Do follow me, my dear."

The viscount was here?

Awaiting her?

The duchess had already turned and was drifting down the hall from where they had come, taking the cat with her. And leaving Elizabeth standing in the hall in her overly large, nearly threadbare redingote and her simple day gown, the heaviness of her valise and heart pulling at her with equal force.

"Miss Brooke?" The duchess paused, peering over her shoulder and offering her a smile of encouragement. "Coming along, if you please. The sooner this matter is settled, the better it shall be for us all."

Elizabeth was more perplexed than ever, and the dread of the unknown awaiting her knotted in her belly. She was keenly aware of the picture she must present. Plain, proper, drab Miss Brooke. Governess in someone else's cast-off clothes. Belonging nowhere and to no one. Wallflower of five failed Seasons, more suitable for scorn than a waltz.

Her fingers tensed on the handle of her valise. She had seen Lord Torrington yesterday in a world of shadows and darkness and candlelight. But she had been suspended in shock and disbelief and fear then. Now, it was daylight. Everything was different.

What did he want from her?

The Duchess of Montrose was continuing blithely on down the hall. And Elizabeth had a choice. She could either leave in a humiliated panic, risking ruining the only possible chance she had to obtain a letter of recommendation from the duchess, or she could follow in her hostess's wake.

One deep breath.

Then another.

Finally, a third.

Elizabeth forced herself to move. Somehow, without truly being aware of her surroundings, she found herself in a cheerful salon, filled with lovely chalk pictures hanging from the wall and gorgeous rosewood furniture and, most eye-catching of all, Viscount Torrington.

Their gazes clashed instantly. Meeting and holding. By the light of day, he was even more handsome than he had been the night before. Without the shadows and darkness obscuring his features, he quite stole her breath. His hair was as dark as the duchess's, a rich shade of ebony that glinted in the sunlight filtering through the windows, and although he was cleanly shaven, the stubble of whiskers shaded his masculine jaw. His eyes were a vibrant Pomona green. His nose and cheekbones were slashing angles. It was as if no time had passed, and she was suddenly an overlooked debutante watching him from her hiding place amidst the potted palms.

Why, oh why, did Viscount Torrington still have to be the most handsome man she had ever beheld?

He bowed. "Madam."

She curtsied, still holding her valise, which was growing heavier by the moment. "My lord."

The Duchess of Montrose turned to the viscount, cradling her cat in her arms, who presided over their odd meeting with sleepy feline eyes. "Shall I remain and act as chaperone, Torrie? I suppose I should, but given what happened last evening…"

Her words trailed away, and Elizabeth felt the sting of embarrassed heat in her cheeks.

"I rather think the damage has been done, Harriet," Lord Torrington told his sister, sounding grim.

With his gaze diverted to the duchess, Elizabeth felt as if she could breathe again. Yes, indeed. The damage had been done. She had lost her situation. She mustn't forget that the viscount's recklessness was the reason.

"Very well. I shall grant you some privacy," the duchess relented.

"There is hardly any need for it," Elizabeth interjected, alarm rising at the prospect of being alone with Lord Torrington.

She still hadn't any inkling why he should wish to speak with her.

But with her protest, the viscount's eyes were once again on her. And the uncomfortable heat that brewed within her at his presence stirred.

"There is every need," he said softly, frowning at her. "Why are you carrying a valise?"

"Because it contains my possessions." Her voice was husky, not her own.

Curse her traitorous body for the effect he had on her.

"I shall leave the two of you to your chat," the Duchess of Montrose intruded with politic calm, giving the cat's fluffy head a scratch.

To Elizabeth's dismay, the duchess took her leave. She watched with a sinking heart and an ever heavier weight of dread lodged behind her breastbone. The door to the salon closed behind her, leaving Elizabeth well and truly alone with Viscount Torrington.

"Put the valise down, if you please."

His voice was deep and sinful and rich, and far too near for comfort. She gave a start as she realized he had moved closer to her during the duchess's escape. His scent of leather, bay, and citrus mocked her.

She didn't obey his request. "Forgive me, my lord, but I fail to understand the need for another meeting between us. Why have you come?"

His brow furrowed, knitting a small line in his forehead. "Is it not apparent?"

"No, my lord. It is not."

Perhaps honesty was the best course. She had no notion of what he was playing at, but she very much desired to be

51

free of his company and the restless yearning that inevitably accompanied it. Why did he insist on further torment?

He came closer, his long-legged strides a trifle stiff, and stopped before her, his countenance stern and yet so sinfully handsome she wished, for a wild moment, to run her fingers through his hair and leave it mussed. Anything to cause an imperfection. To render him less compelling.

"Miss Brown," he said earnestly, "if you would do me the honor of becoming my wife, I would be...pleased."

For the second time in as many days, Viscount Torrington had completely and utterly shocked her. She stared at him, speechless, thinking that she must have misheard. That perhaps she was dreaming, and she would awake in her narrow, uncomfortable bed at the Worthing town house.

She blinked, and no. She was startlingly awake, and Lord Torrington was watching her with the same intent look. He had asked her to marry him. She could not have been more stunned.

Elizabeth had, in the height of her foolish infatuation with the viscount, imagined Lord Torrington offering for her hand many times, and in at least a dozen different ways. But none of them had been in this fashion, the words halting, as if they were poison on his tongue, as he forgot her very surname.

"It is Miss Brooke," she said coldly, astounding herself with her capacity for speech after such a crushing affront.

"Ah, yes, of course." He cleared his throat, twin patches of color painting the sculpted, aristocratic ridges of his cheekbones. "Pray forgive me for misspeaking. Will you marry me, Miss Brooke?"

How desperately she wanted to tell him yes. It was astonishing. Impossible, really, that any lord, let alone this one, would offer for her. Would be willing to marry the governess he had unintentionally compromised the night before. But he did not want to marry her. He hadn't even known her name until she had corrected him.

She was beneath his notice. Beneath his recollection.

"No."

The word fled her lips so swiftly, it surprised him. Elizabeth could see as much in the shift of his expression, the change from awkward, formal invitation—a man resigned to his unwanted fate—to incredulity.

"No?"

"No," she repeated.

Even if it was a mistake, denying him, and even if she was forced to endure some fate beyond her ken, surely anything would be better than forcing this dreadful specter from her past to marry her. To condemn the both of them to a loveless, unhappy union founded on a mistake. He would resent her eternally, and he would find pleasure in the arms of other women, and she would hate him for it.

"You have no home," he said. "No situation. After last night, you will never have another situation. I know the Countess of Worthing well enough to believe she intends to follow through with her threats."

His words were stark. Ominous.

Bitterness rose within her, but she tamped it down, refusing to allow that emotion free rein. "Nonetheless, I will find another situation, my lord. There is no need to offer for me in pity. Even a poor, plain governess such as I must be allowed her pride."

His frown intensified, his entire, august personage rendered austere and forbidding. "No man would ever look upon you and call you plain."

She might have said that he had done so, but he clearly possessed no recollection of ever having crossed her path before last night.

Her stomach curdled, but she forced her chin up, holding his brilliant gaze. "I know I'm no beauty, my lord. I'm a penniless orphan firmly on the shelf, forced to earn her bread. Pray, do not condescend to me. You've done damage enough."

"I have done," he agreed, startling her as he reached out, taking her valise in hand and tugging gently. "Set this down, if you please."

"I'll not," she denied, clinging to it with redoubled effort. "As I said, I'll not accept your pity."

And yet, he refused to let go, the action bringing them closer together than before. Close enough that his warm breath fanned over her lips. He was temptation in a perfectly pristine cravat and spotless Hessians. She wanted to hate him for what he had done, for his carelessness, for his rakish ways, for everything. Yet, a part of her could not.

"It isn't pity which prompts me, Miss Brooke," he said, his voice low and deep, his stare burning into hers, "but guilt. The need to make amends for what I have done."

He was serious, but the realization brought her little joy, even if an old, long-banished part of Elizabeth was sorely tempted to acquiesce. To accept the astonishing turn of Fortune's fickle wheel that would make her the wife of a man she had once longed for desperately.

"You needn't, my lord," she said primly instead.

"I do need." He remained standing in unbearable proximity, his gloved thumb moving over her fingers in a caress that made her heart beat faster.

But no, she didn't dare believe that he would remain steadfast in such a proposal. His reputation was well-known. He was a debauched seducer, a reckless rogue. He was more handsome than any gentleman had a right to be.

Was he in his cups? The sudden suspicion hit her, and she

leaned a bit nearer, inhaling deeply to see if she caught the scent of spirits.

"Are you foxed, my lord?" she asked unkindly.

"I am astonishingly sober."

His thumb moved again, stroking over her knuckles.

"Are you mad?"

It was the only explanation for this morning's bewildering turn of events.

He chuckled softly, but there was precious little mirth in the sound. "Perhaps. But then, aren't we all, just a bit?"

She ran her tongue over her lips, which had gone dry in the course of their unexpected exchange. And his gaze dipped to her mouth, his expression changing, his own lips parting. And she found herself every bit as drawn to that sensual, sinner's mouth as she'd ever been.

Good, sweet heavens above.

"I think that *I* must be mad," she blurted, sounding irritatingly breathless.

Mad because she was considering his offer. Mad because his nearness and his wandering thumb were making her entertain thoughts she hadn't in years. Stupid, imprudent thoughts. Thoughts she had believed herself far too old and wise and world-weary to ever have again.

A small smile turned the corners of his lips up. "Then we shall suit quite nicely."

"I don't think we will suit at all."

"Shall we see?"

Another wicked stroke of his thumb, lingering on her forefinger. There was something ridiculously intimate about the connection, something inherently carnal, and yet it was the simplest of touches.

"We needn't test the notion," she argued, trying to cling to her sense of reason. "You are a lord. I am a governess. We reside in different spheres."

"Let go of the valise," he urged softly, his thumb teasing again.

Elizabeth didn't know why, but she surrendered. She gave in, relinquishing it just as she had the night before when he had spirited her away for the second time, bringing her to the duke and duchess. Solemnly, he deposited the case on the floor at his side.

When he straightened, he bore a look of singular purpose. No man had ever looked at her the way Viscount Torrington was gazing at her now. Heat prickled the back of her neck.

And then, he asked the second-most-longed-for question her former self had dreamed he would one day ask.

"May I kiss you, Miss Brooke?"

Miss Brooke needed coaxing.

That much was apparent.

But it had occurred to Torrie, at some point during their stilted conversation, that Miss Brooke did not harbor a high opinion of herself. Further, that she was quite wrong. She was, by the light of day, far more attractive than the evening's shadows had allowed him to realize. An odd dichotomy, to be sure.

Her mouth was lush and pink and made for kisses, her breasts full and straining against her bodice. Although she was dressed with prim adherence to propriety, the rest of her gown hung oddly from her frame like a sack. She was wearing a dress that had clearly been made for another woman. A much older, much larger woman in everywhere save one. Her hair was covered by an unbecoming cap, and she was shorter than most ladies of his acquaintance.

Equal parts seductress and stern governess. Torrie was desperately intrigued. Suddenly, the thought of sending her away to the country felt like a terrible mistake. There was something about her that drew him.

He wanted to pull off her cap, seduce the starch from her bearing, the severity from her demeanor. He wanted to kiss her and carry her away and peel that dreadful gown off her to see the figure hiding beneath. In the Bedlam of the night, he hadn't allowed himself to fully take note of her. Not truly. But from the moment she had crossed the threshold of his sister's salon, he had been struck by a sudden, forceful attraction. It was palpable, crackling through the air like lightning.

He had won their little battle over the valise. However, he had asked her consent to kiss her, and she was gaping at him as if he had declared his intention to leap out the nearest window. Disbelief crossed her features.

"You haven't answered me," he prompted, taking another step so that there was no distance between them remaining.

Her ugly gown rustled against his trousers, her hems gracing the tops of his boots. She smelled of florals and spring, and his cock twitched to attention.

Her eyes went wide, the rich, brown irises ringed with a fetching circle of gold. Hidden depths, just as he sensed there was far more to Miss Brooke than most others presumed.

"Y-yes," she said, blinking owlishly before hastily continuing. "No. I...I don't know."

She was stammering, a sure sign she wasn't unaffected.

Excellent.

"Yes?" he pressed gently, his hands finding her waist through the shapeless sack, pleased by her hidden curves. She was surprisingly voluptuous beneath the trappings of civility. He found himself deeply attracted to her womanliness, drawn to her in a way he hadn't known with Eugenia. All this time after his accident, and he was still getting acquainted with himself. With his new self, for the old Torrie would never be the same.

From the moment he had regained consciousness after the phaeton accident, waking in his bed in agony, he had been beset by a terrible disinterest. Nothing had intrigued him. No one had moved him. Not even his family, not his friends, not women, although Eugenia and others before her had been pleasant enough bed partners. He'd been seeking distraction every way he could to no avail.

But this stranger in his arms, she felt very intriguing. He thought he could like her. Certainly, he admired her stubbornness, her bravery, her pride in the face of her own ruination and destitution. She was not at all plain, Miss Brooke. He wondered who had ever erroneously told her she was, and then he imagined blackening that stupid clod's eye.

Her tongue flicked over her lips, taunting him. "Yes."

He didn't waste another second in speech. Slowly, lest she change her mind, he angled his head, lowering his mouth to hers. A gentle brush at first. God, her lips were soft and smooth, closed firmly at first. It was the most innocent of kisses, as if she'd never known a man's mouth on hers before.

Torrie found the notion oddly endearing and alluring. Was she truly that inexperienced? She made a breathy sound of need, her lips parting to emit a small puff of air that stirred his already thickening cock. He cupped her cheek, wishing he weren't wearing gloves so that he might enjoy the smoothness of her creamy skin against his palm.

But when he had dressed formally for his call, it hadn't occurred to him that he would be kissing the woman in his arms, let alone that he would wish to. With his lips, he parted hers more fully, his tongue gently teasing until she opened to him. He slid inside, unable to help himself, and tasted the richness of tea she must have taken with her breakfast, along with the sweetness of jam.

Her hands settled on his shoulders at first, and then moved with increasing urgency, exploring his nape above his coat and cravat, her fingers dipping into his hair as she clutched him to her. Such unexpected passion from a woman who appeared to cling to decorum.

Yes, Torrie, thought, they would suit quite well. He hadn't intended to take a wife yet. Not now, not in his present state. However, he knew that after what had happened the night before, and with Eugenia's threats looming, he hadn't a choice. At least they were well matched. She kissed him as if she could devour him, stunning him with her response.

Her lips moved with his and the kiss deepened. It was no longer a chaste brush of one mouth over another. Instead, it was a thorough, steady claiming. But as he held her in his arms, he couldn't say which of them was emerging the victor. Her hands had shifted to his shoulders now, grasping his coat. They fit together almost perfectly, her breasts crushed against him, her hips soft and welcoming.

How right she felt in his arms, how wondrous. Torrie felt as if he were recognizing some new part of himself that had been previously buried. A need he hadn't even been aware had been going unfulfilled. He caressed her jaw, then followed the sleek column of her throat. His other hand glided from her waist to the hollow at the small of her back, pressing her more firmly against him. His hardness burrowed into her softness.

Another sound tore from her, and he swallowed it triumphantly, not ceasing in the sensual onslaught he visited upon her mouth. He would kiss her so thoroughly that she would have no choice but to accept his suit. Nothing less than her agreement would do.

"God's fichu, Torrie."

The Duke of Montrose's voice intruded on their idyll, chasing his ardor.

He tore his mouth from Miss Brooke's and reluctantly stepped away, finding his sister's husband standing at the threshold of the salon, looking equal parts bemused and grim. "Monty," he greeted, finding his voice. "You're intruding."

"At a moment most opportune," the duke countered, his brow raised in comical admonishment.

Torrie didn't remember most of the scrapes he and Monty had found themselves in over the years of their friendship that were lost to him. But he had heard his fair share of tales. He knew that a concern for respectability from the duke was damned hypocritical. But then, this was Monty's house. And he had already ruined the furiously blushing Miss Brooke last night. He hardly needed to do so again.

He cleared his throat, willing his rapidly beating heart to calm itself. "I was attempting to make amends with Miss Brooke for the unfortunate circumstances of the previous evening. You've interrupted before our dialogue has reached a satisfactory conclusion."

"It appeared satisfactory enough to me when I opened the door," Monty drawled, offering no mercy. "Indeed, if the conclusion was any more satisfactory, I shudder to think of the scene I would have walked in upon."

Torrie ground his molars and pinned his friend with a glare. "Have a care for the lady, if you please. Miss Brooke is going to be my wife."

"She is?" Monty asked.

"No, I am not," Miss Brooke said.

"Yes," Torrie answered in the same breath. "She is."

For surely she could see the matter had been settled. There was no question of what must be done. And they most certainly suited. He slanted a look in her direction, finding her cheeks flushed and her lips darkened to a shade of crushed berry from their kisses.

Her brown stare met and held his.

And he quite forgot they were not alone in the room. The urge to kiss her again was stronger than his need for the next breath.

Monty cleared his throat, reminding him they had an unwanted audience. "It would seem the lady is not nearly as convinced as you are, old chap."

Irritation settled over Torrie as he turned back to the duke with a frown of his own. "You seem to forget a similar occasion, when our roles were decidedly reversed."

He was referring to the day he had caught Monty and his sister in a similar embrace during their brief courtship in the wake of his accident. On that occasion, Torrie had been playing the role of protective brother. It would seem that Monty was acting the part for Miss Brooke's benefit. And that irked him, because he wanted to see this matter settled.

"I was a bachelor then," Monty defended, having the grace to look shamefaced at the reminder.

Meanwhile, Miss Brooke was inching closer to her abandoned valise. Torrie caught the motion in his peripheral vision. Blast it, why did the woman insist on being so stubborn? And why had Montrose chosen to interrupt them now?

He was sorely tempted to simply toss Miss Brooke over his shoulder again and carry her away with him. Propriety could go to the devil. As could attempts at quelling the scandal he'd caused.

But he had caused this mess, and he was responsible for resolving it.

"Five minutes more," he told Monty, before reluctantly adding, "if you please."

Monty's lips twitched with suppressed mirth; clearly, the devil in him found this entire tableau amusing. "I'll allow it, but you must know that Hattie will have your hide and mine both if anything untoward occurs. She was most firm in her orders before attending Titus in the nursery."

The mention of his nephew filled Torrie with fondness. The babe made his sister happy, and although many of the years before his accident remained shrouded in mystery, he had slowly forged a new bond with her. Torrie was pleased to see her so settled and contented, and he felt the same for his friend. Could he have the same one day? For the first time, the notion seemed not just possible but almost…pleasant.

"You have my promise as a man of honor," he told Monty, nettled that he needed to do so.

"Five minutes," Monty repeated, his tone bearing all the warning of a protective papa.

Christ.

Miss Brooke didn't have a family. Or a home. And he had just managed to see her dismissed from her situation as governess.

Torrie swallowed hard against a stinging rush of shame as his friend and brother-in-law took his leave from the salon. Miss Brooke was standing behind her valise now, as if it would offer itself up as a shield.

He had five bloody minutes to persuade her that she should marry him. Perhaps if he hadn't confused her surname at the onset, he would have fared better. Still, the kiss ought to have done something.

"Miss Brooke," he tried again. "You must see that the only reasonable solution to your current predicament is marrying me."

She was watching him with wide eyes. "Forgive me, my lord, but it seems far from reasonable or a solution."

"And taking your shabby little valise and leaving here without a roof over your head or a prospective situation does?" he demanded.

Her face fell, and he regretted his hasty words, along with the bite in them.

Torrie moved forward, keeping the valise where it lay between them, allowing her the illusion of safety in a world where he had discovered there was none. He took off his gloves and tucked them inside his coat, offering his bare hands to her, palms up.

"What are you doing, Lord Torrington?"

"Might you not call me Torrie?" he asked. "Everyone who knows me does."

"I do not know you."

"You kissed me. I would say that means you at least know me a bit."

Color rose again in her pale cheeks. "Torrie, then."

He liked the way his name sounded in her prim voice with its slight husk. "Place your hands in mine."

She stared at him solemnly, in the manner he imagined she might regard a stray mongrel, uncertain whether or not she ought to offer her trust. "Why?"

"You'll see." He wiggled his fingers. "Do it."

She heaved a small sigh, but then she relented, placing her hands lightly in his.

And there it was—the sensation. Heat and awareness and something far, far heavier, too. He'd never felt so completely moved by a woman's simple touch before. At least, not that he remembered.

"There," he said slowly. "Do you feel it?"

"Your bare palms against mine?" Her color deepened. "Of course, I do. And it is most unseemly. I cannot think why you would ask it of me."

"To show you that there is something deeper between us. Something more than guilt or pity or necessity. When I kissed you, I felt it. When you place your hands in mine, I feel it, too." With both his thumbs now, he lightly caressed

63

the sinfully soft skin of her inner wrists where she was warm and her pulse beat fast. "Do you feel it, Miss Brooke?"

He wanted to ask her given name, wanted to know it and try it out on his tongue, but he was also cognizant that he had pushed her well beyond her boundaries as it was. And so he didn't press her for another kiss. Nor did he do anything more than allow himself this simple caress. This proximity.

Her body stiffened, her wrists tensing, her supple mouth going taut and pinched with displeasure. "Must you make a mockery of me, my lord?"

Did she think him entirely heartless? Perhaps she did, and Torrie had only himself to blame for her poor opinion of him. But then, what had he done to suggest he was a gentleman, aside from offering to marry her? He had spirited her away in crudest fashion and had cost her the roof over her head. If she'd had a father to demand satisfaction, the fellow likely would have challenged him to pistols at dawn.

"I make no mockery," he hastened to reassure her, keeping his tone as gentle and soothing as possible. "I am in earnest, my dear."

The moment the endearment fled his lips, he wished he could recall the words. She had made her dislike of it known.

"I wish you wouldn't be so kind," she said, her voice low, almost a whisper.

But Torrie wasn't finished. He had more to say, and his time with which he might do so was vanishing by the second. At any moment, Monty would return.

"Everything that happens to us in this life is for a reason," he told her. "I'm in need of a wife eventually, for I require an heir. You're saving me the effort of having to search for someone who would not please me nearly as well as you do."

"How can I please you when you do not know me?"

"I know you well enough."

He knew there was far more to her than she allowed the

world to see. He knew he liked her. She possessed courage, his Miss Brooke. Already, she had intrigued him far more in their short acquaintance than anyone had since his accident.

"I am astonished you believe knowing someone for the span of a frantic carriage ride and one short call is sufficient," she said tartly.

There it was, her stubborn nature returning. Her spine straightened, as if she were receiving a fresh round of courage. And despite his deep appreciation for her spirit, desperation prickled at his neck.

Damn and blast. He'd thought he was winning this latest battle between them.

"I'm afraid we haven't the luxury of more time," he said honestly. "After everything that happened last night, we must make our decision now, with all haste. In scarcely any time at all, the Duke of Montrose is going to return to this salon. I would prefer to have your answer before then."

Proposals without an audience were preferable, he was certain.

And yet, still, she remained hesitant.

She caught her lower lip in her teeth, worrying it. "I thought I had given you my answer already."

"You had. The wrong one."

She sighed heavily. "My lord…"

"Torrie," he supplied. "And you cannot think to tell me that wandering about London, with no home to call your own and scarcely any hope of finding a suitable situation, is preferable to becoming my wife. I am not a poor man, Miss Brooke. I promise to see to your comfort and provide for you. I promise to weather the storm of the scandal I have caused. What more can you wish?"

Miss Brooke hesitated, an emotion he couldn't define flickering over her face. "What more, indeed? My life has been a series of disappointments, and the future you offer me is quite beyond the realms of anything I ever previously imagined possible."

He didn't like the solemnity in her expression. Nor the way she spoke about her life before. He wanted to know how the devil she had ended up where she was, a governess to Eugenia's children, wearing ill-fitting and unbecoming gowns and hiding her hair beneath a cap. He wanted to know why she had been left to provide for herself, why she had no one to protect her. He wanted to know the disappointments she spoke of. But first, he had to rectify the damning wrong he had done her.

"Marry me, Miss Brooke," he repeated, his thumbs traveling over the tracery of veins in her hands.

Such delicacy. She was fine boned and lovely, shapely where it mattered. Having this woman in his bed would not prove a hardship by any means.

The door to the salon opened.

And then, at last, the words he longed to hear fled his wary governess's lips. "Very well, my lord. I shall."

CHAPTER 5

"*H*is lordship asked that a bath be drawn for you, Lady Torrington."

Viscount Torrington was seeing to her comfort. The gesture was a simple one. Likely, by rote. Still, it was…unexpected. It made a strange, fluttery sensation take root within her. One she banished promptly, knowing it was nothing more than utter foolishness to entertain any tender emotions at all toward him.

Elizabeth stared at the fire, merrily crackling in the grate. It was a beautiful, warm fire. Her chamber in the Worthing town house had been without a fireplace, and it had only been when she had been a guest with the Duke and Duchess of Montrose that she had discovered the divine indulgence of being warm. Not even Lady Andromeda, with whom she had been fortunate enough to spend her unsuccessful Seasons, had possessed the financial fortitude for excess fires and candles.

"Will you be bathing now, or would you prefer to wait, my lady?"

At the question from her new lady's maid, she turned to

the servant, blinking twice, then thrice. But still, the girl was standing there, her oval countenance pleasant and polite and eager to please. It was the title, more than the servant, however, that astounded Elizabeth the most.

Lady Torrington.

She was Viscountess Torrington. She had a husband. They had married that morning in a small, private ceremony attended solely by the Duke and Duchess of Montrose. It all felt like a dream from which she would soon wake.

Except, it was real. She had wed the viscount she'd once watched from afar. And yet, there was precious little joy, no sense of happiness to be derived from the fact. For he hadn't married her for any of the reasons her former, naïve self would have wished. It had been, despite his polite arguments to the contrary, a marriage made in pity. An act of contrition for the tremendous scandal that had ensued from that perilous evening, thanks to the Countess of Worthing's vicious tongue.

"My lady?" prompted the lady's maid.

Ah, yes. The tub filled with sweetly scented water, gently steaming across the chamber.

"Now is fine," she said, forcing herself to form words. To act nonchalant, as if marrying the lord she had longed for as a desperate, awkward debutante were a commonplace event.

Her confidence, never strong, faltered, making heat creep up her neck. Why did she make the effort of pretense? It would be plain as Elizabeth herself to anyone that she did not belong here. That Lord Torrington hadn't wanted to marry her. That he had shown her mercy, offering her the trappings of respectability after her colossal fall from grace.

She ought to be swimming in gratitude instead of shame, but she couldn't seem to keep her mind from wandering, worry from swirling. What must the servants think of her? Or anyone else, for that matter? She had met the domestics in a flurry of activity upon her arrival at Torrington House. The viscount's mother, the dowager, had been present as well, just as disapproving as she had been for the days during which Elizabeth's rushed marriage to Lord Torrington had been hastily planned.

She couldn't blame the woman for her lack of enthusiasm at the match. What mother would wish for her son to enter a marriage whilst embroiled in vicious scandal?

"Would you like me to assist you, my lady?" the maid asked brightly.

She hadn't had a servant to attend her so personally. Not ever. The prospect of the younger woman aiding her in her bath was foreign. Elizabeth wasn't sure she could accustom herself to such luxury.

"Not this evening, Culpepper," she said, keeping her voice soft to blunt the sting of her refusal.

She didn't wish to hurt the maid's feelings, nor for her to think she had displeased her in some way. The maid dipped into a curtsy, finished with her tasks, and took her leave from the chamber.

When she had gone, Elizabeth let out the sigh she'd been holding all day. Then, she carefully removed all her garments, took the pins from her hair, and settled in the delicious warmth of the bath. She stared into the flames, contemplating the strangeness of her new circumstances— the impossibility of it all—when a tap sounded at the door. Assuming it was Culpepper returning, she called for her to enter without bothering to send a glance over her shoulder.

The door opened, but it wasn't her new lady's maid's dulcet tones she heard next.

"Forgive me. I hadn't realized you were at your bath."

Instead, it was the deep, low voice of Torrington.

With a gasp, she swirled around in the bath to face him, sending water sloshing over the lip of the tub. She crossed her arms over her chest to shield her nakedness from his view, heart pounding hard. He was dressed simply and intimately in a banyan, his feet bare. And the realization of how little clothing he wore did nothing to calm her body's shocked reaction to his appearance.

"My lord," she said, finding her voice again. "Is something amiss?"

She hadn't expected to see him so soon. He hadn't implied he would visit her this evening. Or ever. Other than his kisses the day he'd persuaded her to marry him, he had been the consummate gentleman. She had convinced herself that his interest that day had been forced, that he had been the practiced seducer, wooing her into agreement out of pity rather than desire.

After all, she knew what he thought of her.

She's a plain, plump little partridge, isn't she?

She had been in such a rush to escape, humiliated by those words, that she had hastened from her hiding place and tripped over her hems, falling with the grace of a downed tree at the viscount's feet.

The humiliating laughter of her fellow guests at Lord and Lady Althorp's ball would forever haunt her. She had scrambled to her feet, ignoring the viscount's offer of assistance, and run to the withdrawing room, her vision blurred by embarrassed tears. She'd never recovered from her mortification.

And all these years later, those words still stung. Not just stung; they were a visceral ache deep inside, the confirmation of her every self-doubt and the sound dashing of all her dreams.

Except somehow, here she was. Ironically, being married to Viscount Torrington had once been her sole aspiration. But not this way. Never as a duty he'd been forced into.

"Nothing is amiss at all," he said calmly. "I merely wanted

to make certain you were pleasantly settled for the evening." His gaze dipped to the bath water for a moment before rising politely to hers again. "It looks as if you are. I must apologize. I didn't intend to intrude on your solitude."

What to say to him? He was her husband now, and he had every right to be here. Every right to watch her bathe, to consummate the marriage if he wished. Her mouth went dry, and to her shame, desire she should no longer feel for him unfurled.

"You needn't apologize," she told him, hating herself for sounding so breathless. For being so affected by him, even with the memory of that dreadful jibe echoing in her mind. "Thank you for arranging for the bath."

That had been kind of him, she reminded herself. And thus far, the calamitous nature of their meeting in the library aside, he had shown himself to be patient and considerate. Hardly the unscrupulous rogue she expected him to be.

"I thought it might be soothing."

He had wanted to please her. To calm her.

The knowledge made her stomach perform an odd little flip. What did it mean?

She couldn't allow herself too much time to consider the question, for she was still naked in the bath, and he was yet hovering on the threshold of their adjoined chambers, flustering her. Making her hotter than the heated bath water was. Perspiration trickled down the back of her neck.

Elizabeth swallowed hard. "That was kind of you, my lord."

"I do wish you would call me Torrie." He flashed her a wry smile that somehow rendered him all the more boyishly charming. "Particularly now that we are wed."

"Torrie," she repeated, acutely aware of how vulnerable she was, scarcely any modesty to save her but her crossed

71

arms and legs and the fact that he remained on the opposite end of the chamber.

"Elizabeth," he responded, her given name in his delightfully rich baritone heightening the sensations already swimming through her. "Is that what you prefer to be called?"

No one had asked the question of her before. Not even Lady Andromeda, who had been, for all her faults, the more generous of the benefactors on whom she had found herself foisted. For a moment, she didn't know how to respond. Everyone called her Elizabeth; more commonly, Miss Brooke. But here was her opportunity to shed both those sobriquets. One because she had married, the other because she could choose it.

And she recalled, quite suddenly and with a painful pang of remembrance, how once, long ago, she had been called Bess. She'd been nothing more than a girl then, head full of hopes that would never come to fruition, with loving parents and a wonderful home and a cat she'd adored, neither of which she had seen in years.

Mince Pie was likely long gone now, just like Mama and Papa.

"Bess," she found herself telling Torrie.

"Bess," he echoed, his smile softening along with his voice.

Becoming even more intimate.

For a wild moment, she forgot that he had married her because of one reckless night when he'd mistaken her for someone else. But then she blinked and remembered, and she heard his voice on that long-ago, terrible day too, calling her a plain, plump partridge. She heard his laughter, the dismissal in his voice, and she wondered how he could not recall her when he had so easily and thoroughly devastated her, crushing her fragile heart to dust. When she could not forget him, nor the stupid, futile feelings she'd once possessed for him, regardless of how hard she tried.

"It suits you," he added, further heightening her inner confusion, "far better than Elizabeth, I think."

She hated that he was making her dredge up memories she'd done her utmost to lock away. The past was where it belonged. Her parents were forever gone, and so too was the girlish hope that a handsome, sought-after lord would ever find her attractive. Would ever willingly marry her.

Elizabeth sank lower in the water, until her chin dipped beneath the surface, wishing she could disappear altogether, terribly aware of his stare, his presence in her chamber, the fact that she was now inextricably tied to him.

Married.

"If you don't mind," she forced out, "I should like to continue my bath."

"Alone?"

Surely he didn't think to join her? The tub was hardly large enough to accommodate two.

"That is how one customarily bathes, is it not?" she asked, her voice emerging more shrilly than she had intended.

But the sharpness of her tone didn't appear to perturb him; he remained where he was, the door to his chamber closed at his broad back. "Why is your lady's maid not attending you?"

"I dismissed her for the evening," she admitted, lest he take the poor woman to task for failing in her duties. "Culpepper was most attentive, but I desired to be alone."

He frowned. "And do you still wish it?"

Tell him yes, she urged herself.

Better yet, politely request that he leave.

"No," she said, astounding herself.

Where had that come from?

"I can assist you," he offered, further surprising her.

"You, my lord?"

"I am your husband, am I not?"

His query stole her breath all over again.

"You are, indeed," she allowed, but oh, how odd it felt, that acknowledgment.

For how could it be? Viscount Torrington, her husband? Not truly hers, she reminded herself, and not without a hint of bitterness. They had not spoken of fidelity, and she knew from experience that he was a rake. Heavens, for all she knew, Lady Worthing was still his mistress. The notion sent a wave of resentment washing over her.

"Your hair is quite long," he said, interrupting her tumultuous thoughts. "A remarkable shade of mahogany. I could wash it for you, if you like."

Did she want him to wash her hair? Her gaze caught on his long, elegant fingers, his large and capable hands. And she longed to feel them on her with a sudden desperation that seized in her chest. But if he drew closer, he would have a full view of her body. Her thick thighs and middle, her bountiful breasts. That was not what she wanted, was it? To remind him of the plump partridge he had married?

"I am unclothed," she said primly.

His lips twitched, as if he found her statement amusing. "I'm aware, Bess. I am doing everything in my power to remain a gentleman and keep my eyes above your shoulders. But it's proving deuced difficult, and more so by the moment."

He wanted to *see* her? Impossible.

And yet, he sounded earnest. There was no mockery in his countenance.

Did she dare accept his offer? Doing so felt dangerous. Having him near, allowing for the possibility he might see more of her beneath the water...

"Do you promise to avert your eyes?" she asked.

This time, he gave her a smile, his sensual mouth curving

in a way that made something inside her melt. "If that's what you wish."

She swallowed against a rush of longing, the likes of which she thought she had lost the ability to feel long ago, the day she'd inadvertently eavesdropped on his vicious assessment of her. "It is."

"Then I shall avert them to the best of my ability."

She was still so keenly aware of her nudity. "Your promise as a gentleman, if you please."

His grin turned wicked. "My dear Bess, as you ought to know by now, I'm no gentleman. But I do offer you my promise, just the same."

And just like that, Viscount Torrington was walking across the Aubusson, headed straight for her.

TORRIE APPROACHED the tub containing his wide-eyed and deliciously naked wife with care. He'd startled her, and that hadn't been his intention. Nor had intruding on her bath. But from the moment he'd opened the door between their chambers to find her all creamy and glistening in the tub he'd requested be delivered to her rooms, he hadn't been able to quell the sudden and ferocious tide of hunger rising within him.

Wife.

He had one now.

It made some instinctive part of him swell with pride and possessive furor.

And seeing her thus made another part of him swell, too.

But that would have to wait, he reminded himself sternly as he reached her side, keeping his eyes carefully pinned to the carpet at his feet instead of feasting upon her curves as he would have preferred. She was hesitant, rather like a spooked horse. He had to proceed with caution if he truly wanted to earn her trust. And after the manner in which they had first met, he owed her that much and more.

The scandal which had ensued had been blistering, thanks in part to Eugenia, who had done her damnedest to spread the gossip of how he had run away with her governess and thoroughly debauched her. Her fury, particularly after discovering he was marrying Miss Brooke and ending their affair as he had promised, had been vicious.

There was a small stool placed beside the tub, likely originally for the lady's maid she had dismissed.

"Bess." He tested her name again, liking the way it sounded, the way it felt. Liking, too that she was here with him. That she was *his*. "I'm going to sit on this stool behind you now."

"Very well," she agreed, her voice husky and soft.

He wanted that voice to call his name when he was deep inside her. He couldn't explain what it was about having a wife that made him so bloody desperate to bed her. Certainly, she was lovely, and what he'd been able to discern of her figure beneath the hideous castoff gowns she'd been wearing was delectable. But it ran far deeper than mere attraction.

Torrie sat, forcing himself to keep his gaze trained on her hair. No hardship, that. It was long and shining with a natural wave to it, so many different shades of brown now that he was nearer, the candlelight shining off burnished hints of gold hidden within. He inhaled slowly, taking in the gentle scent of whatever oils her lady's maid had applied to the water. A blend of rose and lavender, he thought, fingers itching to touch.

"May I?" he asked her, the question a thick rasp laden with suppressed longing.

"Yes."

Her quiet acquiescence was like a fist squeezing his heart. He reached for her, fingers tangling in silken strands. For a moment, he weighed the heavy tresses in his hands, thinking it had been a terrible sin for her to have hidden all this beauty beneath an ugly cap. He didn't recall taking the time to admire a woman's hair before. Proceeding slowly, wooing a woman who was new to the art of lovemaking, was its own pleasure.

She held still as he took note of the elegant column of her throat, the tempting skin at her nape, the pale curves of her shoulders. There was something inherently lovely about a woman's naked back, and somehow, he'd failed to take note. Or, at least he had not done so in recent memory, which was all he had to rely on. The pieces of his past he could recall were few and incomplete. So much of his life was shrouded in mystery and the unforgiving shadows of his mind.

As always, he set that frustration aside, for there was no need to dwell upon that which he could not change.

There was a pitcher conveniently placed on a nearby table. He took it and carefully lowered it to the water, allowing it to fill.

"Tilt your head back, if you please," he instructed, reminding himself yet again that he must not steal a peek. "I'll wet your hair for you."

Wordlessly, she did as he asked, tilting her head back toward him, giving him a view of her smooth forehead and pert little nose. Torrie tipped the pitcher, slowly sluicing water over her hair. There was something about the act of helping her bathe that was so very intimate, and yet tender too. He liked the coziness of the fire licking away in the grate, no one else about save the two of them, no fear of discovery or reprisals.

They were Torrie and Bess, husband and wife.

Soon, he hoped, lovers.

But for this evening, he dared not press his suit. Instead, he thoroughly wetted her hair before taking up some soap and working it through the strands. As he did so, they were both silent, no sound between them save the crackling of the logs in the fireplace, the soft sounds of Bess's breaths, the occasional stirring of water as she shifted to grant him greater access to her scalp. He devoted himself to the task, gently massaging with his fingertips until she rewarded him with a heady sigh of pleasure.

The floral scent of the soap reached him, and he was content to tend to her, lathering, working it through her long, wavy hair. He prolonged the contact as much as he dared, this opportunity to be so close to Bess, touching her as he wished, something to be savored. At last, he forced himself to rinse his hands and dunk the pitcher back into the water, pouring it over her hair again.

He studied her face as he did so, for the manner in which she tilted her head presented him with an excellent vantage point. And regardless of how badly he wanted to peek at her naked breasts beneath the water, he had made a promise to her, and he intended to keep it. She was his now, his to protect, to care for, to introduce to the pleasures of the marriage bed when she was ready for it.

That day couldn't come soon enough.

How lovely she was, her long, dark lashes fanned over her cheeks, her full lips pursed as if she were concentrating on something. She was even more alluring like this, without the primness she tended to cling to as if it were a shield. She was at ease, he thought, and the realization pleased him, for it meant she trusted him.

One more dip of the pitcher, a second thorough rinsing. The silly notion rose within, that he could linger here all night under the pretense of washing her hair, just so he could stay close to her. But no, he wasn't desperate, even if his cock was hard beneath his banyan.

It was suddenly as if all the aimlessness which had been plaguing him since he had awoken after the phaeton crash had been cured. He had a focus now, his life had meaning, a true purpose. He wasn't sure what it all signified just yet, but all Torrie did know was that he felt, to his marrow, at peace. It was a sensation that was entirely foreign. All because of her.

The last of the Winters soap had been cleansed from her hair now, and he had no more excuses to continue touching her. He was sorely tempted to offer his assistance in the remainder of her ablutions, but he suspected he already knew what her answer would be.

"There you are," he said, his voice thick, indicative of how much she affected him. "I'll leave you to the rest of your bath."

"Thank you," she murmured, sinking lower in the water and turning to look at him over her shoulder.

The golden depths in her eyes glittered. She was a woman of secrets and mysteries, continually surprising him with new facets he learned and discovered.

"You're quite welcome, Bess." He wanted to kiss her. Wanted her mouth beneath his again so badly that it was an ache in his chest, fierce and deep, a gnawing craving far stronger than hunger. But he knew it wasn't time for that yet, that she wasn't ready. Her wide eyes and hesitation, her cool reserve, told him so. "Sleep well," he added.

With that, Torrie rose, his cock stiffer than a fire poker, and took his leave from her chamber before he did something that both of them would regret.

CHAPTER 6

*E*lizabeth was greeted at the breakfast table by an unsmiling dowager the next morning, her first full day in her new role as Viscountess Torrington. Her husband was notably absent. Just as he had been for the entirety of their wedding night, aside from when he had visited her and washed her hair.

She stifled the rising disappointment and seated herself, forcing a cheerful smile to her lips in an effort to win over the dour-faced woman already breakfasting.

"Good morning to you, my lady," she offered.

"Indeed," drawled the dowager, her tone icy, countenance uncompromisingly chilly. "There have been mornings far preferable to this one."

Apparently, a night of sleep hadn't done one whit to reconcile the viscount's mother to the notion of her son wedding a mere governess in haste and scandal. Fair enough. Elizabeth had been prepared for such an outcome, although she had been secretly hoping the woman's frigidity toward her would thaw now that her union with the dowager's son had come to fruition. But she had been an unwelcome guest at many homes throughout her life. Why should this one be any different?

The sideboard was laden with an array of tempting foods, the scents wafting to her. Her stomach growled, for she hadn't eaten much the day before, her belly being too twisted with anxiousness over her impending nuptials. Her uneasiness, however, had not relented, even if her appetite had returned. She still had no notion of what to expect from her new life, her new husband, her new home.

A fortnight ago, she had been resigned to her fate, secure in the knowledge that she must spend her life in service to others. That she would have neither husband nor a family of her own.

And now? What did she have? What did her future hold? No more service, certainly. But as to the rest of it? She still had no notion.

Her bed last night had been empty.

Distractedly, she rose again and went to the sideboard, fixing herself a plate. When she had it laden with a mouth-watering assortment, she returned to the table, catching the dowager watching her with a severe frown. Clearly, she did not meet with the august woman's approval in any fashion.

"Where did you find that dreadful gown?" the dowager asked abruptly, her lip curling.

Stiffening, she glanced down at another of Lady Andromeda's castoff gowns. The fit of the bodice was poor; her former sponsor had possessed a far sturdier frame than Elizabeth did.

"It belonged to my chaperone," she admitted, knowing the cut of the gown was also outmoded.

"You must visit a modiste at once," the dowager said, her tone sharp and cutting. "It simply will not do for you to go about London dressed in someone else's old rags."

The gown was hardly what Elizabeth would consider old

rags. Lady Andromeda had never spared expense on her wardrobe. At least, not years ago when the gown in question had likely been commissioned. Her pockets had been far more flush then, a fact which Elizabeth suspected had far more to do with Lady Andromeda's love of cards than she had cared to admit.

"My gown is not ragged," she defended quietly, not wishing to quarrel with Lady Torrington. However, she could not help but to feel as if she needed to find firm footing with her husband's mother, or pay the price for the duration of her marriage.

"It's not becoming," the dowager insisted, unimpressed. "A lady of pale complexion and dark coloring should never wear shades of yellow."

Elizabeth longed to inform Torrington's mother that when a lady hadn't any funds of her own, she had been more than happy to wear whatever she had been given, regardless of style or color. But despite her vexation with the woman, she truly did want to have a friend here at Torrington House in this terrifying new world she'd found herself trapped in. Without the kindly Duchess of Montrose about, Elizabeth was undeniably adrift.

Instead, she forced another smile, hoping to melt some of the dowager's ice with her own warmth. "Thank you for your counsel, my lady."

The older woman's nostrils flared in irritation, but she returned her attention to her own plate, directing her next criticism to her hothouse pineapple. "I'll arrange for a modiste. Madame Beauchamp possesses the keenest eye in Town. Bad enough Torrington married a governess. I'll not have it said that she is dowdy as well."

Elizabeth wondered whose reputation the dowager was more concerned with—her own, or her son's. She had a suspicion it was the former rather than the latter, and that the viscountess did not wish to be associated with an ill-dressed governess who had been compromised.

Dowdy. The insult should not have stung; after all, she had been called far worse by the dowager's own son.

It would seem that although time had passed, she could never entirely outrun all her demons and lack of confidence.

She inhaled sharply, old pain merging with new, and then stabbed her breakfast with more force than was necessary.

Lady Torrington dismissed a footman who was attending the breakfast room, leaving the two of them alone. Alarm crept over Elizabeth at the realization. For she very much feared that no good could come of a private audience between herself and the dowager.

"Tell me," drawled the older woman the moment they were alone, proving her correct. "How carefully did you plan my son's entrapment?"

So great was her shock at the question and the barb inherent in the dowager's voice, Elizabeth's fork clattered to the plate, the sound echoing through the stillness of the breakfast room.

"His entrapment?" she repeated.

"Pray, Miss Brooke, do not attempt to dissemble with me. I know you have always harbored a *tendre* for my son. I watched you pining for him from across ballrooms for years."

Dear heavens. She had? Elizabeth had not supposed anyone had ever noticed her marked interest in the viscount. Not even Lady Andromeda, who had been sharp-eyed as a bird of prey, had spoken a word to her of it.

Shame made her ears and cheeks go hot as she forced herself to meet the dowager's questioning stare, and she was sure she was flushing.

"I'm afraid I know not what you speak of, my lady," she said feebly, ever aware that she was a dreadful liar.

Even to her own ears, her voice was unnaturally high-pitched. Her denial sounded all wrong. Because it *was* wrong, and she was lying.

She had loved Viscount Torrington from afar for years, and he had never taken note of her, other than to callously dismiss her. Not one dance, never an introduction, not a word uttered between them. And oh, how devastated she had been by that.

The dowager gave a bitter little laugh, tucking down her chin to pin Elizabeth with a knowing glare. "You're lying. Torrington may not remember the foolish way you mooned over him for your disastrous Seasons, but I do. It is hardly his fault, what with the amnesia he has suffered following his phaeton accident. But *I* know, Miss Brooke. Rest assured that I know you for the conniving jade you are."

Amnesia following his phaeton accident?

The bitter rancor in the other woman's voice, along with her vicious accusations, was lost on Elizabeth. Her mind seized, shock washing over her.

"Do you mean to tell me that his lordship has lost his memory?" she asked, the possibility seeming so vastly unlikely, terrifying almost.

And yet, entirely possible. She thought of some of the cryptic words he'd said, the way he couldn't remember her at all. Of course, she had believed herself so forgettable, the plain, plump girl he'd never noticed. What if, however, there was another reason? Another reason for his kindness, his kiss, his intimations he found her—the partridge he'd scorned—attractive?

The dowager's mouth fell open, and it was plain that she was shocked by Elizabeth's question. "Of course he has lost his memory. It is the only reason, I dare say, why he would so lower himself to marry you. If he had any recollection of

84

how desperately you set your cap at him, he never would have fallen into your trap."

Those words hurt, and she couldn't deny it, but she was still fixated on this monumental revelation. For it changed everything. If Lord Torrington seemed as if he was not the same man who had mocked her appearance, that was because he didn't remember the man he'd been. It was as if he were a different person.

"There was no trap, my lady," she managed. "I don't know what his lordship told you of the incident, but I wasn't at fault for anything that occurred on the evening in question."

No, indeed. The entire affair had been Torrie's doing, from the moment he had bound her, gagged her, and carried away the wrong woman into the night. But surely he hadn't told his mother that she had orchestrated some manner of plot. Had he?

"You may deny it all you like, and I'm certain my son's lack of memory has made him vulnerable to your scheming. However, I know the truth."

It was plain that no amount of protest on her part would persuade the dowager that Elizabeth was innocent of the charges she made against her. However, at the moment, she was far less concerned with Lady Torrington's opinion of her than with the revelations she had made about her son.

"He truly has no memory of what happened before his accident?" she asked, forgetting about her hunger, her breakfast lying abandoned and cooling on her plate.

"Do you mean to suggest you didn't know?" her ladyship asked, disbelief coloring her tone.

"Lord Torrington—Torrie—didn't tell me," she admitted, wondering at his omission.

Perhaps he believed it didn't matter. Or mayhap he was embarrassed by his lack of memory.

Once again, the dowager's nostrils flared, this time her

eyes narrowing in accompaniment. "You'll not repeat a word of it beyond these walls, or you will have me to answer to. I may not have been able to stop this abomination of a wedding, but do not believe for a moment that I'll not do everything I must to protect myself and my son."

There it was again, the dowager's concern for herself, which seemed to overshadow any feelings of protection she bore for the viscount. It occurred to Elizabeth with stunning clarity that the viscountess likely considered her a challenge. Perhaps she was concerned that Elizabeth would usurp her place in the household or in her son's heart. But neither of those would be the case.

"You needn't fear I would ever do anything to harm his lordship," she reassured the dowager now, all too aware of the other woman's icy glare. "I'll not speak of his private matters to anyone else."

"His lordship is sensitive about the accident and he doesn't prefer to speak of it," the dowager continued, voice still frosty as her glare. "That is why I didn't relay my fears to him when he announced his intention to make this dreadful mesalliance with you. But know this, Miss Brooke. I will be watching you. I don't trust you or your motives, and I don't believe a word of your protestations of innocence. Do you have any notion how many debutantes and widows have thrown their caps at him? He could have had his pick of any of the ladies in London, and instead he is saddled with you."

Belatedly, she realized that the dowager was continuing to refer to her as *Miss Brooke*. She might have at least tried her given name, but likely, the slight was intentional and not inadvertent.

With that grim pronouncement, Lady Torrington rose from her chair, sweeping to her feet with the grace of a lady who had weathered the storm of society for decades. "I've had enough breakfast this morning. I do think I shall retire to my chamber."

Elizabeth stared after the viscountess's retreating form, the venom which had been directed at her leaving her unable to form a response. The door slammed loudly, and then she was seated alone at the breakfast table, a fine spread of food and cutlery laid out before her. The ensuing silence was as mocking as it was deafening.

She couldn't eat another bite.

She hadn't anticipated a warm welcome at Torrington House, but neither had she expected such an attack. Nor to be accused of having orchestrated her marriage when the only mistake she had made was to be in the earl's library when she ought to have been abed. For that trespass, she had paid dearly, both with her situation and her reputation.

And now, despite her marriage, it would seem she was even more alone than she had been before. And married to a man who was, in every sense, a stranger to her. A man who had no recollection of the past.

Questions and misgiving swirled, one rising above all the rest to prominence. What would happen if Torrie's memory returned to him?

TORRIE RETURNED HOME that morning from Winter's Boxing Academy tired, sore, and irritable. Decidedly not in the mood for an interview with his mother, who it seemed was waiting for the moment he set foot in the entry hall to spring out at him and demand an audience. Was it wrong of him to have hoped it would have been Bess instead, eagerly awaiting his return?

Yes, likely it was. He had stolen a governess, ruined her, married her, and now he very badly wanted nothing more than to debauch her whilst the rest of London went to the devil.

"Madam," he addressed his mother formally, handing off his coat, hat, gloves, and walking stick, for it still felt strange to call her Mama as Harriet did. For his mind remained eerily bereft of memories of his former relationship with the woman who had given him life. "What is amiss?"

His mother cast a pointed glance toward the butler, Oswald, and the footman who had gathered at his return. "In private, Torrington, if you please. I require no more than a moment of your time."

Judging from experience, that meant his mother wanted to chatter on about inanities for the better part of an hour. Always the need for an heir, an exhortation to attend this or that ball or musicale. A reminder that she expected him to do his duty and make certain no dastardly country booby cousin would inherit the title and cast her from the comfort of her home. The suggestion he court Lady Althorp's eldest daughter.

His back ached from his exertions, his head felt as if it were laden with cobwebs, he was thirstier than a horse in the desert, and the gnawing desire to see his wife again was stronger than any of those bodily complaints and needs.

Wife.

He rather liked the sound of that word, the possessive surge that accompanied it. Better, he was finding, than *mistress*. Here was a woman who was entirely his. Not an experienced, eager seductress as Eugenia had been, it was true, but there was something strangely enticing about claiming Bess.

He sighed as he took in his mother's fretting countenance. "Can it not wait, my lady?"

"You have been asking me to wait for nearly a week, my lord," she reminded him tightly.

Twin patches of color bloomed on her cheeks, a sign he had come to understand meant she was displeased. He often wondered at the mother-son bond they may or may not have shared before his accident. He found her difficult to know, not nearly as kindhearted as Harriet, nor as generous. She spoke of his father with anger, blaming his every fault for Torrie's own sins, and he disliked that as well. Perhaps her hatred of his father, who he'd been told had been dead for some time now, hadn't bothered him before. It was entirely possible that he hadn't cared for his father either.

But it was the damnedest thing, not being able to remember. Not knowing. Sometimes, he hated it.

"Very well," he allowed at last. "To the morning room, I should think. That is your preferred chamber, is it not?"

"It is." Her expression softened. "You remember?"

"You've told me so," he corrected gently, also loathing the weight of everyone's hopes on him.

All those who knew the old Torrie wanted him to recall the facets of his past, the man he'd been, the life he'd led. They wanted him to be the same. But that could never be. He could no more heal his damaged mind than harness a cloud and ride it to the moon.

"Of course," she said, her voice disappointed, expression crestfallen.

He despised that look, loathed knowing he was the source of her frustration. That something which was beyond his control and ken was ruling his life all this time after the brutal phaeton accident which had nearly claimed his life. It wasn't enough that he had somehow lived. No, everyone wanted the man he'd been to return.

Chest heavy with dread, another sensation coiled within him like a snake about to strike, he led his mother to the morning room. When they were within, he waited for her to seat herself at her favored chair and then sat as well.

She appeared ruffled. Distracted. Upset.

"What has happened that requires an urgent audience with me when I've only just returned?" he asked, trying to keep his frustration from his voice.

"You are always so curt with me, Torrington," she said, hurt in her tone. "As if I am an inconvenience to you. Nothing more than a stranger requesting your time and attention. Will you not call me Mama as you did before?"

He tried to form the word, to please her, but could not. The woman before him, who he could admit bore some resemblance to him, still felt like a stranger.

"I…" He hesitated, not wishing to cause further pain to her, and yet unable to claim a familial connection he didn't feel. It was impossible to explain to others, but he felt as if he were an entirely different person. "I'm sorry," he added stiffly.

Her face fell, but she nodded. "Of course. Forgive me for asking. I should not have done so. I don't know what came over me. After the last time you refused, I promised myself I would be more understanding."

The last time she had asked had been mere days ago. Her patience was perilously thin.

"You long for me to be him," he said, feeling odd for referring to his former self as if he spoke of someone else, and yet that was precisely how it felt to him. The old Torrie was a stranger. Someone he had never met and didn't know. A ghost who haunted him at every turn. "I wish I could be him, but I cannot."

The viscountess sighed, the sound weary. "As do I, and never more so than now. I fear that you've made a grave mistake in marrying Miss Brooke."

His mother had attempted to discuss the matter of his hasty nuptials with him prior to the wedding, but he hadn't allowed it. He'd had no wish to delve into the sordid details

90

of precisely how and why he'd ruined his new wife. Nor would the discussion have proven beneficial; he'd already accepted that he had to marry Bess. And now, he couldn't say he was dismayed by the union. He was looking forward to consummating it as soon as she would allow.

"You needn't concern yourself with my marriage," he told the viscountess as gently as he was able.

Her meddling in his affairs was as tiresome as Monty's inventive cursing.

"I'm afraid I must, because you do not see her as I do," his mother continued, fretting with the fall of her morning gown, her white muslin cap vibrating in her agitation. "If only you remembered. Her Seasons were disastrous, and no man would have her."

"You know her," he said, the realization hitting him for the first time.

"I know *of* her," his mother said, her voice frosty. "I wouldn't presume to know her. However, I do know how she grasped above herself, trying to make you notice her in the past. She failed, of course. She made a fool of herself over you, and now she has schemed and plotted to leave you with no choice but to enter this mesalliance."

Bess *knew* him? Torrie's spine went stiff, the impact of his mother's suggestion like a physical blow.

This was news. She'd said nothing of the past. Had given no indication that they had previously been acquainted.

"I don't understand," he forced out. "Please explain yourself, madam."

"You cannot believe it was unplanned, her ruination. She is an avaricious jade who plotted her way out of a life as a governess and always wanted to marry you." His mother paused, her lip curling as she continued her unkind assault on his new wife. "Oh, Torrington. Do you not recall? She threw herself at your feet at the Althorp ball, so great was her desperation."

The Bess he knew was too prideful to throw herself at anyone's feet, and least of all his. None of what his mother had said made one whit of sense. He inhaled deeply, struggling to dredge up any old memories he could, but it was futile. He had no recollection of that part of his past.

"I must insist you refrain from speaking poorly of my wife," he said, striving for a politic tone he little felt. "Regardless of your opinion of her, or whatever past we may have shared, nothing can change what has been done. We are married, irrevocably so."

His mother's shoulders drew back, surprise evident in her expression. "You would defend her to me? I cannot believe it of you, Torrington."

Why did his mother dislike his new wife so ferociously? And just how well did he and Bess know each other? Questions loomed, making his head ache.

"I've kept the true nature of her ruination from you out of regard for your sensibilities," he explained to his mother. "But trust me when I tell you that the fault for this scandal and my ensuing marriage is all mine. Bess is innocent of any scheming. She couldn't have known what would happen that night, and nor could anyone."

Still, he couldn't help but to wonder what had passed between them, the incidents to which his mother referred. The past and its indistinct memories taunted him, always beyond his reach. One matter, however, was abundantly clear.

He needed to speak with Bess at once.

CHAPTER 7

*E*lizabeth was investigating the library at Torrington House, searching for a volume of poetry or anything with which to distract herself, when her husband's deep voice interrupted her solitude.

"Bess."

The name of her youth made a pleasant glow suffuse her.

She turned to find him striding toward her, dressed informally, and curtsied. "My lord." He looked troubled, she thought, his expression pinched, his jaw hard. "Is something wrong? Have I overstepped? I hoped you wouldn't mind if I searched for a book with which to distract myself."

Navigating the course of her new life was treacherous indeed. Particularly given the ugliness of her interaction with the dowager at breakfast. She didn't know what was expected of her, where she was meant to be, what she was meant to do. She felt like an unwanted guest.

He drew to a halt as he reached her, near enough to touch, his green eyes searching hers. "You're more than welcome to be in the library whenever you wish it. This is your home now."

Her home.

The word and the sentiment settled over her. She hadn't had a true home in years. How impossible it seemed that she would finally belong somewhere, instead of being passed between distant relatives, sometimes treated worse than a servant, and later taking a position to secure the roof over her head.

"Thank you," she said, biting her lip against a stinging rush of emotion.

Tears welled in her eyes, and she blinked furiously, intent on keeping them from falling. She had already humiliated herself before Viscount Torrington on enough occasions. No need to do so now, she told herself sternly.

"Tears?" He surprised her by cupping her face in his hands and gently using his thumbs to sweep over her lower lashes. "Why, Bess?"

Dear heavens, she had no wish to unburden herself, and she had long since believed she had banished such inconvenient emotion, burying it so deeply inside herself that it would never again be unleashed. How wrong she had been, and about a great many things, too.

"I haven't had a true home for a long time," she admitted, her voice cracking on the last word. "To have one now is a source of amazement."

She expected him to withdraw, but he did not. Instead, he remained as he was, the warmth and strength of his hands seeping into her.

His brilliant gaze locked on hers. "Tell me, Bess. Did we know each other before that night in the library?"

His question took her by surprise. He had never spoken of his accident or amnesia before, and she couldn't help but to wonder at the reason for doing so now. Had the dowager spoken with him about their uncomfortable interaction at the breakfast table? Her shoulders tensed at the possibility, for what if he believed his mother's suspicions?

"We were never introduced," she said.

He released her, a muscle in his jaw ticking. "Explain, if you please."

She huffed out a small breath, filled with trepidation, the same old shame that had sent her from the Althorp ballroom years ago revisiting her. "Might I ask what the meaning of this is?"

"I don't have any memory of knowing you." He raked his fingers through his dark hair, looking weary. "I should have told you before now, but it is a subject which is painful for me and I don't like to speak of it. I was badly injured in a phaeton accident, and I don't remember much of my past. All I know is that there was a man who existed before the accident, and I am the man who woke up. That other man is a stranger to me. His thoughts, his memories, his family and friends...they've never felt like mine."

His raw honesty made her long to take him in her arms, but she didn't dare. Instead, she kept her hands carefully clasped at her waist. And oh, how her heart ached for him, at the pain he must have experienced. What must it be like to recall nothing of one's past? Neither family nor friends?

"I am so very sorry," she said softly. "It must be incredibly difficult for you."

A wry, half smile curved his lips. "It's far more difficult for others than it is for me. I cannot mourn what I don't miss."

His calm acceptance was humbling, and she knew she owed him the truth, even at the risk that it would force old emotions long buried to the surface.

"We weren't formally introduced," she elaborated, "but I knew of you. We attended several of the same society balls together. We traveled in different sets, however. You were handsome and sought after, and I was a dowdy country girl come to London to find a husband."

His brow furrowed. "What happened between us?"

"Nothing," Elizabeth admitted, her cheeks going hot as her mind returned to that brutally humiliating evening at the Althorp ball. "The extent of our interaction was when I was hidden in a potted plant and I overheard you telling some of your friends that I was a plump, plain partridge. I was so embarrassed that I attempted to rush from the ballroom and instead tripped over my hems and fell at your feet. You offered to help me, but I was too humiliated to accept, and I spent the remainder of the night hiding in the lady's withdrawing room until my cousin Lady Andromeda found me and took me home."

There it was, the brutal, hideous, mortifying truth. A truth she'd hoped never to have to relive.

"My God." Torrington was staring at her, his expression inscrutable, passing a hand over his rigid jaw. "I said that?"

She rolled her lips inward and dropped her gaze to the patterns on the Aubusson. "Yes."

"Bess, I'm sorry."

Of all the words he might have spoken, those three were the least she'd expected. His contrition warmed her. Chased some of her embarrassment. Wrapped itself around her heart like a fist.

"You needn't apologize," she hastened to say, jerking her eyes up from the carpets to find him watching her intently. "It happened years ago."

"I do need to," he countered, taking another step closer, so that there was scarcely any distance at all separating them. "I hurt you, and I'm sorry for it."

She swallowed hard against a new rush of emotion, needing to look away from his handsome, earnest countenance.

She focused on a place over his left shoulder, a picture hanging on the wall. "As I said, it was long ago. I'd prefer not to speak of it further."

But the memory of flying to the hard floor at his feet would never leave her. Nor the bursts of laughter from the other revelers which had trailed her to the withdrawing room.

"Bess." Once again, his big, warm hand cupped her cheek. "Look at me."

He was being so kind. So tender. And it was difficult indeed to gird her heart against this version of himself, this inexplicably new Viscount Torrington. But there had been shades of the old rogue in him, hadn't there been? After all, he had been attempting an assignation with his mistress when he had taken her from the library instead. She mustn't forget that, nor allow her old feelings for him to be resurrected. She couldn't bear to be so vulnerable.

"Please," he added softly, and that lone exhortation broke her resolve.

She looked at him, and what she saw in his expression stole her breath and made her heart beat faster. Made molten heat glide through her and longing blossom to life.

"I cannot make excuses for the man I was, but I can promise you that I'm nothing like him. Do you know how I would describe you now?"

She certainly knew how she would describe herself.

Foolish. Weak. Far too generously curved in all the wrong places. Thick-waisted and big-hipped. Her nose too pointy, her mouth too large, her eyes a nondescript shade of brown, the same as her hair. And she was short. Vexingly so. Unfashionably so.

"I'll tell you," he continued when she didn't offer a response. "I would describe you as resilient and strong. Beautiful in a way I've never seen in another woman, with the figure of a Venus hiding beneath your gowns. Tempting and lovely and filled with mysteries I dearly long to solve. A woman I very much want to kiss."

And yet again, she could not seem to find either her wits or her tongue. He'd rendered her speechless. He wanted to kiss her? He thought she was beautiful and tempting and lovely?

Perhaps he felt guilty, knowing that she'd overheard his unkind description of her. Yes, that had to be the answer. She hadn't had a single suitor in five Seasons, and she knew quite well that a beautiful woman would have had her share of beaus to choose from instead of none, even with her lack of dowry. But oh, how she had wanted to believe his kind words, even if for just a moment.

She took a step in retreat, breaking his hold on her, her cheek feeling oddly bereft when his hand was no longer touching her skin. "You needn't flatter me, my lord."

A self-deprecating smile curved his sinful lips. "I'm not flattering you, Bess. I'm telling you the truth."

"Please don't feel as if you must somehow atone for what was said so long ago. Years have passed, and I've mostly forgotten it." Elizabeth forced herself to laugh lightly. "Besides, I'm more than aware of my appearance, my lord."

"Apparently not, because if you were, you'd know I'm right."

The confidence in his voice gave her pause. He didn't sound as if he were lying to appease her. He didn't look like a man trying to assuage his own guilt. Rather, he appeared genuine, his eyes burning with fierce intensity. And the way he had touched her, the way he had kissed her before. She could almost dare to believe him.

"I wish you would forget about what happened," she told him quietly. "It hardly signifies any longer."

But that was a lie. It did matter. To her. It always had. Just as *he* always had, from the moment she had first seen him waltzing with another beneath the glittering chandeliers. She had done everything in her power to banish the old yearning, to force herself to accept that all the times their gazes had clashed across a crowded room, she had been the only one of the two of them so moved.

"But it does," he countered. "I wish you would have mentioned it."

She unclasped her hands, and needing something to do with them, dug her fingers into the voluminous muslin of her morning gown instead. "Some things are best forgotten."

The moment the words left her, she wished she could recall them.

"Pray forgive me," she hastened to say. "I didn't intend to sound so flippant about a matter that must weigh on you each day. I cannot imagine how difficult it is for you, not being able to remember."

His countenance changed, his expression softening, the look he wore laden with such tenderness that it made something inside her melt. "Bess?"

"Yes?"

"I need to kiss you now."

Her heart thudded. Heat pooled in her belly. Her body's reaction to his declaration was instant.

Her fingers twisted in the soft, worn muslin. "You do?"

He nodded, moving forward. One step. Two. Until their bodies were nearly flush, her breasts just grazing his hard frame, his scent enveloping her, the heat from him emanating, almost burning her.

"I do. May I?"

Her breath caught. Here was the moment where she ought to remember who she was and who he was. To recall that, regardless of the kindness he was showing her now, he had once been the source of so much pain and shame. She should tell him *no* and return to the safety and loneliness of her chamber.

"Yes," she whispered instead.

HE WAS GOING to kiss away the pain she'd suffered. Kiss her until they both forgot about the man he'd been before, and there was nothing and no one between them. Until they were Torrie and Bess, husband and wife, no complicated past to burden them. He hadn't known how much her feelings mattered to him, nor how badly he had hurt her before, until he'd heard the humiliation in her voice as she described overhearing him calling her a plain, plump partridge.

Christ, what a bastard his former self had been.

Slowly, he reached for her, drawing her into the circle of his arms, pulling her into him. The heavy fullness of her breasts crushed into him, and her hips were soft and tempting as they molded to his body. His cock was already hard, springing against the fall of his trousers and jutting into her belly.

"What's about to happen isn't about him," he said, before elaborating, "the man I was. It's about us. Do you believe me?"

Torrie needed to know. Needed her to understand. He had been right when he had thought that someone had made her feel undesirable. But he hadn't known it had been him. He wished he could plant a facer on his former self. Because there was nothing about the woman in his arms that was plain or unpleasing. How the devil had he ever supposed he was going to send her off to his country seat and never think of her again?

"I…" she began, then faltered, catching her lower lip in her teeth, her expression turning worried.

He was damned glad his mother had told him what she had; though her revelations had decidedly had the opposite of their intended effect. Anyone who could believe Bess capable of scheming to force him into marriage had never taken the opportunity to get to know her.

"Believe me," he urged her. "I'm not the same man I was. I haven't his memories. I haven't his personality, so I'm told. I'm different now, a new man. My mind may be broken, but I would never hurt you that way again. This, I vow to you."

He wanted her trust. But also, he wanted her to believe in herself. To know the effect she had on him—the effect she'd have on any man if she'd but give them half the chance to show her. And thank heavens she hadn't, because now she was his.

"I believe you," she said, her gold-brown gaze burning into his.

He could read the depth of her sincerity in her eyes. With careful deliberation, one of his hands moved to the small of her back, splayed and resting in the hollow there. Anchoring her to him.

"You are nothing short of lovely to me," he added, because she was, and he wanted her to know that. He wanted her to carry herself with the confidence she deserved.

"My lord," she protested.

But he was done with her refusal to believe him. He would show her with actions instead of words. The time for speaking was done.

"Torrie," he reminded her. "I'm your husband now, and you're my wife."

Her lips parted. Her pupils went rounder. Her hands, which had been wringing her skirts when he had taken her into his embrace, had found their way to his shoulders.

Bess's head tipped back. And there was her mouth, the

ripe-berry lips he had been yearning to take from the moment they'd spoken their vows.

He bent, inhaling her sweet scent as he did so. Taking his time even as he longed to devour her. A soft sound fled her, surrender or anticipation—he couldn't be sure. But he held her gaze until the last moment, when their lips touched, and he allowed himself to close his eyes and savor the lushness of her mouth beneath his. This kiss seemed to matter more than any he'd ever given, those he could remember and certainly every one that had been lost to him.

Because he'd never had a wife before.

For the man he had once been and for the man he was now, there was only one woman he could truly call his own. Bess was his. And she was responding, her lips moving against his tentatively at first, and then with greater enthusiasm. Until suddenly, it was as if a dam inside her had burst, and a waterfall of passion broke free. Her arms twined around his neck and she rose on her toes to press herself more fully against him, all her beautiful curves melding into his hardness.

He teased her lips open, and then pushed into the lush wetness of her mouth with his tongue, tasting her. Tea laced with sugar. Sweeter than before, even. God. He couldn't get enough.

A growl tore from him as he angled his mouth over hers, deepening the kiss, plundering her mouth. Showing her with his tongue and lips and teeth just how badly he wanted her. Everything he wanted to do to her. How thoroughly he wanted to claim her.

Another needy sound, and now her fingers were tangled in his hair, fingertips dancing over him in tantalizing touches, nails scraping against his scalp. Her tongue writhed against his, wet and smooth and greedy, as she consumed him too, kissing him with a carnal abandon that took him over the edge.

He hadn't intended for the kiss to progress to anything more, but now that their mouths were fused, his ability to control himself dissolved. He moved them as one, Torrie forward and Bess backward, until he had her pinned against a wall of bookshelves. And then he thoroughly devoured her some more.

But he couldn't stop at her lips. He buried his face in her throat, kissing the silken smoothness, finding her pulse beating hard and fast, just like his. Good. She desired him, too. He wanted her with a ferocity that startled him. Had his hips moving into hers, pressing his length against her softness. And still, it wasn't enough.

Had he thought to woo her? To slowly seduce her?

It seemed the worst idea he had ever had by the light of day, with her pliant and warm in his arms, her abundant breasts a delicious torment as they spilled into him. He sucked on her throat, his need for more of her bare skin thwarted by her prim decolletage. He would give his left arm right now to peel her gown and suck on her nipples.

Lifting his head, he gazed down at her, pleased by the way her lips were plump and swollen from his kisses. Pleased, too, by the glazed look in her eyes. But none of these small triumphs were sufficient. Nothing, short of burying his cock deep inside her, would be. He needed her more than he needed air to breathe.

"Come to bed with me," he said. "Let me show you how desirable you are."

"Torrie."

Her voice was a husky blend of desire and prim censure, and he loved it. He couldn't tell if she was protesting or acquiescing. But in the next moment, her response failed to matter, for the door to the library opened, and the voice of Harriet intruded on the fog of lust clouding his mind.

"Torrie, Mama said you were... Oh dear! Forgive me. I hadn't realized you were... Perhaps I ought to just go."

Grinding his molars, he turned to his sister, taking care to shield the flushed and thoroughly ravished Bess. Not that Harriet would gossip, and nor did he believe she would disapprove, but he was stunningly protective of his wife after what he had just learned.

And the irony in that was he was the bastard who had hurt her. He hated the man he'd been for that. Hated the absence of so many memories that forever plagued him.

"Harriet," he greeted, attempting to keep the irritation at her untimely intrusion from his voice. "I hadn't expected you to pay a call."

His sister's eyes were wide. "Of course you didn't. I should have sent word. I'm desperately sorry. I merely thought to see how Elizabeth is settling in here at Torrington House."

He raised a brow. "As well as can be expected."

She would have been settling in even better if he'd had five minutes more to persuade her to join him in his bedchamber. But that wasn't the sort of comment a gentleman made to his sister, so Torrie kept it to himself, even as he struggled to rein in his overwhelming desire for his new wife.

"It is kind of you to pay me a call," Bess said, moving to stand at his side, looking as if she had been ravished.

He would have preferred to make her even more flushed and rumpled. To get her out of that travesty of a gown and have her naked in his bed.

Who would have thought he would be this enamored of his unexpected wife? Certainly not the Torrie of several days ago. But then, no one knew how quickly everything could change better than he did.

Harriet smiled wryly. "The next time I decide to call on you on a whim, I'll be certain I'm not intruding."

"You could never intrude," Bess insisted politely.

"Yes," Torrie growled, still vexed at the lost opportunity to seduce his wife, "you most definitely could. And did."

Harriet sent him an apologetic glance. "Am I forgiven, dearest brother?"

"You're forgiven," he allowed grudgingly, for he liked his sister. She was tenderhearted and good. Quite the opposite of their mother in every way.

"I'm so pleased to have a sister," Harriet added, smiling. "You must forgive me my enthusiasm. I never thought to see the day you married, Torrie. You were always far too content in your rakish ways."

He winced at the reminder and wished he could change the circumstances under which he and Bess had met. Eugenia had been doing her utmost to spread gossip and fan the flames of scandal at every opportunity, and he feared the effect it would have on Bess. To that end, he did need his sister's help with blunting the wagging tongues and earning Bess some acceptance in Society. He needed to speak with her about that. But first, he had to direct the conversation into safer waters, lest he drown.

"I'm no longer that man," he told Harriet coolly.

Bess's bearing had grown stiff at his side. His sister seemed to recognize her error, for she hastened to add, "And now you shall be quite content with our Bess, I know. For look at the two of you. I don't believe I've seen a couple more besotted with each other."

Torrie felt the novel sensation of his cheeks and ears going hot. Besotted? Well, hell. Perhaps he was. He certainly could think of no one but Bess. Was that what this feeling was?

He cleared his throat, wondering at the newness of it all, the queer sensation lodged deep in his chest. "Since you are here, Harriet, I would like your suggestions for weathering the gossip storm. Shall we all find a more comfortable room in which to sit?"

Preferably a chamber in which their mother was not present, he added silently.

"Of course," his sister said, and whether it was his countenance that gave him away or she merely shared a similar vein of thought, he couldn't say. But when she added a suggestion that they seek the drawing room, he was relieved.

He offered his arm to Bess and then escorted her from the library, her hand on his arm burning him through his coat with each step.

CHAPTER 8

*E*lizabeth emerged from her bath that evening exhausted and disappointed.

Her first dinner at Torrington House had been a frigid failure.

The dowager had remained mostly silent for the duration, but her disapproval of Elizabeth had been plainly written on her face. Torrie had attempted to interject some humor into the abysmal affair, but by the meal's conclusion, the three of them had fallen into grim silence.

But she was dismayed to realize her greatest source of discontent. Torrie had once again sent a bath for her, and yet, this evening he had failed to join her. She pulled a clean night rail over her head now. It was one she had been carrying with her for years and which bore the neatly stitched repairs she'd had to make. The Duchess of Montrose—Hattie, as she had insisted Elizabeth call her—would take her shopping to replenish her admittedly disastrous wardrobe.

Her fingers found the buttons, sliding them into their moorings one by one, as she told herself that it didn't matter if Torrie's mother despised her. Telling herself that even if the gossip swirling about her amongst the *ton* was as dreadful as Torrie suggested, and even if the Countess of Worthing continued to hatefully spew her bile, that at least she was no longer a governess.

At least she had a home. A chance for a future.

A husband.

She reached the final button as a knock sounded on the door.

It was him. Unbidden, his words from earlier in the library returned to her. *Let me show you how desirable you are.* An ache began between her legs and blossomed outward, making her feel heavy and flushed. Combing her fingers through her long, wet hair, she took a deep breath, attempting to calm her galloping heart.

"Come," she called softly.

The door opened, and Torrie swept over the threshold, barefoot and in a banyan just as he had been the night before. So handsome, he stole her breath.

She swallowed hard, keenly aware that she was clad in nothing more than the threadbare night rail, without a dressing gown to offer her modesty. His vibrant, green gaze swept over her like a caress.

"Good evening, Bess."

His voice was equal parts sin and seduction, a husky rasp that filled her with longing.

"Good evening," she returned, feeling unaccountably nervous and eager all at once.

Would he wish to consummate their marriage tonight? His actions and words earlier certainly suggested so. Her breath caught at the thought.

"You've finished your bath already?" he asked, closing the door at his back before striding toward her.

She noticed that his hair was wet.

"Yes." Her bare toes curled into the thick woolen carpet beneath her feet. "And you?"

"I did." He stopped before her, a smile on his lips that reached his eyes, unlike the strained smiles from earlier at dinner. "I'll admit, however, that I was hoping to catch you yet in your bath, that I might help wash your hair again."

The scent of him swirled around her, fresh soap and citrus and bay.

"I would have liked that," she admitted, all too aware of this man in every sense.

Because now that he was her husband, she wanted nothing but him. Nothing but everything he had to give. How quickly her foolish, fragile heart had become involved. One full day as his wife, and she was in the palms of his hands.

"Shall I brush it for you?"

His question surprised her. "You want to brush my hair?"

"I want to tend to you," he said softly, tenderly. "It pleases me to make you happy."

What to say to that?

"That is kind of you," she forced out, feeling dreadfully awkward and wanting nothing more than to kiss him again. "Particularly given the nature of our marriage."

He raised a brow. "The nature of it?"

"A marriage founded in necessity rather than romance," she elaborated, feeling her cheeks go hot at the last word and the images it conjured.

"Do you regret marrying me, Bess?" he asked, frowning down at her.

The rich, dark ebony of his banyan made his eyes appear bolder and brighter in the low candlelight. He was so handsome that looking at him created a physical ache deep within her. How was it possible that the beautiful rake she had yearned for from across so many ballrooms was now hers, within reach?

"I regret the circumstances. I regret the resentment you must feel toward me, having to marry with haste, all the scandal which has plagued us both. I regret that your mother dislikes me."

"I don't feel resentment toward you, Bess. And the scandal is my fault alone." His frown deepened. "My mother's opinion is unwarranted. She needs to know her place. My relationship with her is complicated, given that I don't remember her. I can't help but think that some of her frustration with me is falling on you instead of where it belongs. I'll speak with her."

He didn't remember his own mother? Good heavens, how painful his amnesia must be, not just for Torrie, but for his family as well. She well understood the shadows in his gaze. Elizabeth thought of what it would be like to have no recollection of her parents, and it was as if someone had torn a gaping hole open inside her.

"No," she hastened to say, not wanting to be the reason for further discord between Torrie and the dowager. "Don't speak with her, please. I would prefer to do so myself, should it come to that, although I fervently hope to prove myself to her."

"You're certain?" His gaze searched hers.

Such consideration for her. She could scarcely reconcile this gentle, caring man with the rogue who had swept her from the library. And the man she had overheard speaking of her with such callous dismissal.

"Bess?" he pressed, breaking her from her whirling thoughts when she failed to answer him.

"Yes," she said firmly. "I'm certain. Likely, she sees me as a threat to her position. Perhaps even to her relationship with you, such as it is. I want her to know that I pose her no challenge. It is my greatest wish to befriend her, for my recollections of my own mother are cloudy at best."

He tilted his head, still studying her with the same intensity that set her instantly aflame, and yet in a different manner as well. Almost as if…

Well, as if he *cared*.

And what an astonishing notion that was, Viscount Torrington caring for Miss Elizabeth Brooke, plain, plump partridge.

"You lost your parents some time ago, did you not?" he asked.

"When I was a child." Sorrow washed over her, along with bittersweet memories, and for the first time, it occurred to her just how truly fortunate she was that she had those years of happiness with her mother and father to cling to forever. Unlike Torrie, who had lost almost all his life in one blow.

"I'm so very sorry, Bess. How terrible it must have been for you, being left alone in the world. I cannot fathom it." He reached for her, nothing more than his hand on her upper arm, the gesture meant to be a comfort.

And yet, that lone touch was so much more than solace. His hand was firm, his fingers wrapping gently around her, searing her through the linen of her night rail.

"Thank you. I am grateful for the time I did have with them. For the memories."

He nodded, his expression changing, and she wished she would not have added the last words. How insensitive of her. She hadn't meant to remind him of his lack of memories at all. What had she been thinking? Clearly, she had not been, and therein was the problem.

"I'm sorry, Torrie." She caught her lower lip in her teeth and studied his countenance, looking for any hint of vulnerability and finding none. "I didn't wish to…that is to say, forgive me. Please."

"You needn't apologize," he said smoothly. "I'm glad for you, for the recollections you have, particularly if they give you comfort. In some ways, I wish it were different for me. And in other ways, I'm content in my life now, in the man I am. I'm not certain I could reconcile the two. It is likely better this way, with me not remembering most of my life before. The more I learn of the man I was, the less persuaded I am that I would like him."

A self-deprecating smile quirked his mouth into a mocking half smile then, and she was not impervious to the effect of that smile, that look. That *man*.

Good, sweet heavens, he was more handsome than any gentleman had a right to be, whether rake or rogue or honorable, and she was the focus of all that masculine beauty, all that sensual intent.

"I like the man before me," she admitted, startling herself with the revelation.

"Good." His smile deepened, making the corners of his eyes crinkle. "I like the woman before me as well. Now then, where is your brush?"

Ah, yes. His offer to brush her hair. She'd nearly forgotten. Elizabeth moved toward a nearby rosewood table, where her lady's maid had laid out the necessities for her toilette in neat array. Extricating herself from Torrie's touch felt wrong. She mourned the loss of his warmth. Liked the way it felt, his fingers encircling her arm, his touch burning into her.

But here was a moment to remind herself of the necessity that she guard herself against falling in love with him all over again. The first time, she had been young and foolish. Despite the fact that he was now her husband, she didn't dare allow herself to entertain tender feelings for him.

He had married her to save her from gossip and the inability to find another post as governess. Theirs was a marriage of convenience, a far cry from a love match. And despite the kind and tender words he offered her, Elizabeth knew he never would have lowered himself to marry her if his sense of honor hadn't demanded it.

Belatedly, she realized she was staring at the implements arranged before her. She took up the brush, then hastily turned about, startled to find that Torrie had followed her. He was perilously near, his tall frame looming over her petite one. Unsmiling now, his expression guarded, his jaw tense.

Slowly, as if he feared she would shy away from him, lest he move too quickly, Torrie took the brush from her. She relinquished it, their fingers grazing each other as she did so, sending awareness sparking through her.

"Turn," he said simply.

And, lackwit that he had turned her into with such devastating ease, she obeyed, spinning on the ball of her foot and presenting him with her back.

"We've been talking for so long that your hair is drying," he rumbled behind her. "You must tell me if I get caught in any snarls. I have no wish to hurt you."

"I'll tell you," she lied, knowing full well that even if the brush became helplessly entangled in her wavy locks, she would never breathe a word of protest.

Viscount Torrington, the man she had pined for, yearned after, dreamt of, stood at her back, giving hope to the awkward debutante she had once been. Hope that there might be happiness awaiting her after all, despite the odds that suggested strongly otherwise.

She held her breath as the brush passed through her hair slowly.

"How is this?" he asked near her ear.

They weren't touching, and yet, they might as well have been pressed together for the intimacy of the moment. It took Elizabeth a few seconds to gather her wits and find her tongue.

"It is quite lovely, thank you."

"Hmm," he hummed, sounding unconvinced. "Better than your lady's maid?"

The brush made a few more passes through her hair, stroking from root to end. The patience with which he attended her did strange things to her ability to resist him.

"I can't compare the two of you," she confessed with a smile, "since I've been dismissing her each night. She has never brushed my hair."

"You prefer to tend to yourself," he observed as the brush traveled slowly through her hair again. "But you needn't now. You're not a governess any longer. You are the lady of the house. *My* lady."

The emphasis he placed on the last was not lost upon her. And Elizabeth couldn't lie to herself. She liked the thought of belonging to him. The possession in his voice made her weak in all the ways she had previously believed herself to have overcome where he was concerned. Oh, yes. Let there be no doubt about it. She wanted very much to be his. In every way.

"It will take me some time, I suspect," she allowed, the admission torn from her. "To accustom myself to the change in circumstance. Not long ago, I accepted the fact that I must be a governess for the rest of my life, until I became too aged to keep my charges under control, and now, I am a married woman."

The brush went through her hair a few more times, her husband silent behind her. And then, he leaned forward, replacing the ivory-handled brush on its polished table. The action made his chest press fully against her back. There was nothing but the muscled wall of him, the heat of his body, his scent, heady and decadent.

And the undeniable prod of his manhood, rising to prominence against the small of her back.

He wanted her. The realization was gratifying. Heady.

Terrifying and exhilarating, too. She wasn't sure how to feel, what to do. What to expect. Lady Andromeda had attempted to explain the marriage bed to her once, and she had stumbled over her words, growing so flushed with embarrassment that she had ended the discussion prematurely, never to revisit it.

Elizabeth's heart wanted to leap from her chest, but she forced herself to remain calm. To inhale slowly, and to exhale carefully.

His fingertips grazed over her nape as he moved the heavy curtain of her hair to the side. And then, just as quickly, she felt the scorching heat of his lips on her bare skin. His hands moved to her hips, his fingers sinking into her softness, keeping her where she was.

"Speaking of marriage," he murmured, raking the coarse bristles of his cheek whiskers over her sensitive skin, "when do you want to consummate ours, Bess? I confess, I've been desperate for you all damned day."

He had?

His words sent a heavy, hot arrow of desire shooting through her.

"Oh," was all she could manage.

Hardly coherent. Scarcely a response. But his hardness was pressed against her, and she could feel every inch of his muscled, masculine body warming and tempting hers. Her breaths were falling heavily, and desire burned to life. Her every defense against Viscount Torrington, tormentor of her failed Seasons, handsome, perfect rakehell, sinner, and scoundrel, was disintegrating in helpless fashion.

His lips found the curve of her ear. "Bess?"

"Yes?" she managed, half sigh, half whisper.

"I want you. If you aren't ready, tell me now, and I'll return to my chamber and we both can forget this conversation ever happened. I'll wait if I must."

She inhaled swiftly, then exhaled slowly. He wanted her. Torrie wanted her.

Did she dare to believe him? Was he being honest with her?

Apparently, Torrie sensed her concern, for his lips glided over her ear first, then her temple, kissing her softly. "Trust me, Bess. This is just as new for me as it is for you."

Trust him? Trust the man who had once disparaged her with such ease? Trust the scoundrel who had kidnapped her, mistaking her for his mistress? Trust the handsome devil for whom life had been so irritatingly easy, aside from his phaeton accident and loss of memory?

She should resent him. She should deny him. By no means should Elizabeth surrender to her longstanding desire for him, regardless of how tempting he was, no matter how kind and caring and melting his words were. He had called her plump and plain. A partridge.

She tried to remind herself, but her body was woefully traitorous at the moment, and the man she had married was not the same man of that long-ago day.

He caressed her hips as if he were committing the lines of her figure to memory. "Bess? Do you trust me?"

No, she didn't. Yes, she did. It was complicated and horrible, and she wanted him and loathed him at the same time.

"Yes," she whispered, the concession leaving her before she could rethink it. "I do."

"Good." His lips were on her nape, soothing, kissing. "Because I've been thinking about making you mine from the moment you agreed to marry me."

At his possessive words, her knees went weak. They trembled, and she would have sprawled to the floor in an undignified heap had he not caught her, holding her to him, his face buried in her hair, his mouth on her throat. He kissed her neck, his lips demanding and smooth as they worked over her greedy flesh, the heat of his breath sending a shiver through her that had nothing to do with a chill.

She angled her head, giving him more access to her throat. His mouth trailed a path of fire to the edge of her night rail, then he rubbed his face against her, the prickle of his whiskers making her nipples hard.

"You have?" she asked, breathless and yet doubting.

His hands smoothed over her waist. "Of course. I've scarcely been able to think of anything else. Why do you think I went to Winter's Boxing Academy this morning?"

So that was where he had been.

"For sport?"

"For distraction." He spun her slowly so that she faced him.

Her hands settled on his broad chest, and she couldn't help but to notice how well-muscled and firm it was. "Oh." She thought suddenly of the Countess of Worthing. Was he continuing to see her? Was she still his mistress, or had he taken another?

"You're thinking," he guessed. "What is amiss? Have I pressed you too soon?"

"I was thinking of Lady Worthing," she blurted. "Is she still your mistress?"

"I gave her the congé the day after that night," he said solemnly.

Relief washed over her. More questions clamored inside her. Would he take another mistress? Did he intend to be a faithful husband? Somehow, these worries had not weighed on her before. But now they were like a waterfall, raining down on her.

117

Still, she didn't know how to ask them. Wasn't sure she could bear the answers.

"Thank you," she said instead.

He cupped her face, his thumb brushing reverently over her jaw. "You needn't thank me, Bess."

He was frowning, studying her face as if it possessed the answer to a complex mystery. Now, he was the one who was thinking, and she wondered what thoughts were roiling through his capable mind, causing his brow to furrow.

"What are you thinking?" she asked.

"That I don't ever remember wanting to kiss a woman as badly as I want to kiss you right now."

His low, raw confession chased the last of her doubts, filling her with inexorable warmth.

"Then kiss me," she whispered.

SHE DIDN'T HAVE to tell him twice.

Torrie took Bess's lips with his.

And they were silken and full and hot. She responded instantly, tentatively at first and then with greater confidence. He gathered her in his arms, their bodies flush, all her sweet curves melding against him. His cock was painfully hard, and although he'd been doing everything in his power to proceed slowly, he wanted her so desperately that he feared an unhurried seduction would be impossible.

Because now that she was kissing him, the threads of his restraint were fraying fast. Her mouth beneath his felt so very right, her hands on his chest perfection as they glided over his banyan to curl around his neck. She clung to him, her breasts spilling into him, her nipples tight little points he could feel through the thin barrier of his robe. He wanted to

118

lift the hem of her night rail, to carry her to the bed, to bury himself inside her.

He wanted to mark her, take her, make her his.

All the need was boiling inside him, threatening to spill over before they'd even begun. And she was a virgin. God.

He tore his mouth from hers, his breathing ragged and harsh. "You must tell me, Bess, if I proceed with too much haste. Tell me what you like, what, if anything, you don't like."

"I'll try," she murmured, her breathing as affected as his. "I've never…this is all so new for me."

"We'll learn together, learn each other." He kissed the tip of her nose where it turned up. It was positively endearing. The more he looked at her, the more he found to admire.

Kidnapping her that night was gradually proving to be the best mistake he'd ever made.

"Together," she echoed. "Yes."

He kissed her temple, her cheek, holding still as he inhaled deeply, drinking in her scent. "Come to the bed with me," he breathed into her ear.

Without waiting for her response, he withdrew, taking her hands in his. He linked their fingers, before pulling her across the chamber to where her bed beckoned. When they reached the mattress, he drew her against him again, releasing her to cup her nape beneath her unbound hair.

Angling his head, he kissed her again. Slowly, deeply. His tongue traced the seam of her lips and she opened with a sigh, her fingers clenching on the silk of his banyan. He licked into her mouth, and she followed his lead, her tongue sliding against his, wringing a moan from him.

How strange and yet how perfect it was, this kiss, her surrender. The supple give of her body curving into his. He was going to pleasure her until she was wet and breathless and desperate, and then he was going to sink inside her slowly, carefully, and join their bodies just as they were joined in marriage.

He kissed her and kissed her, allowing her to grow accustomed to him. Familiarizing himself with her responses. When he increased the pressure of his mouth on hers, she made a small, needy sound deep in her throat, her breasts rubbing against him in a way that made his cock-stand even more painfully rigid. But he had to try to control himself.

He would make the night, their lovemaking, about her.

With his other hand, he allowed himself to explore her body, the only barrier between them her thin night rail. She was soft and warm and lovely. He found the full curve of her hip, the swell of her bottom. His fingertips flexed on the soft-ness with a mind of their own, and as he kissed her, he urged her body more fully against his, so that his cock was prod-ding her belly.

Not enough, every part of him screamed. He needed bare skin. Needed her out of her night rail, naked and flushed and ready for him. She was wearing far too much fabric. Inwardly, he cursed the white linen keeping him from what he wanted, the high collar thwarting him from creamy curves.

He took his lips from hers, his breathing more ragged than before, his fingers tangling in the well-worn billow of her night rail. "May I take this off you?"

Her eyes, which had been closed, fluttered open, reminding him of how many hues were hidden within their brown-gold depths.

"My night rail?" she asked, eyes widening farther.

Had she imagined she would remain fully clothed while he bedded her?

"Yes," he told her gently. "I want to see you, all of you. Touch you, kiss you."

Everywhere he could, but he kept that bit to himself, lest he alarm her further.

Her kiss-stung lips parted. "You do?"

"Can you doubt it?" Torrie kissed the corner of her mouth, then her ear, speaking softly. "Do you not feel the effect you have on me, Bess?"

He swept his hand down the delicate tracery of her spine, stopping at her rump to grab another delicious handful. Slowly, he pressed into her, allowing her to feel how hungry he was for her, his hardness burrowing into her softness with agonizing intent. A pale imitation of what he intended to do.

"Oh my," she murmured, swallowing hard. "All that is...you?"

He grinned. She was adorable.

"All me," he confirmed. "We'll go slowly, love. We'll take all the time you need."

She nodded, his words appearing to reassure her. "Yes, slowly."

He was going to have to seduce her out of that bloody shapeless night rail. Never mind. More excuses to touch and kiss her. No hardship there.

Releasing his grip on her bottom, he lightly trailed his forefinger down the line of prim buttons on her high-necked nightgown. "One at a time. Tell me if I should stop, and I'll stop."

She exhaled, her hot breath fanning over his hand, giving him a nod of acquiescence. She was nervous, and understandably so. Lovemaking was new to her. But oh how he would enjoy showing her the pleasures of the marriage bed.

His fingers found the first button and slid it from its mooring with ease. A small swath of creamy skin was exposed, and he set his lips there, kissing her reverently. Her skin was smooth and soft and sweetly scented from the bath she had taken. The effect it had on him was instant and thunderous, but he reined in his desire and reached for the second button with a trembling hand. This button slid open as easily as the first. One by one, just as he had promised, he continued, kissing each new patch of skin he bared.

Until he reached the valley between her breasts. Stopping there, he couldn't resist cupping the heavy globes in his palms, weighing their fullness. They were larger than he had imagined, hidden away in the dreadful, ill-fitting garments she wore—this nightgown included. Thank Christ Harriet had offered to take her shopping. He would spend every last ha'penny he possessed to see Bess properly clothed, her lush figure lovingly outlined by the fashionable gowns she deserved.

Her nipples were hard buds tempting him to take them into his mouth and suck. Reverently, he pressed a kiss between her breasts. "Beautiful." He kissed each mound, nuzzled the peaks through the thin impediment of her night rail. "More beautiful than I could have guessed."

"I am no beauty," she whispered, sounding fretful.

"Blasphemy," he countered, showing her how lovely she was by kissing her again and not stopping until she was once again soft and pliant in his arms, her body melting into his as all fears and worries fled her.

A few more buttons to go, and he undid them with ease as his tongue played with hers, until he had finally reached the last in the daunting row, and there was nothing save a knotted belt securing her modesty. He made short work of it as well, prolonging the kiss for a few moments more before lifting his head.

Her simple white linen gown billowed around her, the swells of her breasts visible through the fabric he had opened. And Torrie couldn't stop himself from reaching inside, parting the gown to reveal the fullness of one pink-tipped breast. Nor could he stop himself from sucking on her nipple.

She moaned softly, body bowing as he flicked his tongue over the turgid bud.

"Perfection," he murmured, then gave her nipple another hard, lusty suck. "My God, Bess, you make me ravenous for you."

The admission was torn from him.

"You make me feel the same," she said, her voice so low he almost couldn't make out her words.

"How do I make you feel? Tell me." He slid the other half of her nightgown to the side, leaving both her breasts exposed.

"I ache."

He blew a stream of air over her nipple. "Where, Bess? Tell me where you ache."

He gently nipped her, tugging the beaded tip of her breast with his teeth and earning another moan from her.

"Tell me," he pressed when she didn't answer.

"In my belly, and...lower," she said, gasping when he sucked again, tormenting them both.

"Here?" he asked, daring to cup her through the cloth of her nightgown, the heat of her sex searing his palm.

Her hips pumped against him, seeking more.

"Yes," she whispered.

"Your cunny." Slowly, he rotated his palm over her mound, applying a bit of pressure. "This is where you ache, isn't it, Bess?"

"Mmm," came her incoherent response.

"You're aching for me here, aren't you? I can feel it through your gown."

God, she was wet, the linen of her night rail dampened instantly. She was so responsive. The discovery made a fresh onslaught of lust go roaring through him.

He rocked his hand against her some more, loving the slack expression on her face, her eyes glazed with desire. "I can't wait to have you completely naked, to bury my face between your pretty legs and lick you until you come on my tongue."

Wicked, filthy words. Words that were not fit for the ears of a virgin. But he was beyond control now, and Bess didn't appear to mind. She was gripping his banyan, moaning softly, her body arching into his.

"Oh," she said, clutching him as if she would pitch to the floor without him to keep her upright.

He didn't wait, lest she cling to her prim sensibilities once more. Torrie peeled her nightgown down her shoulders, past her waist, until it fell to the Aubusson around her feet.

And she was naked.

Gloriously, beautifully naked.

The full effect of her curves—all pale and pink and haunt-ingly lovely—rendered him speechless. For a moment, he could do nothing more than stare, drinking in the sight of her.

When he found his voice, it was little more than a husky rasp. "Get on the bed."

She did as he asked, seating herself on the edge, looking uncertain and yet just as hungry for him as he was for her.

"Good," he praised. "Now hold on to the bedclothes, love."

She swallowed hard, her fingers clenching on the coun-terpane.

Torrie went to her, dropping to his knees on the carpet. Her legs were firmly pressed together, keeping him from the full sight of her pink, glistening folds. His hands found her calves, caressing past her knees to her thighs.

"Relax for me, Bess."

Gently, he guided her knees apart, and she allowed him the intrusion. He kissed her inner thigh, the scent of her filling his head with roaring flame. He could lick and kiss every inch of her, and it still wouldn't be sufficient to slake his need.

His hands found their way to her hips, caressing up and down, and she came to life beneath his touch. He felt the tension seeping from her, the last of her worries giving way to desire. Her hesitance fled, and his prim, proper governess slowly faded away. His lips moved with a will of their own, chasing every bare expanse of skin he could kiss. Up her inner thigh, her legs parting more fully in welcome. And then higher still, until he had her just as he wanted, in full bloom, her cunny pink and so very wet, glistening in the candlelight.

He couldn't wait another second.

Bowing his head like a true supplicant, he licked her slit, then kissed the plump bud at the top of her sex. The taste of her was floral and musky. Woman and abundance and spring blooms bursting to life. *Perfection.* Sweet, sleek perfection. His tongue dipped, teasing her clitoris, running over and around as he lapped her up.

She gasped above him, seizing his shoulders, fingernails biting into his muscles in painful pleasure. "Torrie!"

She sounded scandalized. He didn't give a damn if she was; this was what he had been born for: pleasing this woman. Pleasing *his* woman. With his head firmly buried between Bess's thighs, it was as if everything in his life—all the frayed ends and jagged pieces—had somehow formed together. He didn't feel broken. He didn't care about the past he couldn't remember. All he felt was alive. Gloriously, thoroughly, recklessly *alive*. Heart thundering in his chest, cock pulsing, her cunny rocking rhythmically against his mouth as her instincts took over.

He sucked hard on her pearl, then ran his teeth over her until she bucked beneath him, moaning. She was wet, decadently so, her juices dripping down his chin. And it made him harder than stone. He groaned, licking into her, rubbing his face deeper into her cunny until he didn't know where he ended and she began. He savored her, the sound of his feast echoing in the stillness along with her labored breathing.

It was all so good. Too good. Too much.

He rocked back on his bent knees, gazing up at her, wiping his chin with the back of his hand. "You're so wet, Bess."

He meant the words as praise, but he realized his error when she frowned, her knees moving quickly back together. "Forgive me. I'm sorry."

"My God, don't be sorry." He kissed each of her knees, caressed her upper thighs. "It is a good thing, love."

"It is?"

He hated the hesitance in her voice and could have kicked himself for momentarily forgetting just how innocent she was.

"A very good thing," he told her tenderly, trying to quell the need to get to his feet and fuck her properly, sinking his cock deep and not stopping until he filled her with his seed. "It means you want me as much as I want you."

"Oh." A flush tinged her cheekbones, and she managed to look as proper as any governess just then. "I…yes. I do want you, Torrie."

She caught her lower lip in her teeth, and he could tell that the revelation was one she hadn't intended to make.

"Never be embarrassed with me." He swept his hands over the seam of her thighs, urging them apart. "You couldn't please me more. Let me show you how much. Let me worship you as you deserve."

Bess made a tiny huff of sound—part sigh and part moan. But she relaxed for him, legs opening and giving him what he wanted most. Torrie didn't waste another moment. He was ravenous now. He kissed his way up her silken inner thigh, using his palms to spread her open even more. Pink, glistening perfection awaited him. He sucked the pouting bud, then worried it lightly with his teeth, gratified when her hips jumped off the bed toward him.

She was intoxicating. Her scent, her responsiveness, how soaked she was. It was all making him wild. He pleasured her with his lips and tongue and teeth, intent on making her lose control, learning what pleased her most just as he had promised. She came apart without warning, shuddering against him with a cry that echoed through the chamber. And he stayed where he was as she rode his face, surrendering to pleasure with complete abandon.

When she was limp and breathless, only then did he rise to his feet, tearing at his banyan in his eagerness to remove it. His hands were trembling and the taste of her was on his lips, and he was going to bloody well explode if he didn't have her beneath him in the next minute.

Strike that—the next fifteen seconds.

Somehow, he was able to rip away his banyan and settle them both on the bed, Bess under him. He stared down at her, taking in the comely flush tingeing her cheeks and throat, the sight of her so lush and naked and ready for him.

And his, all his.

Was this what it was like to be whole again? He felt omnipotent. As if he could heft the entire world in his own hands. He felt as if he had finally found what he'd been searching for since that damned phaeton accident.

He felt as if he might lose his heart to this woman and not regret it for a single moment.

Torrie kissed her then, feeding her the taste of herself on his tongue, and she moaned into his mouth, wrapping her arms around his neck, her body rising up to meet his. Ah,

SCARLETT SCOTT

Christ. He had to rein himself in because he didn't want to hurt her.

Reluctantly, he ended the kiss, lifting his head to stare down at her again as he leveraged himself on one forearm and gripped his cock in his other hand. "Are you ready for me, Bess?"

Her lips parted, eyes widening as she nodded, her hair a dark, wavy tangle around her lovely face. "Yes."

No other word had sounded sweeter from her lips.

He guided his cock to her wet heat, slicking himself in her dew before finding her entrance. Calling on all the restraint he possessed, he pressed forward slowly, giving her time to adjust. She gasped softly, her hands finding his shoulders now, nails nipping into his bare skin. Such torture, holding still when all he wanted to do was drive forward.

He dropped a kiss on her throat, nuzzled her ear, his heart pounding ever harder. "I want you desperately."

"Yes. *Oh.*" She turned her face toward his, seeking his mouth, and he gave it to her, kissing her deeply, open-mouthed and lusty.

She undulated, hungry hips seeking more. Still kissing her, he allowed himself a thrust, meeting with her body's natural resistance as she tensed and stiffened. Her cunny was gripping him tightly, so tightly.

Torrie lifted his head. "How does it feel?"

"Different," she murmured. "Overwhelming. Is it over?"

A chuckle almost escaped him at her query, but he kissed her temple instead, another surge of affection for her washing over him. "It's hardly over, darling. I'll show you the rest if you'd like."

"Please."

He kissed her cheek, her nose, thrust again. Not as gentle this time. She clenched on him, and he ground his molars. *Control*, he reminded himself. *Control.*

128

"How is this, love?" he asked, his voice a strangled growl as he struggled to contain his raging need.

"I want..." Her words trailed off as she moved under him, hips urging him deeper. "I want more."

Thank God.

One more pump, and he gave her the rest of his length, sinking into her drenched cunny to the hilt.

And it was so good, too good. She was impossibly tight and hot and wet and he was lost. Helplessly, hopelessly, happily lost in her. He remained as he was, their bodies perfectly aligned, her breasts a soft seduction against his chest, and he swore there could be no more perfect moment than this. Until she shifted, and pleasure hit him like a wave, rolling down his spine, and the temptation to move was too irresistible.

He buried his face in her throat and slid his fingers between them. Unerringly, he sought her pearl, rubbing over it in small, quick circles that had her sheath gripping him. He withdrew, then sank in again slowly, deliciously, savoring the way she clung to him, the way her hips chased his.

Together, they found a rhythm, moving together sinuously, frantically, each of them seeking the completion their bodies so desperately craved.

"Come for me, my sweet Bess," he urged, dotting kisses down her neck to her collarbone. "Come on my cock."

More firmly, he circled her swollen bud, gratified to find her wetter than she had been before, throbbing. She moaned again and arched her back as he sucked a nipple into his mouth while driving in and out of her slick cunny. He was already close, and so was she if her body's responses were any indication. She rocked with him, nails trailing down his shoulders and back, as if she intended to mark him. Some primitive part of him hoped she did.

In and out, he drove, losing some of his ability to be

gentle, losing any control he'd managed to retain. There was nothing but the soft, breathy pants of his name on her lips, her hard nipple in his mouth, the wetness of her cunny bathing his rigid cock, the pounding of his heart, the roaring in his ears as he strove to hold off his looming orgasm.

His ballocks were drawn tight. He was there. But she had to get there first. He wouldn't allow himself to spend without her. Torrie released her nipple with a carnal pop and kissed the swell of her breast, the valley between them, fucking in and out of her with fast, deep thrusts.

"Let yourself go," he crooned. "Fly with me."

"Yes," she cried out, tensing beneath him as her body shook with the heady tremors of her release.

Her cunny tightened on him viciously, deliciously, squeezing him from her. Taking himself in hand, he sheathed himself in one quick thrust, until he was buried ballocks deep again, and there was nothing left to do but spill himself inside her. Taking her mouth in an open-mouthed kiss, he came so hard that little black stars exploded before him.

He collapsed against her, breathless and utterly spent and happier than he could recall ever being.

CHAPTER 9

*V*iscount Torrington had put his head between her legs and had kissed her there.

And she had liked it.

These bewildering thoughts were dancing through Elizabeth's mind as she traveled through the trivialities of her day, making her grow flushed and uncomfortable. Unfortunately, she was neither alone nor with her husband, either of which scenarios might have proven less embarrassing. Rather, she was on her promised shopping expedition with the Duchess of Montrose.

"We shall certainly be needing ball gowns, Madame Beauchamp," Hattie was telling the modiste as Elizabeth stood patiently in her chemise, allowing for all her measurements to be taken by one of Madame's seamstresses.

"And some new chemises and petticoats, I presume?" Madame asked, casting a withering eye over Elizabeth's worn, oft-repaired undergarment.

A different kind of flush rose to her cheeks at the question. She was more than aware that none of the garments in her possession were fashionable or well-suited to her form. However, she'd never had a choice in the matter. Not that she had one now, for it seemed as if the duchess and the modiste were more than happy to take command of her new wardrobe without her.

"She will require everything, Madame," Hattie confirmed, directing a sympathetic smile in Elizabeth's direction. "Your beauty deserves to shine rather than be hidden away, my dear. Torrie will approve, trust me on the matter."

"Thank you for saying so," she offered, growing weary of holding herself still and remaining on display, even if it meant she would soon have a host of new gowns at her command.

For Elizabeth could scarcely wrap her mind around the cost of an entirely new wardrobe, and one to be created for her with all haste. Madame Beauchamp had assured Hattie that she would have her team of seamstresses working on Elizabeth's new wardrobe day and night.

Nothing but the best for the Duchess of Montrose and Viscountess Torrington, Madame had added smoothly, her words lightly tinged with a French accent that could have been feigned or real. Elizabeth wasn't certain. And Hattie had responded with perfect grace while reminding the modiste that she would prefer not to share her dressmaker with the Countess of Worthing and was willing to pay handsomely to see that she didn't have to do so. Madame had also been happy to accept the offer, and Elizabeth had been touched by her sister-in-law's loyalty.

"By the time I'm finished, that dreadful woman will be fortunate if she can find a sack to wear," Hattie had told Elizabeth with a wink, *sotto voce*.

If only the dowager had possessed such an easy and welcoming nature as her children did. Breakfast that morning had been as frosty as ever, although blessedly without further accusations that Elizabeth had intentionally caused the scandal that had led to her marriage. Perhaps the other woman's ability to hold her tongue had been down to the presence of her son at the breakfast table. Torrie had been pleasant and cheerful, sharing no shortage of stolen glances with her after he had procured her a plate laden with food.

Now that their marriage had been consummated, she felt...

Different.

She felt rather like a wife instead of a mistake, and Elizabeth couldn't lie that the former was far preferable to the latter.

"Just a few more measurements, my lady," Madame Beauchamp chirped, no doubt pleased herself at the notion of what her commission would be. "Tell me, what colors would you prefer for the evening gowns? Shades of blue and green would suit your coloring well, *je pense.*"

Green, like Torrie's eyes.

Elizabeth bit her lip as a rush of longing swept over her at the thought of her handsome husband. For with it, inevitably, came more memories of the night before. Good heavens, she was going to be red as a beet again. She hoped no one could tell what she was thinking by looking upon her.

They couldn't, could they? Dear God, what if they could? What if everyone knew he had used his tongue on her and said such wicked things?

Wicked things she'd liked far, far too much.

She cleared her throat, feeling suddenly dizzied. "Pomona green is a favorite of mine, Madame."

"An evening gown in green, then," Madame decreed, "and a ball gown in celestial blue."

"Both would be lovely on you," Hattie agreed, smiling. "A few others as well, Madame, in whatever you think would be best for Lady Torrington."

"How many ball gowns and evening gowns does one woman need?" Elizabeth wondered aloud.

Hattie chuckled, the sound infectious. "As many as she can have, my dear."

"An excellent answer, Your Grace," offered Madame slyly.

"Certainly, I'll not be attending so many balls, however," she countered, realizing she hadn't truly thought about what the rest of her marriage to the viscount would entail.

The *ton* and all its glittering fêtes and wagging tongues and condescending, judgmental stares. She swallowed hard against the dread bursting open like a seed within her. She had never been accepted, not truly, in that world. Five failed Seasons of misery as a wallflower no one wanted haunted her as proof.

"Of course you shall," Hattie said brightly. "Torrington will want to have you on his arm, and not just at the ball he is hosting in your honor."

A ball. In her honor?

Trepidation joined the dread as she swayed, prompting the seamstress at her feet to give her chemise hem a chiding tug so that she remained still.

"I knew nothing of a ball in my honor," she said weakly.

"It will be the event of the Season," Hattie reassured her warmly. "And if you require any help, you have me, of course. You're family now."

Family.

Somehow, that lone, precious word and all the inherent meaning it possessed banished the doubts and fears rising within her and filled her instead with gratitude. Elizabeth blinked the sting of impending tears from her eyes and sniffed.

"Thank you, Hattie," she managed softly without weeping.

She hadn't had a family since her parents had died when she'd been a girl. And the notion of finally finding one now—she, the spinster governess no one had wanted—filled her heart so full that she swore it could burst.

"You needn't thank me, my dear." Hattie reached out, giving her hand a sisterly squeeze. "That is what sisters are for."

∼

"My God, you've gone mad." Torrie issued his pronouncement as he stared at the assortment of wood and canvas which Monty had proudly invited him to view at Hamilton House.

"One has to have been sane in the first place to go mad," his friend quipped, utterly unaffected by Torrie's grim assessment of his wood-and-canvas device.

A device that rather resembled a bird.

Or perhaps a bat.

"What do you think of it?" Monty asked, grinning proudly like the lunatic he was.

A reluctant chuckle tore from him, for he would never be surprised at the antics of his old friend. "This isn't a flying machine like the one you intended to fly from the turrets of Castle Clare, is it?"

Monty jolted as if Torrie had landed a blow, his spine going stiff. "You remember my flying machine story?"

He laughed again. "How could anyone forget? Who else would be enough of a Bedlamite to think he could actually fly from the turrets of a bloody castle as if…"

His words trailed away as he realized what he was saying in the same moment that his friend's astonished expression occurred to him.

"You remember," Monty repeated, his tone awed, as if Torrie had just revealed a miracle to him.

And perhaps he had.

Because as he stood in Montrose's study, staring at the hideous, ridiculous flying machine, he realized that he *did* remember. He remembered Monty regaling him with the story one night at their club. He remembered laughing uproariously at Monty's tale of a gust of wind catching the wings he'd fashioned, sending the flying machine crashing to the ground before he'd been able to test his efforts at Castle Clare. And thank Christ for that. Monty likely would have broken his fool neck in the fall.

Everything inside Torrie froze.

He *remembered*.

"I do," he said, rubbing at his jaw, searching the murk in his mind for more. "You told me about it, and I laughed until I cried. You're the only man I know who would have the ballocks to attempt to fly off a castle turret."

"Do you remember anything else?" Monty asked, sounding hopeful.

He sifted through the memories, those he had since the accident, and the few which had come before. Hattie's fat cat old cat, Miss Pudding. Laughing with Monty. Drinking with Monty. Racing Monty in their phaetons.

"I remember racing you," he managed. "In our phaetons. It was dark and raining, and you told me you'd give me an early start because your phaeton outmatched mine."

Monty went pale. "That was what happened the night of the accident. I don't recall it in great detail because I was sotted, but it was raining that night, and I remember giving you the lead. What else do you recall?"

Torrie shook his head as if it would dislodge more pieces of his old life and all would be revealed to him. But there was only a great, blank wall of nothingness where once there had been more.

"Nothing," he admitted, disappointment and frustration rising. "Not a goddamn thing."

And today had been going so well, too. He had begun it by waking in bed with his wife after making love to her for the first time last night. He had kissed her softly and then used his mouth to soothe all the places where she ached until she'd been writhing against him and coming on his tongue once more.

Those memories were worth at least a hundred thousand others, so he would rejoice in them.

"Beelzebub's earbobs," Monty muttered. "I was hoping there would have been more. I miss you. Not *you*. You're here, quite obviously, but the Torrie you were. Old Torrie enjoyed my oaths. New Torrie sneers at them."

He blinked. "I find it difficult to believe I enjoyed your cursing in any state, old or new."

Monty shook his head with a heavy sigh. "You see? Old Torrie bloody well loved my curses."

"Perhaps Old Torrie was humoring you."

His friend raised a brow. "Don't you think New Torrie might then as well?"

His lips twitched. The Duke of Montrose was entertaining, Torrie would grant him that.

"New Torrie might perhaps do so," he relented, unable to suppress his grin. "But only if he's in an extraordinarily good mood."

"How considerate of him," Monty said, grinning back at him. "Now, about my flying machine. What do you think of it?"

"I think that my sister will tie you to the nearest piece of furniture if you express any intent of taking it off a roof," he drawled. "Hattie won't stand for it, particularly not now that you have Titus."

"And another son or daughter on the way," Monty added.

"Another?" Once again, Torrie was shaking his head, but this time, it had nothing to do with his lost memory and everything to do with surprise. "Hattie didn't mention it to me. Does my mother know?"

"We haven't told anyone else yet," Monty said, shoulders going back and chest puffing up like the proud, doting father he was. "I wanted to tell you first, Torrie."

"Me?"

"Of course you. Who else? I've told you often enough that you're like a brother to me."

There were only so many occasions when Torrie remembered those words. Half a dozen, mayhap more. He found himself frowning as other memories seemed to filter into his mind, like dust motes in sunlight. Dancing about, almost impossible to discern.

Monty clapping him on the shoulder.

Riding with Monty.

Laughing with Monty.

Causing all manner of trouble together.

Skipping balls and suppers to gamble.

Like my own brother. You're a brother to me, old chap. You are my brother.

Yes, always those same sentiments, those same phrases, the corresponding feeling deep in his chest. But it hadn't only been Monty telling him that. Torrie had spoken those words as well. Monty had always been like a brother to him, too. He'd felt it then, over the years. He felt it now again.

More memories, small and imprecise, but they were returning.

Slowly, gradually returning.

"Torrie? Are you well, old chap? You look pale." Monty's

voice sliced through his thoughts, bringing him back to the present with another jolt. "You're remembering more, aren't you?"

"I think so," he admitted, too afraid to hope, uncertain of what it meant. Was it Bess who was responsible for this change in him, for the memories which had been locked away now seemingly being freed?

"This is bloody wonderful news, old chap," Monty said, striding across the study floor and clapping him on the shoulder as he had done so many times before. "It's only a matter of time until you remember everything and we have Old Torrie back where he belongs."

Torrie stared at Monty's silly flying machine, which, now that he thought on it, resembled nothing more than the carcass of some mythical bird, and wondered if his friend was right. After all, much time had already passed since the accident, and the memories he had regained were few and far between. Would he ever truly remember?

And, more troubling of all, what would happen between himself and Bess if he one day did?

He didn't want to dwell on any of those unsettling questions just now. He couldn't for fear of where they would take him.

Instead, he turned to his friend. "A hearty felicitations to you and Hattie on my impending, newest niece or nephew. I'm happy for you both."

"Thank you, old friend. And you've called her Hattie instead of Harriet several times." Monty was still grinning as if he'd just been told his flying machine would send him soaring through the air like a bird.

"So I have," he said, bemused and unwilling to think of the matter of his amnesia any longer. "Now, tell me about this latest flying machine of yours."

"I thought you'd never ask..."

But as Monty explained all the materials he had used for his machine, Torrie couldn't shake the odd premonition—a feeling in his chest heavy as a boulder—that the past he hadn't been able to remember for all this time would soon return in full. And that with it would come a whole host of other problems he wasn't prepared to face.

CHAPTER 10

"*B*ess."

At the fervent note in her husband's voice, Elizabeth looked down at the gown she was wearing, one of the new creations from Madame Beaumont, and her heart fell to her slippers. "It's far too scandalous, isn't it? I'll ask Culpepper to lay out a different frock for this evening."

They were attending a supper being held by some of Torrie's friends. It was to be her first toe in polite Society waters since everything had changed for her. But the dress was all wrong.

Yes, she had known too much of her breasts were on display. For one thing, it made them look shamefully large. For another, she had never, in all her life, had so much of her skin on shocking display. Well, aside from when she had been naked with her husband, or bathing or dressing, that was. Neither of which she was doing now.

No, indeed. She was standing in her bedchamber, half her breasts open to the wind.

"It's not scandalous." He was moving nearer—the sound

of his voice told her that he was—but she couldn't bear to look up and see his expression.

Likely, he was horrified that his wife would dare to wear such an appallingly brazen gown.

"It is worse than scandalous," she lamented, heaving a sigh that did nothing to lessen the effect her new stays and the cut of her gown were having on her breasts. Heat crept up her neck. "I look like a woman of ill repute."

"Bess," he repeated her name, stopping before her and gently placing his forefinger under her chin, tipping it up so she had no choice but to meet his gaze. "It is a beautiful gown, and it looks lovely on you. But more importantly, *you* are beautiful. You look like a viscountess, not a woman of ill repute. You look like *mine*, and I couldn't be prouder to have you at my side in this dress."

His words had an instant effect on her, chasing all her worries. Making her feel as if she were as beautiful as he suggested she was.

"Truly?"

"Truly." He smiled, his green eyes glinting into hers with sensual intent. "And I cannot wait to peel you out of this gown later."

"You mean that you approve of it?" She glanced down at herself again, taking in the way the bodice clung to her, the relative transparency of the gossamer fabric of her skirt, which was a perfectly lovely Pomona green just as she had asked. "I've never worn a gown so revealing before."

"That is because you've been hiding your glorious curves in dowdy, shapeless sacks given to you by some distant, ailing relative who squandered everything and left you with her castoffs," he pointed out.

Not incorrectly, even if his assessment of Lady Andromeda was rather harsh.

"Lady Andromeda was kind to me," she felt compelled to defend. "She chaperoned me through five Seasons."

Five failed Seasons.

Never mind that, for it, like so many other parts of her past, still stung.

"She gave you her old rags and then abandoned you when it suited her, leaving you to the mercy of others, earning your bread as a governess," he countered, his voice bearing an unusual harsh edge.

"She hadn't a choice," Elizabeth insisted. "She gave me a roof over my head and the opportunity for a Season for years."

"According to my mother, it's common fame that Lady Andromeda was a dreadful gambler who lost her entire fortune through her own vice. And, I suspect, funds which were rightfully yours as well."

Elizabeth shifted, feeling disloyal for even acknowledging the truth in the dowager's words, delivered by Torrie. "She did have a propensity for making wagers, but I fail to see what funds of mine she could have spent. I had nothing and no one. What she did for me was more than I could have asked of anyone. My parents left me with a pittance, not even enough to pay for my care by the time she took me in."

His expression changed, hardening. "Is that what she told you?"

Elizabeth frowned, thinking of that long-ago day when she had found her way to the last of her distant familial connections, at least a London cousin this time, and gentry too. "She said there was nothing left by the time I came to her. I had been staying with my mother's cousin and her family before that."

"My solicitor advised otherwise. It was hardly a pittance that your parents settled on you. I made some inquiries on your behalf before we married." His tone gentled, his hand cupping her face. "Look at me, love."

She did as he asked, holding his gaze. "You're saying that Lady Andromeda lied to me?"

"It wouldn't be the first time someone lied to another for their own gain, and nor will it be the last," he said softly. "Your trust provided for you according to Lady Andromeda's demand, and considering there had been a not-insignificant sum settled on you by the Marquess of Buxton, you should never have been reduced to rags. Not ever. By all accounts, your trust still possessed hearty funds when you went to Lady Andromeda."

His words brought more confusion rather than explanation. She struggled to make sense of what Torrie had just told her.

"The Marquess of Buxton? But why would he place any funds in trust for me? I've neither met the man nor heard of him."

His countenance shifted again, his jaw tensing, a flicker of something like surprise flaring in his vivid eyes. "You didn't know then, Bess?"

"Didn't know what?" She searched his gaze, trying to understand how the man she had only recently married could know more of her past than she did, when he didn't even recall his own. "What are you trying to tell me?"

"Ah, Christ," he muttered, his thumb running over her cheekbone in a gentle sweep. "I thought you knew. I'm sorry, love. If I'd had an inkling, I wouldn't have told you now, not like this."

"You wouldn't have told me what?"

"That your father was a by-blow of the marquess," he explained patiently. Kindly. Painfully. "Buxton apparently settled a significant sum on his son, which rightfully became yours after his death. The funds were held in trust. But it would seem that you were passed from one relative to the next, each of them culling every last ha'penny they could from you, until there was nothing left."

Elizabeth reeled. She was utterly astounded by this revelation, for her father had never spoken of the Marquess of Buxton. Not once. Nor, as she thought of it now, had he spoken often of his own father, aside to say that he had died. Before that, once, when she had been a very small girl, a man had paid a fleeting call to them. His carriage had born a crest, she remembered now, and she had watched from a window in awe at the sight of the matched horses pulling that tremendous conveyance. It had been apparent from the way in which her mother and father had welcomed him that the stranger had been someone important. A lord.

My God, had it been the Marquess of Buxton? Could it be true that her father was his illegitimate son? And if so, why had no one ever told her? And if there had been funds aplenty for her care, why had she never had a chamber with wood in the grate and a fire with which to warm herself? Why had her slippers always been threadbare, her dresses castoffs from others? Why had she spent miserable winters sleeping in attic garrets, often playing the role of chamber maid for her mother's cousin until the family had grown too much in size, according to Mrs. Pettigrew, and she had been sent away?

"Bess? Say something. You're frightfully pale."

Torrie's voice intruded. She blinked, and he was there, his face concerned and sinfully handsome as he hovered over her. His thumb had never stopped stroking her cheek, and she found herself leaning into that touch now, taking comfort from his compassion, his concern.

"I never knew," she admitted, feeling foolish.

And utterly shocked.

Her father had been the illegitimate son of a marquess?

She hadn't been relying on the generosity of distant relations all this time?

No, instead, if what Torrie had just told her was true, they had been relying on *her* funds to provide themselves the lives of comfort they wished, until they had grown tired of her.

"My God, Bess." He took her in his arms then, holding her tight.

And she could do nothing but cling to him in response, wrapping her own arms around his lean form and falling into his by-now-familiar warmth and strength. It struck her suddenly, how much she trusted him. How much she relied on him.

How much she cared for him.

"I'm sorry," he whispered, his lips moving over her hair.

And she realized she was weeping. Fat tears rolling down her cheeks that could not be stopped. Why she cried, she couldn't say. Surprise? Hurt? Confusion? Or perhaps a blend of all three and more. It would seem she'd been lied to for most of her life by everyone around her. Not even her own mother and father had told her the truth. And when they had died unexpectedly in a carriage accident, she'd been left to the mercy of a world that had taken advantage of her.

"They were lying to me," she sniffed. "All this time. They made me leave behind my cat, Mince Pie. She was a tortoise shell, her coat all black with small flecks of orange, and she was so sweet and trusting, the only friend I had in the world after my mother and father died, and they said that I came to them with nothing, so they couldn't possibly afford to feed one more hungry belly."

Just as swiftly, anger rose as she recalled the way she had been made to labor for Mr. and Mrs. Pettigrew, treated no better than as if she were a maid laboring for the family. The pain of leaving behind Mincey. Those cold, terrible winters. And Lady Andromeda, always wearing fine jewels, a roaring fire in her own chamber to keep her warm, dressed to perfection whilst Elizabeth had her old, worn gowns to mend and wear. She thought of all the times Lady Andromeda had reminded her how grateful she ought to be, for all the generosity which had been bestowed on her.

"I don't like seeing you weep." His voice was a low rumble against her ear, his hands moving in comforting motions up and down the small of her back. "My sweet Bess. You're too kindhearted and trusting, and they took advantage of you. Every last one of them."

They had, and how silly she felt too, for believing without question. For trusting.

"I was a fool," she muttered into the perfect fall of his cravat. Very likely, she had marred it with her tears, but she was feeling too distressed to care at the moment.

"No. You were a girl alone in the world, preyed on by the people who were meant to protect you." There was a sharp edge in his voice she'd never heard before. True fury.

On her behalf.

His outrage melted some of the anger inside her. How fortunate she was to have somehow found herself married to this man—to the man he was now. He had been nothing but honorable, patient, considerate, and caring with her from the first.

"Thank you," she said, leaning her head back to gaze up at him through watery eyes.

His brow furrowed. "For what?"

"For telling me the truth. For championing me."

Years ago, when their circumstances had been so dissimilar, he had not. But he had been a different person then. Nothing like the Torrie she had come to know.

"I'll never stop, Bess. You deserve nothing less."

She believed him.

And she was beginning to believe in herself, as well.

Impulsively, Elizabeth rolled to her toes, setting her lips to his. He made a low sound of approval, responding instantly, deepening the kiss until it was hungry and carnal.

They were both breathless when he tore his mouth from hers. "If we don't stop soon, we won't make it to supper."

She wouldn't have minded missing the evening, for thinking about spending a few hours in the presence of Torrie's friends still made her feel desperately uncertain. However, she had no wish to cause more scandal than they already had with their hasty marriage.

"I suppose we must, in that case," she agreed with the greatest of reluctance, releasing her hold on him.

Her sinful husband winked. "There's always the carriage, my dear."

THE HOUR WAS QUITE late as their carriage rocked over Mayfair roads, returning them to Torrington House.

"You did splendidly tonight," Torrie praised, his eyes burning with intensity in the low light of the lamps illuminating the interior.

Elizabeth wasn't certain she had done splendidly. However, she hoped that she had made at least a passable presentation of herself as his viscountess. For their parts, his friends the Earl and Countess of Rayne had been welcoming hosts, and within moments of their arrival, she had realized she had been fretting over the night without cause.

"Thank you," she murmured, pleased by his compliment nonetheless. "Everyone was so kind to me."

"Rayne is an excellent chap," Torrie said easily, settling his hand over hers in her lap, lacing their fingers together. "And the countess is Monty's sister, so she's a good sort as well."

"How long have you known them?" she asked, before

realizing she had misspoken and hurrying to amend her question. "Forgive me. That was dreadfully rude of me. I didn't mean to bring up an unsettling subject."

He gave her fingers a squeeze. "You needn't apologize, Bess. I'm accustomed to questions like that by now. At first, after my accident, it was more difficult for me to accept than it is now that most of my memory is gone. I've had ample time to live with it."

"How long has it been since the accident?"

"Two years." His thumb found the sensitive skin of her inner wrist beneath her kid glove and sleeve, playing over her in light circles.

"Do you suppose your memory will ever return?"

The question fled her before she could think better of it, motivated by her own fear. Because if her husband *did* remember everything, she had no notion of where it would leave the two of them and this fragile truce they'd struck thus far in their marriage.

What if he remembered everything one day, and he would once again think of her as the plain, plump partridge? What if he regretted marrying her?

"Pray don't answer," she rushed to say. "I shouldn't have asked you."

"I don't know if it will," he answered, voice low and decadent, like velvet to her senses. "At first, I wished for nothing more than for it to be restored. My friends and family knew a life I didn't. I looked at them and saw strangers. It was... odd in a way I cannot explain. But over time, that changed for me. Now, I try not to be as concerned with what I've lost as I am with what I've gained."

The look he gave her was pure sensual intent.

Her breath caught. "And what have you gained?"

"I've rebuilt friendships." He gave her hand a gentle tug. "And I've found a wife." He brought her hand to his lips for a reverent kiss, and she wished she weren't wearing gloves. "Now tell me, how are you feeling after my dreadfully thoughtless revelation before supper?"

She had been doing her utmost not to think of it during the carriage ride to the earl's town house and the subsequent meal they had shared. If she thought about it for too long, her emotions swelled to an uncomfortable crescendo. She was still shocked, she supposed, and equal parts angry and sad.

"It changes nothing for me," she said slowly, struggling to sort out her complicated tangle of feelings. "My parents are gone, Mince Pie is gone, Buxton is gone, and anything that remained of the trust he left is long gone as well. I cannot go back in time and right the wrongs which have been done. All I can do is move forward."

He kissed her hand again. "Have I told you how much I admire your strength?"

She hardly felt strong.

She felt, most days, desperately weak. Especially where he was concerned.

"You're too good to me," she said thickly, moved by the expression on his face, the careful way he had been at her side all evening.

It was far more than she had ever dared to hope from him, particularly given the nature of their marriage.

"Oh, but I could be better." He gave her a wicked smile that sent smoldering heat straight through her. "Would you like that?"

She forgot about the past at once. Forgot about her fears for the future. All that mattered was this moment. This man.

"Yes," she said, breathless again. "Please."

"Come here," he invited, patting his lap.

Fresh heat pulsed between her thighs. Her body was more attuned to his than ever, and she had spent much of supper longing for his touch rather than paying attention to the conversation or the food on her plate.

"How?" she asked, eying his lap and thinking there was scarcely sufficient room for her there.

"I'll show you."

With his tender guidance, she found herself astride him, her gown and redingote pooled about her, her thighs on either side of his, knees bent on the Moroccan leather squabs. The position left her open to him, the texture of his trousers over his muscled thighs pressing shockingly— delightfully—into her most intimate flesh.

"There we are," he said, sounding infinitely pleased as he removed his hat and placed it on the seat she had vacated. "I told you there is always the carriage, did I not? And I must confess, I've been thinking of nothing but this from the second you left my arms earlier this evening."

He had?

"You have?" she blurted.

"Oh, yes." His smile turned her insides molten as he fingered the closures on her redingote, plucking them open one by one, just as he had the buttons on her night rail the night before. "And it was nothing short of torture, being seated at the dinner table tonight, staring at you in this dress without being able to do with you as I wished."

She swallowed, licking lips that had gone suddenly dry at his words. "What did you wish to do?"

He had finished opening her outer garment, which was still Lady Andromeda's castoff. Madame Beauchamp had managed to send the evening gown and some undergarments, but Elizabeth's new wardrobe was far from complete.

"I wanted to do this," he said, giving her bodice a swift tug.

So swift that her nipples popped free, her breasts completely exposed.

"And this." He bent his head and sucked hard on one pebbled bud.

Her breath left her in a quivery sigh. His mouth was so hot and wet, the suction making an answering need throb to life between her legs. Her hands settled on his shoulders for purchase as the carriage rattled over a bump in the road.

"I can understand why you didn't wish to do this at the dinner table before Lord and Lady Rayne," she managed.

He chuckled against her breast, before giving her nipple another lusty suck. "It would have been desperately rude, would it have not?"

"Quite," was all she could manage as his wicked lips latched on her other breast and one of his hands crept beneath her skirts, unerringly gliding over her bare inner thigh.

"Are you wet for me, Bess?" He scraped the swell of her breast with his teeth, his fingers venturing higher.

"Yes," she hissed as those fingers parted her folds and glanced over the sensitive nub he had so thoroughly pleasured the night before.

How good it felt, his touch.

"I've been wanting to do this, too," he murmured, eyes hooded as he watched her while he stroked her sex. "I've been wanting to pet this pretty cunny of yours, to feel how slick and drenched you are. Tell me, Bess, were you this wet all during dinner and polite conversation?"

His sinful words only served to heighten her need. She thought in that moment that she would do anything, say anything to please him, if only he would promise to keep touching her this way.

"I," she began, then faltered when he rubbed rhythmically over her pearl before his fingers traced a trail of fire lower.

Words eluded her. So, too, the capacity for thought.

He parted her, his touch dipping to her entrance.

"So wet, love," he praised, probing her lightly.

"Mmm," was all she could manage, a guttural plea. She didn't know what he intended to do with those clever fingers next, but it hardly mattered. All she wanted was more of it. More of him.

He sank inside her. One finger, stretching, entering her. The sensation was exquisite, sending a sharp spike of dark desire through her core.

"Ah, Christ, I love the way your cunny feels, so tight and hot." He stroked deeper. "So perfect, gripping my finger. So greedy."

She loved the way he felt inside her. She would have told him, but in the next second, that lone digit sank all the way inside her, reaching a place where pleasure bordered on the painfully exquisite.

She bore down on him, rocking against his hand in help-less agony, loving the fullness, the pressure. His thumb stroked over her bud as he worked his finger in and out of her with slow, maddening pumps. The sound of her wetness filled the carriage above the familiar jangling of tack and clattering of wheels and hooves. It was obscene and somehow even more rousing at the same time. She rode his finger, her breasts bouncing and swaying, her nipples hard and pointed.

"There's my girl." He caught a stiff peak in his mouth. "I wanted to do this, too." He withdrew his finger suddenly, bringing it to his lips and sucking it clean before pulling it free with a rumble of pure masculine satisfaction. "And this. God, Bess, you taste so good. I want to eat your cunny when we get home. But first, I want to make you come."

She was close already. The combination of his knowing touch and filthy words was all it required. If anyone had told her that she would be bare-breasted, riding her husband's lap on her way home from a staid supper with the Earl and

Countess of Rayne this evening, she wouldn't have believed them. And yet, here she was. No match for her husband's stunning sensual abandon.

His hand was beneath her gown and petticoats and chemise again, finding her center. Caressing her lightly, teasingly. Making her impatient.

"Torrie," she bit out. "Please."

"Tell me what you want," he urged.

Oh, how wicked. He wanted her to say it aloud. And she wanted to please him.

"I want you to make me come," she forced out quietly, her cheeks going hot and a corresponding rush of wetness rushing to her sex.

"Good girl." He swirled a caress over her bud, making her hips jerk in response. "Time for your reward."

And oh, what a reward it was. His thumb circled her clitoris, while his fingers slipped through her folds, sinking into her with exacting finesse. He stroked, filling her, stretching her wider. It had to be more than one finger inside her now. *Oh God.* It was so thrilling, so wicked, the illicit allure of making love like this in a carriage under the cover of darkness as they rode through Mayfair. His tongue flicked over her nipples, his attention divided evenly between both breasts as his hand worked furiously beneath her skirts. He sucked, licked, bit. Sank in and out of her, his fingers curling, finding that wondrous place again.

And the tension that had been coiling inside her finally burst free. Her pinnacle seized her with a violence that couldn't be contained. She came on his fingers, rocking hard on his hand to keep him in place, deep inside her where she wanted him, and he suckled her breasts as she threw back her head and cried out her devastating pleasure to the night.

So intense was her spend that there was a great rushing in her ears followed by a dim ringing. She felt delirious, out of her head as she collapsed against his chest, breathing as if she had just run the entire distance from the Earl of Rayne's town house instead of being comfortably seated on her husband's lap in a carriage.

When the last wave of her release undulated through her, he gave her pearl another little rub and withdrew his fingers. In the low light, the evidence of what he had been doing glistened as he extracted a handkerchief and discreetly wiped his fingers on it before tending to her bodice. A few sturdy yanks, and all was back in place just in time for the carriage to sway to a stop as they arrived back home.

With a sinful grin, he claimed her lips with his again, and then helped her, weak-kneed and breathless and sated, from his lap.

She would never look at a carriage in the same way again.

CHAPTER 11

*A*lthough a week had passed since his marriage to Bess, once again, breakfast was proving a frigid affair. One in which his mother largely ignored his wife's presence at the table, refused to refer to her directly, and had Torrie's ire rising until he was clenching his jaw so hard he began to develop a headache.

He turned to Bess, who was looking delightfully fetching in a morning gown that—fortunately for his ability to concentrate—was far more modest than the delightfully fetching supper frock and some of her other new gowns thus far had been. "What are your plans for the day, my dear?"

"Hattie invited me to pay her a call," Bess said shyly, a becoming tinge of pink in her cheeks as she studiously avoided his gaze.

He wondered if she was thinking about their wicked carriage ride.

Christ knew he'd been thinking of nothing but ever since she had writhed in his lap and come all over his fingers. Later, she had come on his cock as well. And the next day, and the day after. It had rather become a habit for the two of them.

He cleared his throat and shifted in his chair, reminding himself that the breakfast table with his dragon of a mother was not the place for a cockstand. "Perhaps Mother and I will join you, if you don't mind having company."

It was, he acknowledged, a desperate attempt to force the dowager into melting some of her ice where Bess was concerned. With Torrie to serve as chaperone, he reasoned, his mother would have to be on her best behavior. And paying a call to his sister and nephew would be an added incentive. Titus was a delightful baby, always smiling and never screaming, his temperament good-natured and pleasant.

"I'm afraid I have other commitments for the day," his mother said coolly, chilling the heartwarming notion of the three of them visiting Hattie and Torrie somehow managing to forge a truce between his mother and Bess.

Having a wife was glorious.

Having a scowling mother who followed him about like a cloud of doom with a bee in her bonnet was...decidedly not as glorious. And a mother who was rude to his wife as well? Well, here and now, in this moment, he was deciding that was the end of it. He'd rather had enough of her bad temper and dreadful behavior.

He pinned his mother with a searching look. "Indeed? What commitments can be of greater import than paying a call to your daughter and grandson with your son and his wife?"

His mother sputtered, looking uncharacteristically ruffled by his directness. "I'm calling on Lady Althorp."

The Countess of Althorp was one of his mother's oldest friends. They saw each other regularly.

He was unmoved by the excuse. "Can you not call on her a different day?"

His mother's expression became pinched. "No, I am afraid not. I have already made it known that I shall be calling. I cannot help but to think she would be hopelessly insulted should I suddenly send a note that I won't be calling after all."

"I'm sure she would recover," he drawled.

"But I am not certain that *I* would," his mother countered. "It is bad enough that our family has been tainted by scandal. What shall be left if I go about insulting my greatest friend as well? Lady Althorp is all I have left. Already, I fear that I shall be given the cut by others."

She was referring, of course, to his hasty nuptials with Bess and the reason for them, to say nothing of the insidious gossip Eugenia had been doing her utmost to stir.

"If our family has been tainted by scandal, the fault is mine alone," he told his mother pointedly. "Direct all your ire toward me, where it belongs."

A bitter smile curved his mother's lips. "I am not certain it belongs solely to you."

He was weary of her refusal to accept Bess. Or to, at the least, treat her with the kindness she deserved.

"Who does it belong to, if not solely myself?" he demanded curtly, keenly aware of his wife's gaze on him.

Yes, she had asked him to not to speak up on her behalf. However, his patience for his mother had been worn threadbare.

"I'm sure you know," the dowager said frostily. "The one who orchestrated this entire sordid mess. It rests solely on her shoulders."

That quickly, his anger boiled over. Torrie's fist slammed down on the table, rattling the cutlery and eliciting a gasp from his mother.

"No one orchestrated any of this," he said succinctly. "My marriage to Bess was caused by my own failures. However, I am doing everything in my power to make amends for my past mistakes. My wife has been compassionate and understanding throughout this entire ordeal, which is more than I can say for you."

By the time he had finished his tirade, his mother was gaping at him, mouth open like a fish. He was dimly aware of the presence of a footman at the sideboard, doing his best to blend in with the wall coverings. Blast. It wasn't done to argue in front of the servants, but he'd endured quite enough of his mother's ill treatment of Bess, and he would be damned if he allowed it to carry on for another moment without putting her in her place.

Belatedly, he dismissed the fellow, who hastened from the breakfast room as if his arse were aflame.

"You are not the woman of the house any longer," he added sharply when the footman had gone. "Bess is now, and you will treat her with the respect she deserves."

"Torrie," Bess protested quietly at his side, reaching for his sleeve in a staying gesture, as if to keep him from saying more on her behalf.

But he would not stop until he had reached an understanding with his mother. This could not continue. She had to accept the fact that Bess was his wife and he would not allow her to insult or otherwise be unkind to her.

"This needs to be said," he told Bess gently, hating the worry knitting her brow, the concern in her voice.

His mother suddenly stood, with such violent haste her chair overturned to the floor behind her.

"How could you?" she spat at him, tears brimming in her eyes. "The son I know would never treat me so horridly. He would never choose a greedy, grasping governess over me."

He stood as well, recognizing that there was more to his

mother's anger toward Bess than the circumstances of their marriage. It was almost as if she had chosen Bess as the scapegoat for their failed relationship. For his absent memory. For the changes in him and the man he had become after the accident.

"Bess isn't at fault for my amnesia, Mother," he said calmly. "The phaeton accident was two years ago. I know you want me to return to the man I was then, to the son you knew so well, but *I* don't. Because the more I learn of the man I was, the less I like him. Before Bess came into my life, I was in danger of becoming him again, that same, aimless scoundrel without purpose. She saved me from that, and she's made me a better man in the short time I've known her. A better man than he ever was or could have been. If you can't accept me as I am now, and if you can't accept my wife and treat her well, then perhaps the time has come for you to retire to the country."

His mother was staring at him, mouth still agape, and he wasn't sure if it was shock or outrage reflected on her countenance. He wasn't certain he cared. She had pushed him to the edge of reason, and had been gradually doing so with her impatience to return to things as they were before. He would never be the old Torrie again. Not even if he regained all his memory.

He had changed, and for the better. He wanted—*needed*— her to understand that. But he wasn't certain if she could.

"I cannot countenance it," she said at last, shaking her head. "She has fooled you and taken you from me."

Damn it, there was his answer. He wondered if a single word he had just spoken had permeated her stubborn mind. Why did she insist on clinging to her wrongheaded belief he would miraculously change and go back to being the son she'd known? When would she accept that Bess was her daughter-in-law?

"You are placing the blame where it doesn't belong," he repeated sternly. "Apologize to my wife for the disrespect you have shown her."

His mother's chin tipped up stubbornly. "I'll not apologize to her. You cannot force the words from me."

The remaining threads of Torrie's patience snapped.

He held his mother's stare, unflinching. "If you won't apologize, then I'll see to it that your belongings are packed and sent to my country seat, where you can go and reflect on the decisions you've made. You may return when you are willing to be reasonable."

She jolted as if he had struck her, but Torrie didn't regret what he had said. She had crossed a final boundary with him, and he wouldn't stand for Bess being mistreated. She'd endured mistreatment enough in her life from everyone she had known.

His wife was on her feet now as well, her hand on his coat. "Torrie, please. You needn't do this on my behalf."

"I do need," he told her firmly, before turning back to his mother. "The choice is yours, madam."

His mother's lips tightened, her fury toward him still palpable. "Forgive me."

The apology sounded painfully insincere, but he was willing to accept the gesture she had made for now. It was a start, at least.

He inclined his head. "Thank you, Mother."

"If you'll excuse me," she said. "I must return to my apartments to prepare for my call to Lady Althorp."

She didn't wait for him to respond before sweeping from the chamber, still in high dudgeon. Still refusing to accompany them on a call to Hattie. Torrie waited until the door had closed with more force than necessary at her back to turn toward Bess.

"I'm sorry for her coldness toward you," he said, regret

filling his chest with heaviness. "She has been having difficulty accepting my lack of memory and the changes in me for a long time. Unfortunately, my marriage to you appears to have further strained the relationship between she and I. However, the fault is not yours, and I'll not stand for the disrespect she continues to pay you."

Bess's fingers tightened on his sleeve. "Thank you. You must know that I don't wish for there to be any discord between yourself and your mother. Certainly not on my behalf."

Christ, even after the cutting words his mother had issued concerning her, Bess was still capable of such kindness. It was humbling. He would protect her with his dying breath. The depth of feeling he had for this woman astounded him. She was so good, so compassionate, so caring. And how he hated that she had been overlooked and taken advantage of, used and ignored and derided and abandoned for so much of her life. It ended with him, this he vowed.

"No one was there for you in the past, to stand up for you, to champion you," he said past the rising lump in his throat. "But I'm here for you now, Bess. Now and forever."

She surprised him by rising on her toes to press a chaste kiss to his cheek. "I am so grateful, Torrie. If you don't mind, I think that I should like to go and speak with her, just to clarify matters between us if I'm able."

Once more, she amazed him. "After that dreadful display, you would still wish to speak with her?"

"Yes." Bess gave him a small, sad smile. "Her heart is hurting. She is my mother-in-law now, and I would hate for her to feel uncomfortable in her own home because of me."

How good she was. How kind. He felt like the world's greatest cad in her shadow, knowing what he had done to her and having just born witness to his own mother's treatment of her.

He took Bess's hand in his, raising it to his lips for a kiss, her compassion lighting an answering warmth deep inside him. "If you wish it. But be forewarned, if she is unkind to you, it won't go well for her."

Torrie could only hope that, in the face of Bess's kindness, his mother's ice would at last begin to melt. If anyone could manage such a feat, he had no doubt it would be his lovely wife.

What had he ever done without her?

ELIZABETH KNEW she was taking a tremendous risk, seeking out the dowager after what had happened in the breakfast room. However, she had hated seeing the pain in the older woman's eyes. And she knew that she had to, at the very least, make an effort to forge some manner of truce, if there could be one. Now that she and Torrie had been married for the span of a week and she'd had the opportunity to settle in to her new life and home, she was feeling far stronger than she had upon her initial arrival.

She reached the dowager at the top of the stairs after hastening from the chamber in her wake and leaving Torrie to finish his breakfast alone.

"My lady," she called to the dowager's departing back. "Wait, if you please."

Her mother-in-law stopped and spun about to face her, resembling nothing so much as an angry stray feline attempting to defend her territory. "What cheek you have, following me. What can you possibly wish? The opportunity to gloat at how you have won my son and I am left with nothing?"

Elizabeth rushed forward, thinking that she finally understood the other woman, in a way she hadn't been capable of doing before. For the dowager viscountess, it didn't matter that Torrie's accident had happened two years before and Elizabeth had only just entered his life. Their sudden marriage, coupled with the scandal that had been the cause for it, had driven a further wedge between the woman and her son.

"Don't you see?" she asked, stopping when she reached the dowager, her breath ragged from the haste with which she had departed the breakfast room. "You are hardly left with nothing. Torrie is still your son."

"A son who doesn't remember me and is a shell of his former self," the dowager said with a sniff. "That is what I am left with, a son who takes the side of his scheming governess wife at the first opportunity, who chooses you over me. How can that be any less than nothing?"

Tears glittered in the other woman's eyes, but she blinked furiously, clearly too proud to allow them to fall.

Too late, for Elizabeth had seen them, and it was a sure sign that the dowager was not unassailable. Rather, she was all too vulnerable.

"I am sorry for all you have lost with him," she said quietly. "I can imagine how difficult it must be for you. I lost my parents when I was a girl, and I mourn them still, every day. There isn't a sun that rises or sets without me remembering them fondly, wishing they were still here. But you haven't lost Torrie. He's not dead."

"He may as well be," the dowager snapped, her linen cap bobbing wildly in her distress. "I kept hoping that with time, his memory would return. The physician said that it was a possibility. But as time has gone on, and he has scarcely remembered anything of note, my hopes have waned. And then when he married you, I knew for certain that he would never be the same son I knew again."

"I'm not to blame for his amnesia," she reminded the other woman gently. "The accident was two years ago."

"Don't you see? You are the symbol of everything I've lost. His mesalliance with you signaled the end of my last dream for him. I had such high aspirations for his marriage. Lady Althorp's eldest daughter would have made him a perfect match. Such a lovely young woman, in her second Season, a veritable diamond of the first water, her lineage impeccable." Her voice broke, and she pressed a hand to her mouth, as if she were too broken to continue.

Long ago, when she had been a child and her parents had still been alive and everything had been right and wonderful in Elizabeth's world, she had been running wild in a field. Quite against the advice of her mother, and without any shoes. Barefoot and giggling, she had raced through that flower-dappled field without a hint of care for the consequences.

Until her bare foot had landed soundly on a bee, and she had been stung.

The dowager's refusal to relent was akin to that sting, only it was lodged deeper. And she knew that she didn't have her mother waiting to soothe her and remove the stinger. This time, she was alone. But not unlike that day, she had gone heedlessly rushing into something she never should have.

She could see that now.

The dowager wasn't ready. Perhaps she never would be. Her hurt was too great, and in her mind, Elizabeth was partially responsible for dealing the last of the painful blows.

"I am sure Lady Althorp's daughter would have made Torrie a lovely bride as well," she agreed, pleased with herself at the steadiness of her voice. "I am certain her bloodlines are faultless and she is the loveliest of debutantes. I have no doubt I cannot match her beauty or grace. However, I am the woman your son has married. And one day, I hope that you will be able to see beyond the pain to which you cling. When you do, I'll be waiting, and so shall he." She dipped into a curtsy—the finest one she had ever performed. "I bid you a good day, my lady, and I do hope you enjoy your call on Lady Althorp."

With that, she turned away again before the other woman could spy the sheen of tears in her own eyes. Defeat sat heavily on her heart as she made her way back to the breakfast room.

CHAPTER 12

$\mathcal{E}$lizabeth was in the music room, playing the pianoforte, a skill which she hadn't had the opportunity to practice for her own pleasure in years. Lady Andromeda had been forced to sell her pianoforte some time ago, and then Elizabeth had spent her time in service, as a governess. Her every occasion to play had been teaching her charges.

Now, here, at last, was yet another small freedom she'd been denied. Gradually, one by one, they had amassed. And she hadn't realized how much she had missed these tiny parts of her former self until one day, they had simply all been gone. She had packed her meager belongings, bid Lady Andromeda farewell, and she had gone on to her post.

Warming to her cause, she played on. Song after song, until her fingers grew tired from the effort, and at last she finished with a lively tune that had always been one of her favorites. At the last note, she sighed happily, feeling that same sense of deep contentment that washed over her when she was in Torrie's arms.

It felt right, being here.

Being his wife.

Too right.

Everything in her life that had been good had always been stolen from her too soon—her parents, her childhood, her freedom, her happiness, the only true home she had ever known. Heavens, even the funds left in trust to her by her parents had been depleted without her knowledge. It stood to reason that it would be no different with Torrie, and that she would lose him and this fledgling happiness as well. Perhaps he would grow tired of her. He would take a mistress. He would regain his memory and recall her as the plump, plain partridge he had once derided.

The thought of it made guilt slice through her. For she knew that he suffered, living a life he couldn't remember, even if he had told his mother that he preferred the man he was now to the man he had been.

Surely, the weight of not remembering was a mantle he wore heavily, for the way it affected his relationships with his friends and family. She had no doubt that if he could recall his past, a burden would be lifted from his shoulders. And she wanted that for him. Wanted the conflict which had been brewing between himself and the dowager to fade.

And in the same respect, she hated herself for being so greedy and selfish, for also wanting him as he was instead of as he had been. For fearing he would no longer want her if his past were suddenly restored to him.

"That was a heavy sigh following such a spirited reel."

At Torrie's deep voice behind her, she gave a jolt, spinning to find him crossing the room to her, the door closed behind him. She hadn't heard him enter, nor had she heard the door snap shut.

Elizabeth rose from the bench, feeling more vulnerable and awkward than she did when they were naked and alone together, her feelings so raw and close to the surface. "How long were you standing there, listening to me play?"

"Since several songs ago now." He gave her the slow, intimate smile that never failed to make everything inside her melt. "You are exceptionally talented, Bess. I hope you don't mind. I intended to make my presence known, but then I also hated interrupting. Listening to you play soothes me."

His words filled her with warmth. His gaze burned into hers.

"I missed you," she blurted.

Stupidly.

Had she not promised herself that she would control her emotions where he was concerned? That she would not open herself to hurt any more than was utterly necessary?

But Torrie's sensual mouth quirked into an instant smile, and he closed the last of the distance separating them, taking her into his arms as if it were the most natural of actions.

And to Elizabeth, it felt as if it were. In his arms was her favorite place to be. It occurred to her suddenly, with potent power, that Torrie felt more like a home to her than any of the roofs she had ever had above her head.

"I missed you too, love." He kissed the tip of her nose—the pointed tip she despised—in a tender gesture that made her heart skip a beat. "It's been years since I left your bed this morning, and I couldn't bear another second from your side."

A giggle slipped from her at his extravagant declaration, meant in jest, for that was another side of her husband she was coming to know—he could be lighthearted as well as charming when he chose. And heaven help her, she liked every new side of him she met. Liked them all far, far too much.

"It has only been hours, not years," she corrected gently, twining her arms around his neck.

He was tall and handsome and so deliciously strong

everywhere. How she admired him and his ability to regain his strength after his accident. He had confided in her that it had taken him some time to recover following his phaeton crash. But when he had been able, he had thrown himself into the one way he could heal himself, if not his mind: through physical exertion. His efforts certainly showed in the breadth of his shoulders and his lean form.

Torrie lowered his forehead to hers. "It may as well have been years. All I've been able to think about is you."

More warmth crept over her. Tentative. Hopeful. Contagious. She couldn't stop it any more than she could force rain to cease falling from the sky. The way she felt for him was inevitable.

"You have?"

"Yes. Thinking about your lips and how long it has been since they've been beneath mine. An eternity, I vow." His mouth found hers for a long, drugging kiss that stole her breath before he ended it far sooner than she would have preferred. "And holding you in my arms." The band encircling her tightened in emphasis. "And fucking you."

At the last wicked statement, her ears went hot. "Torrie!"

Her husband also possessed a shockingly vulgar tongue when in private. One she had discovered she secretly enjoyed.

His grin deepened, unrepentant. "And burying my face in your sweet cunny."

Now her entire face was hot. "You put me to the blush."

He winked. "You like it."

The audacity of the man. But he was not wrong. She *did* like it. She liked him. She liked the easiness they had settled into together. She liked everything they did, intimate and otherwise.

Also too much.

The nagging sense of fear crept over her once more, but she tamped it down.

"How was your session at Winter's Boxing Academy this morning?" she asked, seeking to distract herself from the inconvenient emotions churning within her.

"Punishing. Winter has one hell of a fist. I was thinking about you when he landed a blow to my jaw that is still smarting."

Concern rose, her gaze dipping to the strong, whisker-stubbled slash of jawline. "Are you injured?"

"My pride, yes, and quite dreadfully." He kissed her again swiftly. "Would you care to kiss it and make it better?"

Her lips tingled from his mouth, and yearning burned through her. "Your jaw or your pride?"

"I was rather thinking of my cock." His grin deepened at his outrageous pronouncement.

She laughed, but then the laughter swiftly died, because she was thinking about what he had said. Not long ago, she would have been shocked by such a suggestion, such a notion. She wouldn't have even been able to make sense of it. But now, she understood. And it fanned the flames of her hunger.

"Here?" she asked, daring to glide a hand between their bodies, over his taut abdomen to the fall of his trousers where she found his cock with ease. He was thick and eager and long, so very long, as she wrapped her fingers around his length through the fine fabric separating them.

"Bess." He swallowed hard, his Adam's apple bobbing over the simple knot in his cravat. "I was teasing you."

"I know you were." She held his gaze, feeling bold. Feeling needy. Feeling as if she were invincible. "But I want to. I want to pleasure you the way you do to me. Tell me what to do."

They had been married for several weeks now, and he had introduced her to so many ways the marriage bed could

SCARLETT SCOTT

be enjoyed. But like everything where Torrie was concerned, Elizabeth was greedy. She wanted more.

Beneath her questing fingers, he thickened, growing harder. The effect that her words had on him pleased her immensely. Heightened her own desire. She was already wet and throbbing, pressing her thighs together to stave off the rising need.

"Christ," he muttered, hips rocking into her touch, lowering his face to her throat where he nuzzled her, then sucked on the delicate cord there, so hard that she suspected he might leave a mark. Likely she ought to be scandalized by such a prospect, but at the moment, she was too caught up in her own need to care.

"What are you doing to me, wife?" he added in a low growl.

She stroked him again, her touch firmer, finding the sinful words and the boldness within her that he had brought to life. "Making your cock hard."

"Ah, damn it. You're frightfully good at that, aren't you, love?" He chuckled, nipping at her ear.

An excellent compliment. One she accepted with secret pride.

How powerful it made her feel, to know he desired her. To know she could make him feel as weak with wanting as he made her.

"Tell me what to do," she urged him, wickedness surging.

And her husband liked it, for he groaned. "Now?"

"Oh, yes." She gave him another taunting stroke through his trousers. "Tell me."

"Damn it." He kissed her jaw, her lips, then lifted his head, considering her with a smoldering stare before he nodded, apparently satisfying himself with whatever he had been attempting to see in her countenance. "You want my cock in your mouth?"

Something deep in her core fluttered at the crude words, the images they brought to her mind. "Please."

He kissed her sweetly, deeply, and just when she thought she would burst with the sheer beauty of the sensations he evoked, he ended it and raised his head. "Come with me, Bess."

His voice was rough with desire and yet soft as velvet, and she was instantly aflame. When he looked at her as he was now, and when he spoke to her thus, she knew she would follow him anywhere he asked.

Even to the gates of Hades itself.

He took her hand in his and led her from the music room.

TORRIE HADN'T INTENDED to return from his bout at Winter's Boxing Academy, covered in perspiration, jaw aching from his lack of attention, and perpetual back pain gnawingly persistent, to a wife offering to suck his cock.

But he had.

And she had, thank Christ for that.

And now here they were, in the nearly overflowing tub together, Bess on his lap, his aching length nestled firmly against her soft bottom. He cupped her generous breasts and thumbed her nipples as he kissed the delicate shell of her ear.

"I could grow accustomed to taking all my baths with you," he murmured, wondering to himself why he had never thought of bathing with her before.

Had he known how delightful and rousing it would be to have her in his bath, he wouldn't have bloody well waited several weeks into their marriage to give it a try. But now he knew, and he intended to bathe with Bess as often as possible.

Any excuse, really, to have her naked and at his mercy.

"I was certain we both wouldn't fit in the tub at the same time," she said breathlessly, arching into his hands so that his palms overflowed.

"And I was equally certain we would," he said, rolling the hard peaks of her breasts between his forefinger and thumb, then tugging at them until she made a soft, breathy sound and writhed in his lap.

He had taken great pleasure in soaping every inch of her body, and she had done the same for him. When she had been bold enough to ask to take him in her mouth earlier, a bolt of lust had gone straight through him. But although he had been eager, he hadn't wanted a hurried shag in the music room.

No, indeed. He wanted a thorough, prolonged bedding.

His cock pulsed at the thought, ready.

"The water is nearly overflowing," Bess pointed out, giving him a sidelong look that made him want to kiss her.

So he did, showing her without words just how badly he wanted her. When the kiss ended, they were both breathless and overflowing water was the last thing on either of their minds, he had no doubt.

His hand glided down her smooth, slippery belly, not stopping until he was parting her folds and finding her pearl, swollen and eager for attention. "We could *make* it overflow, if you'd like," he suggested wickedly.

This new domesticity with Bess had him in a state of perpetual readiness. Following his accident, he had been adrift, seeking bed partners to slake his need and not remind him of how broken he was. But with Bess, everything was different. He didn't long for anyone else, and everything that happened between them was founded in something far deeper and more potent than mere lust and bodily needs. Nor, it seemed, could he have his fill of her. He wasn't bedding her to forget that he was broken. He was bedding her because she made him feel, for the first time, utterly whole.

She chuckled, the sound low and throaty, landing directly in his cock. "Why should we wish to make such a mess of the chamber? The poor maids would not be happy with us."

She cared about the servants, and that pleased him too. Her kind heart extended to everyone. Including, he had discovered, to animals. Her growing bond with Hattie's cat Sir Toby, coupled with the story she'd told him of the tortoise shell cat she'd been forced to abandon, had persuaded him that Bess ought to have a feline of her own to keep her company. Not a replacement for her Mince Pie, but a new friend. One with whom she would not be made to part.

But cats fled his mind as his fingers slid lower, finding her entrance and teasing her.

"We could sop up the mess ourselves afterward if that absolves your conscience," he said, wondering at the mechanics of fucking her in the tub.

He didn't know if his old self had made love to a woman in the water, but the notion of doing so with Bess was deuced tempting. He could spin her about on his lap, he thought, so that she could ride him…

"Oh," she breathed with feeling as his finger slid deeper, her inner muscles clenching in welcome.

"You're contemplating it now, aren't you?" he teased, stroking her pearl simultaneously.

"You are…Torrie…"

Her words drifted off as he traced the whorl of her ear with his tongue. "I am, indeed, Torrie. How astute you are, wife dearest."

Wife.

Damn, no matter how many times he called her by that title, it never failed to make him hard. In this instance, harder than he had already been, with her delightful arse snuggled against him and his forefinger buried inside her to the knuckle.

Who would have thought that being married would become such a potent aphrodisiac? Not Torrie. But here he was at a quarter to midday, naked with his wife in the bath, and happier than he had ever been.

"I didn't mean...that..." Bess was panting now, her words once more drifting away as he continued to play with her.

A bit more pressure on her clitoris. He strummed as if she were an instrument, adding a second finger and working both deeper.

He bit her earlobe. "What did you mean, then?"

She shifted, water rippling over the edge in truth now, the crevice on her bottom sliding along his aching cock. Narrowly, he avoided the urge to thrust. To rub himself all over her in any way he could.

"I meant..."

He tongued the hollow behind her ear and she faltered again.

"What did you mean then, love?" he asked innocently, all while continuing to destroy them both with his fingers and tongue.

He couldn't bloody well wait to have her on the bed, naked, legs spread, so he could feast on her delicious cunny. For the moment, he would have to settle for playing with her under the water and making her squirm, which had its own rewards. Oh how he adored watching his prim governess unravel and surrender herself to desire.

"Mmm," was all she said this time.

A sign that he was succeeding in his intention to undo her thoroughly. He wanted her breathless and desperate, and if she still wanted to pleasure him after that, then good God, he strongly feared there would be nothing left of him. He would combust into a pile of ash.

Sated, well-pleased ash.

Yes, he could happily die with Bess's lush lips wrapped around his cock. There was no conceivable better way to go.

He kissed her damp throat, sucking on a place that he knew always drove her to distraction, and was gratified when she moaned and rocked against his erection.

"Have I rendered you speechless?" he asked against her skin.

"Mindless," she said with a sigh.

He could work with that.

Torrie bit the smooth curve of her shoulder. "Do you want to sit on my cock and ride me in this tub? We'll splash water all over the carpets and you can fuck me until you come, and then I'll carry you to the bed and slip inside your sweet cunny and fuck you some more."

Her cunny quivered around his fingers as he spoke the naughty words, making him smile. He didn't know where this new wickedness within him had emerged from. All he did know was that it was wild and uncontrollable. He loved saying the filthiest things to her that his mind could conjure and watching a flush turn her creamy skin rosy. And feeling the effect it had on her? That was the most delightful part of all. She was so wonderfully responsive, and he thoroughly enjoyed bringing her wicked side to life.

"That would be very bad of us, wouldn't it?" she asked breathlessly.

His smile deepened. His minx was intrigued.

"It would be very, very bad." He pulled her heavy hair to the side and kissed her nape as he sank his fingers deeper inside her, curling them just so. "But perhaps you wouldn't mind being bad with me, would you? Just this once."

"Perhaps," she said, turning her head to meet his gaze.

He was struck by her artless beauty. Hers was a face with such expressive character, her every emotion flitting over her features and bringing her countenance to life. There was strength in her jaw, stubbornness in her chin, a delightful bit of rebellion in her pointed nose. Her eyes were glistening, the golden lights burning, her dark lashes long. The lips he had been longing to see wrapped around him were parted, the color of summer berries. And he had never wanted to kiss her more.

How had his former self failed to be entranced by Bess? He couldn't fathom it now. This woman was perfect for him in every way. But then, perhaps it was a boon that he had failed to realize what a gem she was in the past, because the clod he'd once been certainly hadn't deserved her.

Hell, he wasn't sure that he deserved her *now*.

But he was selfish enough to keep her forever. And damned glad she was his.

"What say you, love?" he asked, unable to resist following the determined line of her jaw with his free hand, leaving water droplets in his wake.

Curiosity flickered in her gaze. "How would I…"

He bit his lip to stave off a chuckle at her shyness. She was a delectable combination of prudishness and wanton. He adored both.

"How would you ride me?" he asked, taking pity on her and finishing the question on her behalf.

She nodded, then wrinkled her nose. "Do you suppose it would make a terrible mess? Perhaps we could ring for some towels afterward."

She was still fretting over the servants.

"We can do whatever you wish, Bess," he told her, humbled by her compassion.

Everyone in her life had abandoned or used her. But here

178

she was, concerned over making the Aubusson damp for the chamber maids.

She nodded. "Very well, then. Show me, if you please."

Her words sent a sharp current of lust straight through him. He cupped her cheek and brought her mouth to his for a long, thorough kiss that left them both breathless.

"Do you remember the carriage?" he asked, referring to the night they had gone to supper and he had pleasured her on the way back to Torrington House.

"I do."

Her eyes darkened with desire.

"Just like that." He withdrew his fingers from her and took her waist in a gentle grip beneath the warm water.

Torrie guided her until she was facing him on bent knees, her legs on either side of his. Her wet hands settled on his shoulders, then caressed down his chest, making his cock twitch. Her breasts were full temptations in the water, but her nipples were submerged. A situation he rectified immediately by lifting her higher so he could draw one taut bud into his mouth.

Her nails scraped his chest. "Torrie."

Fuck, he loved it when she scratched him and moaned his name. And he loved her nipples in his mouth and the way she arched her back and thrust more of her breast into his face. He loved the way she smelled and the divine temptation of all her curves above and below the water's sweet-scented surface. He released her nipple with a lusty-sounding pop and inhaled a deep breath, trying to calm his raging need.

"Take what you want from me," he urged. "Touch me."

One of her hands glided beneath the water, down his chest and past his abdomen. When her fingers wrapped around his cock in a firm, sure grasp, he groaned, his head falling back against the lip of the tub.

"Like this?" she asked hesitantly.

"Hell yes," he managed as she began stroking him from base to tip. "Just like that, love. Don't stop."

Never stop, he thought.

Torrie wanted to surge inside her, but he also wanted her hand on him. Wanted her to take control of the moment and himself and her own desire, too. Being at her sensual mercy was the most exquisite seduction.

As was watching her settle into her own sensual power. And oh, what power she had over him. Not just in this, the carnal. But in other ways, too. Since their marriage, he had spent his days thinking about her, wanting to make her happy. Living for her, not just for himself.

Her hand glided up and down his cock with greater confidence, swiftly banishing his ability to concentrate on anything other than Bess. Her touch. Her body warm and slippery atop his. Her breasts bobbing temptingly in the water between them. Her mouth awaiting more of his kisses. Her fingers working him, pulling and gripping and twisting until he was almost ready to come in the water instead of inside her where he belonged.

She leaned into him, pressing a kiss to his jaw that undid him, before her lips grazed over his ear as she spoke. "I want you in my mouth."

He groaned, those words his complete ruination. Being a gentleman and bringing her to spend first no longer mattered as Torrie was gripped with a violent need. He wrapped his hand in her wet mahogany waves and cupped her nape, pulling her to him for a voracious kiss. Their tongues tangled, their frenzy bringing their teeth together. But it didn't matter. There was no finesse in this kiss: only the affirmation of their mutual desire.

When it was over, their breaths were equally ragged.

"My lady always gets what she wants," he told her.

And then, he rose from the tub, water dripping down his

naked body, hard and readier than he had ever been. She stood as well, and there was no more beautiful sight than Bess rising from the tub, glistening and pink, all womanly curves and bright-eyed desire. Her confidence pleased him; in just a few weeks, she had come a long way from the shy, uncertain governess who had been embarrassed by her own body and needs.

Together, they stepped out of the tub, and he took a moment to towel her off thoroughly so that she wouldn't take a chill despite the merrily crackling fire in the grate. He did the same for himself, so quickly that he was still damp by the time he discarded it.

But it didn't matter. Nothing mattered but her.

"You're sure?" he rasped, trying not to allow his eagerness to supersede all else. "You needn't, love. I'm already desperate to take you."

"I'm sure. I want to." Her tongue flicked over her lips, nearly drawing another groan from him. "Tell me what to do."

Ah, hell. She was tearing him apart in the best way possible.

"Get on your knees, Bess."

She did instantly, dropping before him on the towel-shrouded Aubusson, her hair a dark curtain falling down her back. And it required all the restraint he possessed to keep himself under control. Because the sight of his beautiful wife on her knees for him was almost enough to unman Torrie right then and there. His cock jutted between them, thick and hard.

She took him in hand, and he groaned as she slicked her fist up and down his damp length before slanting him a sultry look. "What do I do now?"

His fingers tangled in her hair, holding her, sifting the

heavy, cool strands. "Whatever you want. You're in control, love."

Slowly, hesitantly, she kissed the tip of him, then dragged her lips along his shaft. "Like this?"

Before he could answer, her tongue darted out, licking his length, then finding the head where his seed had already beaded. She licked it up, and he fought against a crushing tide of need to slide his cock down her throat.

"More, please," he managed tightly, begging, and he didn't give a damn. "Take me in your mouth."

Obligingly, she brought him to her lips, opening and taking him inside. Hot wetness bathed his cock head, and if he hadn't known better, he would swear he was going to die. His heart was pounding, his body was coiled as tightly as a watch spring, and he was holding his breath. She didn't take him far, but her tongue whorled against him, making his hips desperate to pump. He wrapped her hair around his hand again as he had in the tub, watching as his cock slid deeper into her mouth.

It was heaven.

It was hell.

Exquisite torment.

He slid free and she rocked back on her heels, staring up at him with such undisguised desire that his knees threatened to give out.

"Do you like it?" she asked, her lips glistening.

"I like it too much," he ground out.

"Tell me what to do," she said. "I want to make you feel the same way I do when you pleasure me."

He swallowed hard. "Take me in your mouth again and suck."

She didn't hesitate. Still holding the base of his cock firmly, she brought the tip of him to her mouth, opening.

And damn, the sight of her crushed-berry lips wrapped around his cock…

He held his breath and counted inwardly to ten to maintain control.

She sucked, and he feared his head might fly off. Pleasure licked up his spine. His ballocks tightened. His fingers grasped at her hair.

"Touch yourself, Bess," he managed to order. "Touch yourself as you take my cock."

She moaned around his shaft, and he felt the rumble of her desire deep within him. As she sucked harder, taking him deeper into the velvet recesses of her mouth, her free hand did as he had commanded, her fingers dipping between her legs to pleasure herself. The sight of her hand working, the soft breathy sounds she made as she swallowed a mouthful of his cock, and the knowledge that she was petting her perfect cunny whilst it all unfolded proved too much for him.

As gently as Torrie could manage, he disengaged, slipping from her eager mouth.

She was still on her knees, her fingers glistening from her swollen sex, blinking up at him as if in a drugged state of lust and confusion. "Is something amiss?"

"Nothing, love. You please me far too well," he hastened to reassure her. "I have to be inside you now."

Somehow, he managed to gently haul her to her feet and get the two of them the rest of the way across the chamber. They fell into bed together, Bess on her back, Torrie between her parted thighs, his throbbing cock pressed to her center. He took her lips, tasting the muskiness of himself in her kiss, as he thrust inside her.

Her muscles clenched in welcome, and he lost himself to the beauty of their lovemaking. They were one, bodies aligned, breaths merging, lips fused. She met him thrust for thrust, just as eager as he was, and all it took was his thumb pressing on her swollen pearl for her to come. Harder, faster he rode her, until the spasms of her own release proved too much. He sank inside her deep and spent, filling her with the hot lash of his seed.

When coherent thought returned, he was breathless and helpless, the heavy weight of him pinning her to the bed, his heart pounding with the relentless fury of a galloping steed.

"I'm crushing you," he murmured into her ear, body still awash with the intensity of his release.

"Stay." She wrapped her arms around his back, holding him tightly to her. "I love the way you feel on me, inside me."

"I'm too heavy," he protested anyway, although his cock did feel bloody good buried inside her, still pulsing.

"You're wonderful," Bess said.

And when she said it, he believed it.

So, he stayed as he was, his face burrowed into her neck, thinking himself the luckiest damn man alive. Feeling as if they were invincible together. That nothing and no one could separate or break them.

It was a feeling that terrified him, because he couldn't help but fear that it couldn't possibly last.

CHAPTER 13

"Don't open your eyes just yet."

Elizabeth sighed at her husband's decree, but she couldn't keep the smile from her lips. He was being so secretive this morning, and it was as endearing as it was maddening. She had awoken to find herself alone in her bed, which was quite unusual since they had fallen into an easy routine of spending each night together.

Waking without him had been unsettling. She had rolled to her belly, stretching an arm out to touch him as she always did, and had met with empty bedclothes instead of warm, hard man. But as quickly as she had risen and begun performing her morning ablutions, he had returned, looking unfairly handsome whilst her hair remained a wild tangle from the night's sleep.

When she had asked him where he had been at such an early hour, he had told her she would have to be patient. He had then directed her to a chair by the hearth, telling her she must close her eyes and await a surprise he had procured for her.

A gift.

For her.

No one had given Elizabeth one since she had been a girl, and that Torrie had ventured from bed early this morning just for her filled her with warmth.

"Why must I keep them closed?" she asked now, wondering where he was in the room. "It's rather disconcerting to remain as I am for so long. I'm beginning to feel quite dizzied."

The last was an exaggeration, but when Torrie had instructed her to close her eyes and not peek whilst he went about whatever mysterious task he was currently conducting, she had been obliged to sit and do as he had asked. Her sense of anticipation was getting the best of her.

"You're dizzy?" There was instant concern in his voice. "You aren't taking ill, are you?"

She wasn't accustomed to someone taking such an interest in her welfare. But he did. He was attentive, attuned to her, it seemed. Whether they were alone in bed or at a societal obligation surrounded by others, Torrie made certain to put her at ease. When she was feeling shy, he'd offer words of encouragement. When she was nervous, he made a silly joke. When she feared her gowns were too revealing or daring, he told her that she looked lovely.

"I'm not taking ill," she reassured him, careful to keep her eyes still firmly closed regardless of how badly she wished to open them. "I'm merely eager to see whatever it is you've been so secretive about."

"Thank God. You had me worried there for a moment."

He was farther away from her, on the opposite end of the room, if she had to wager a guess. And a curious sound reached her then, one that could not have possibly emerged from Torrie.

"What was that?" she asked, more curious than ever.

"What?" he called, sounding harried, his voice muffled as well.

Almost as if he were on the floor.

"That sound," she clarified. "Was it a cat?"

"Come here, you scamp," he muttered instead of answering her question.

Elizabeth couldn't resist tipping her head back and raising her lashes ever so slightly, revealing Torrie, who was indeed on his hands and knees at the other end of the chamber, peering beneath a table. Just what in heaven's name was he doing?

She hastily lowered her lashes. "Torrie?"

"Yes, love?" His voice grew strained on the endearment, as if he were extending his arm and reaching with all his might.

Meow.

The feline protestation echoed in the chamber, undeniable. There was most definitely a cat in the vicinity.

"That wasn't you, was it?" she asked, and then rolled her lips inward to stifle her smile.

"It was one of Beelzebub's minions," he said grimly. "Why did I allow Monty to persuade me he would know what he was talking about? The man thinks he can build a flying machine."

Oh dear. This mystery grew more interesting—and entertaining—by the moment.

"Montrose is building a flying machine?" she ventured, intrigued by that as well, and having no wish to spoil Torrie's secret.

He had seemed so pleased with himself when he had poked his head into her chamber and asked her to sit and close her eyes.

"Monty *thinks* he is building a flying machine. And it isn't the first, either. The man is a menace to society. Did you know that he once got into an argument with a familial bust?"

A burst of startled laughter fled her. "An argument with a familial bust?"

"He broke the nose off the first Duke of Montrose," Torrie confirmed, his voice sounding even more strained than it had before. "Come here, you bloody devil. I promise not to hurt you."

"He isn't hiding under the rosewood table, is he?" she ventured.

"No, and thank Christ for that," her husband confirmed. "No, now that I think upon it, I've confused the stories. He tripped and fell on the first duke's statue. It was a portrait of his father that he found himself in a shouting match with. To say nothing of the time he attempted to paint the second-floor hall in the midst of the night. Or the time he mistook a potted palm for a spinster at the Oxley ball... Christ, I had forgotten all about that."

Elizabeth forgot that she was still meant to have her eyes closed. They flew open, finding him still on all fours, peering beneath the elaborately carved table's solid base.

"Are you remembering?" she asked.

Torrie's head came up with sudden swift haste, and before she could warn him, he struck it soundly on the underside of giltwood decorating the outer edge of the furniture. The impact echoed in the silence of the chamber, and a small blur of black-and-orange fur darted across the Aubusson before disappearing beneath Elizabeth's bed.

She rose from her chair, going to him. "Have you hurt yourself?"

Torrie was rubbing the top of his head and grinning at her with boyish charm. "I'll live. However, my attempt at surprising you with a cat of your own has, I quite fear, failed utterly."

She dropped to her knees at his side, a rush of tenderness for him bursting inside her at his revelation that he had been trying to surprise her with a cat.

"It *is* a cat, then," she said, touched by his thoughtfulness.

"And you were meant to remain in that chair with your eyes closed, madam," he reminded her pointedly. "Although in truth, I'm not certain if it is a cat Monty has found for me or a tiny, furred demon. The thing had dreadfully sharp claws, and they cut through layers of garments like an assassin's blade. That is all I can say."

Upon closer inspection, Elizabeth discovered angry, red scratches on Torrie's neck above his neatly knotted cravat, along with drops of red marring the snowy linen. "Has the cat scratched you?"

"Yes, the little beast has," he confirmed, frowning. "I meant to fetch her out of the covered basket and carry her to you and place her in your lap. But I suspect the carriage ride here scared the devil out of her, and she wasn't willing to oblige me."

Her eyes burned, emotion making her throat go tight. "I should clean the scratches for you," she decided, rising to her feet in search of her wash basin.

Needing something with which to busy herself. A way to hide her face until she could gather herself sufficiently that she wouldn't turn into a watering pot.

Torrie hadn't brought her just any gift. He had brought her a cat.

A tortoise shell cat.

Like Mince Pie.

But she had only told him about Mincey once, on the day he had told her the truth about her father and the trust which had been squandered without her knowledge. It hardly seemed likely that he would remember, and with such attention to detail. That he would intentionally seek out not just a

189

cat for her as companion, but that he would find a cat which looked the same.

She dipped a clean strip of linen into the basin and then wrung the excess water from the cloth, tears blurring her vision. She sniffed, trying to keep them at bay.

"Bess?"

Torrie's hand was on her shoulder. She jumped, flinging water everywhere.

"Yes?" She sniffed again.

"Have I upset you? You sound as if you're weeping. Do you not want a cat? If not, I have no doubt Monty and Hattie will take her in. Hattie has always been tenderhearted where felines are concerned."

She blinked furiously, trying to clear away her tears, and then turned to face her husband. He towered over her, all lean grace and effortless handsomeness. But it wasn't his masculine beauty that struck her as she drank in the sight of him, the sunlight gleaming in his dark hair and his green eyes glittering into hers.

Rather, it was his heart.

The way he cared for her, in a way no one ever had. It was humbling, astonishing.

Breathtaking.

She couldn't speak, so she dabbed at the scratches on his neck with her cloth, cleaning away the specks of blood. The scratches were shallow—merely the effect of the cat being desperate to escape a stranger.

"You're not saying anything." Torrie cupped her face, his palm a warm, reassuring touch that brought her back from her tumultuous thoughts. "I know she isn't a replacement for Mince Pie. But she looks like her, and when Monty said he knew of a cat in the mews who had recently had a litter of kittens and I went to investigate and saw her, I thought she would be a perfect fit for you."

"You remembered," she blurted stupidly, still keeping her gaze firmly fixed on the scratches on his neck for fear she would burst into tears anew if she met his stare.

"Of course I did, Bess. I remember everything you tell me."

A tear rolled down her cheek.

She finished her task and forced herself to look back up at him at last.

"Thank you," she whispered, grateful for far more than the feline presently hiding under her bed.

Grateful for him, for the caring he continually showed her. Grateful that fate had somehow chosen for her to be in the library at Lord and Lady Worthing's town house at the wrong time. Which had somehow, impossibly, become the right time.

"You don't want the cat?" he asked again, his brow furrowed, vibrant gaze searching.

"I *do* want the cat," she reassured him, voice still thick with suppressed emotions. "Of course, I do. Does she have a name?"

"Evildoer?" he suggested wryly. "Furred Assassin? Demon With Claws?"

She laughed. "I think she's fearful."

"Understandable. I wouldn't wish to be stuffed inside a basket and escorted through Mayfair by a stranger either," Torrie drawled. "Shall I attempt to lure her out from under the bed for you now?"

He fully intended to crawl on his hands and knees and try to cozen a terrified cat from under the bed.

"I think that perhaps we should ring for my lady's maid and ask that some meat scraps from the kitchen be found," she suggested. "That will likely help."

"Ah, bribery." He grinned and kissed her soundly. "I like the way you think, Lady Torrington."

Lady Torrington.

Yes, that was her. And here and now, as she stood with him in the sunlight streaming through the windows and a cat he had managed to find for her hiding under her bed across the chamber, she truly felt, for the first time, that she was indeed Lady Torrington. That she was his wife rather than a usurper.

That she belonged here.

Specifically, that she belonged with *him*. That she was his, and he was hers, and that perhaps this marriage of convenience between two opposites—founded in scandal and unintentional mishaps—might actually work.

So she wrapped her arms around his neck, rose on her toes, and kissed her husband again, showing him all the happiness that was overflowing in her heart.

Torrie watched Bess happily petting the sleeping cat who was curled up in her lap, looking adorably innocent and not at all like the beast from hell who had scratched his neck and clawed his chest and shoulder earlier. From where he reclined amongst pillows on the floor of Bess's chamber, the soft sound of the cat's contented purrs reached him.

They had finally tempted the stubborn feline from her hiding place in the shadows beneath the bed using a plate of cooked chicken livers. After the little menace had begun eating, Bess had won her over easily. Not that he was surprised. Bess had a way about her that tended to win everyone over.

Except his mother.

But that was another story, and one he refused to dwell on as he watched the happiness radiating from his lovely wife. Despite the injuries to his person—which he would gladly sustain again just to make Bess happy—he was ridiculously pleased to do nothing more than watch her. At her direction, he had fashioned this mound of pillows and blankets, creating a cozy nest in which they had settled with the cat.

"What will you name her?" he asked, careful to keep his voice low and soft lest he wake the sleeping beast and send her racing back beneath the bed.

"I am trying to decide what she looks like," Bess said, glancing up at him with a smile that melted everything inside him.

"She looks like a cat," he pointed out, just to distract himself from the way Bess made him feel.

It was akin to the way he had felt earlier when he had spied the tears in her eyes. Like he wanted to haul her into his arms and bury his face in her sweetly scented hair, and never let her go. Like she was everything he had been searching for in this aimless life of his, without ever knowing it.

"Of course, she looks like a cat," Bess agreed, her smile deepening. "That is not in dispute. But I want to give her a name that suits her. It needs to be the right name."

She was putting a great deal of importance on the cat's name. Upon the cat itself as well. And he was doing his damnedest not to feel jealous of the way she gazed on the furry little scamp.

"I've only had Mincey," she added, her smile fading. "I wasn't able to keep one with Mr. and Mrs. Pettigrew or with Lady Andromeda."

The reminder of the selfish, greedy distant relatives upon whose grasping mercies she had been unceremoniously thrust made his jaw clench. Sent anger on her behalf slicing through him. He had investigated whether there was any recourse for Bess concerning the misappropriation of her trust, but Pettigrew had drunk himself into an early grave, and his wife had taken ill soon thereafter and had died as well, leaving their own children orphaned. Lady Andromeda had lost everything as well, including her health. She was living with friends, and it was unlikely she would ever return from Bath.

It infuriated him to think there was no way he could regain what Bess had lost for her. That there would be no punishment for those who had hurt and used her. But Bess had been calmly accepting of the news. And in true Bess form, she had fretted over the Pettigrew brood, until he had reassured her the children had made a home with their maternal grandmother.

"I dislike thinking about the suffering you endured without reason," he said now. "You should have had a dozen bloody cats if you'd wished."

Her gaze caught his and held, searing him. "I have one now. That is all that matters. And she has to have the finest name I can possibly fathom. Do you have any ideas?"

He raised a brow. "Paws of Doom?"

Bess laughed quietly.

And dear God, that sound. He loved her laughter. Loved her happiness. He would never grow tired of hearing it, nor of being the reason for it.

"I was thinking of something far more formal."

"Lady Razor Claws?" he suggested next.

"Too undignified," she said, stroking the cat's head as she slept. "She told me that she is embarrassed that your acquaintance began in such a regrettable fashion, and she is strongly looking forward to the opportunity to reform her reputation."

It was his turn to chuckle now. "That is rather a mouthful for such a small cat, is it not?"

As if it were the most rational, reasonable act, pretending as if a sleeping cat possessed the ability to speak.

"She has much to say," Bess offered with a small smile playing at the corners of her lips again. "She says she is sorry for scratching your neck."

"And for causing my lifeblood to flow onto my cravat?" he asked.

Bess scratched some more. "She says you're exaggerating the nature of your injuries, and she reassures me that the scratches you suffered were scarcely deep enough to bleed. Only look at what an angel she is."

"She is indeed an angel," he agreed pointedly.

But he wasn't thinking about the cat. Rather, he was thinking of the kindhearted beauty on whom the feline was slumbering in peaceful respite. He raked his fingers through his hair, continuing to watch her, soaking in the quiet radiance she exuded. The happiness. Her legs were curled beneath her, skirts pooled and keeping her limbs hidden from view. The cat was snuggled where Torrie himself longed to be, and again, he had to tamp down an inconvenient rush of envy.

"Perhaps that is what her name should be," Bess said, pulling him from his thoughts.

"Angel?" He stroked his jaw thoughtfully, contemplating the appellation. "Seems a bit of an exaggeration, particularly considering the state of my neck and shoulder."

"Your shoulder?" Bess's eyes flew to him. "You never said anything about an injury to your shoulder. What happened?"

"Her claws," he said wryly. "But at least I had the protection of a few layers of garments. The same can't be said for my neck."

"Poor darling," she murmured, stroking the cat's back. "Shall I kiss it for you later?"

Damn it, the effect his wife had on him was criminal.

He was lusting after her whilst she held a cat in her lap.

A small, relatively innocent feline who had been so terrified by her journey that she had nearly clawed him to ribbons, it was true. Nonetheless, watching his wife bonding with the cat had proven more than worth every drop of blood he had shed.

"You may kiss me wherever and whenever you like, wife," he told her, giving her a teasing wink.

As predicted, his words brought a charming flush to her cheeks. He could have said more—would have, likely—had they not possessed the audience of the feline. Somehow, saying vulgar things to Bess felt wrong when there was a cat involved.

"I'm a fortunate woman indeed," she said, no trace of humor in her voice.

She was all seriousness, and he wondered if she was thinking about what had happened between them in the past. When he had been someone else, and she had been a wallflower he had so ruthlessly mocked and ignored. Although he and his mother had not spoken of Bess's past affections for him since the day of their dreadful argument, he had found himself contemplating it often. He was curious, he couldn't lie. What had she felt for him, if anything?

"Is it true?" he found himself asking at last. "That you set your cap at me all those years ago?"

Her flush deepened, her gaze dropping from his to the blasted cat, and he regretted his question instantly. Her discomfort was palpable, and he hadn't intended to ruin this blissful idyll with her by dredging up painful memories.

"Forgive me," he hurried to say. "It was unkind of me to ask, and it hardly signifies. I'm not the man I was then. It is merely that...sometimes I think about the past. I wonder about it. I wonder if I'll recall more, or if I'll only ever have a trickle of random, incoherent memories to string together in remembrance of the man I was before."

"You needn't apologize," she said quietly, head still bowed over the cat. "I can well understand your curiosity. I can't begin to understand what it must be like for you, not knowing, not remembering. Having no notion of when or if the rest of your memories will return."

Amnesia was its own kind of hell, and he was trapped within it. But thanks to Bess, he was beginning to find a place where he truly felt as if he belonged.

"I've had time to make my peace with it as best as I'm able." He flattened his palm on the pile of pillows and used it as leverage to haul himself nearer to her. The cat shifted in her lap and stretched, offering a tiny pink yawn, but promptly resumed her sleep. "It's only that sometimes I find myself angry with him. Jealous of the time he could have had with you, had he not wasted it so thoroughly."

She looked up again, giving him a sad smile. "Perhaps it is selfish of me, but I'm glad you are the man you are and not the man you once were. When I was younger, I was foolish. I saw you from across a crowded ballroom and our eyes met, and I fancied you were... I had this foolish notion... It doesn't matter. It's all best forgotten now."

He leaned forward, resting his weight on his arm, needing to be closer to her. "What were you intending to say? What did you fancy?"

The most astonishing thought occurred to him then. Had she been in love with him, when she had been a debutante and he'd been a devil-may-care rakehell tearing about London with Monty? A new stab of jealousy accompanied the thought.

Envious first of a cat and then of his former self, the man he could scarcely recall having been.

"It is nothing," she repeated, eyes firmly pinned to the cat.

197

Did the cat have a name? Was it Angel? He wasn't sure, but his greatest concern for now was unraveling a piece of his past, with his wife's help. He needed to know.

"Bess." He reached forward, brushing a tendril of hair away that had fallen across her silken cheek. "Tell me. Please. I want to know."

"Oh, Torrie." She bit her lip, glancing up at him again, looking uncertain. "It's embarrassing, my foolishness. I was dreadfully naïve, and I know that now."

He frowned, another uncomfortable thought occurring to him. "Was I unkind to you in other ways? Aside from the terrible things you overheard me saying at the Althorp ball, that is. I want—nay, need—to know."

He fervently hoped that she hadn't kept the truth from him to make him feel better about what a cruel arse he'd been. He wouldn't put it past her. That was just how goddamned selfless and good his Bess was.

She sighed, and the cat stirred again, the heaviness of their conversation apparently disturbing her sated slumber following the chicken liver feast. "Very well. If you must know, I had an idea, which was quite wrong-headed, that you must have felt the same connection sparking within you that I did when your eyes had met mine. I fancied myself in love with you. But I recognize my feelings then for what they were—a girlish infatuation, nothing more. Please don't think you gave me any reason to have hopes, or that you were otherwise unkind to me, aside from that one remark."

In love.

Bess had been *in love* with him. With the old Torrie.

Why that knowledge produced such a sudden, vicious ache in his chest, he couldn't say. But it was there, swelling, growing stronger, tearing him apart. Other emotions rose, too. So much emotion. The strong, kind, beautiful, resilient woman before him had been in love with him, and he had been too stupid and thoughtless and careless to notice. What manner of man had he been, to have Bess looking at him the way she did now, and fail to see her for the magnificent woman she was?

How had he failed her, failed them both?

"I didn't say anything else that was hurtful to you, then?" he pressed, wanting to be certain.

She shook her head, a wistful smile playing at her lips. "As I said before, you never spoke a word directly to me. Even when I fell at your feet, I believe you were too astounded by my lack to do anything other than offer me a hand. You never took notice of me after that, and then Lady Andromeda could no longer keep her town house, and I abandoned my hope of becoming a wife and mother and became a governess instead."

The reminder of the injustices visited on her rankled.

He ground his molars. "You should never have been reduced to such circumstances. That you were will forever be a mark upon the souls of everyone who should have been caring for your welfare instead of lining their avaricious coffers."

Pettigrew and Buxton deserved retribution, but that was beyond his reach now. As for Lady Andromeda, he had no doubt she would soon meet a similar fate. Her lot was to suffer in relative penury, living off the generosity of friends as she had once forced Bess to live.

"I hope to God that Lady Andromeda is being made to wear someone else's castoffs," he added for good measure. "I hope she has naught but sacks and rags that are three times her size."

And far worse things, but he was gentleman enough not to say any of them aloud.

"I suppose I should be far angrier with everyone than I am," Bess surprised him by saying, her tone contemplative.

"It isn't that I wished for them to take advantage of me, of course. But if they hadn't, I wouldn't be here with you now. I never would have been in the Worthing library that night, and little Angel wouldn't be sleeping comfortably in my lap."

He swallowed hard, startled anew by the stinging pinprick of tears against the backs of his eyes. Torrie couldn't recall when he'd last wept. Nor if he ever had. But a wave of feeling hit him now. Hit him harder than a fist.

Despite his questionable introduction to the cat—Angel, it was decided, then—he reached out and gently stroked the feline's soft, thick tortoise shell coat. Slowly, gently, his fingers grazing Bess's.

"I'm not grateful that they stole from you and mistreated you," he said, voice low and thick with suppressed tears. "But I will be forever grateful that fate found you in the library that night, and that I carried you away in my carriage. I should have done it long ago, when you fell at my feet at the Althorp ball, but I reckon I wasn't ready for you then."

He wasn't sure he was ready now. He was forever aware—acutely so—that she was his better in every way. Kinder, gentler, more thoughtful and caring and forgiving. She was everything a woman should be. Everything he wanted in a wife.

All he wanted, forever.

"I wasn't ready for you then either," Bess said. "Not for that man."

His old self, she meant.

Their fingers grazed again and he looked up, their gazes meshing, emotions snapping to life like a spark turning into flame. He knew what she had been referring to, the connection he felt to her, deep in his chest, when their eyes met and held. How had he failed to see it before?

"Are you ready for this one?" he dared to ask.

Angel purred loudly between them, the only answer for far longer than his pride preferred.

And then at last, Bess spoke.

"More than ready," she said quietly.

He leaned into her, unable to resist stealing a kiss that was meant to be hasty but turned into something longer and deeper. Something that said far more than any of their words or revelations could.

Perhaps, he reasoned as he tore his lips from hers, that was life's truest mystery unraveled, one that even a man who had lost much of his memory could understand. Life was just a series of moments, strung together, and all good things took time. All good things came when one was truly ready.

And like Bess, he was more than ready for anything and everything there was to come with her at his side.

"Thank you for Angel," she said, such tenderness in her voice and in her eyes, directed toward him alone.

For a moment, he found it difficult to find his tongue. But at last he did, giving her a teasing smile first.

"I still think we should have named her Lady Razor Claws instead. It's far more apt."

His wife's musical laughter was her only response, and he tucked this memory—the two of them surrounded by pillows on her bedchamber floor, a sleeping kitten in her lap—into his heart. For it was one that he bloody well never wanted to forget.

CHAPTER 14

*T*orrie had made a vast, inexcusable mistake in encouraging Bess to procure an entirely new wardrobe. He could see that now.

Because from the moment he'd first spied her in that frothy green frock with her breasts spilling temptingly over the decolletage several weeks ago, he'd been walking about with a perpetual cockstand. Bess in a snug new riding habit? Cockstand. Bess in a fetching morning gown with the sunlight gleaming in her mahogany hair? Cockstand. Bess in a transparent night rail trimmed with lace, her hard nipples poking the linen in sinful invitation? Cockstand.

Cockstand, cockstand, cockstand.

And the devil of it was, there was not always a convenient empty chamber, bed, or carriage in which to debauch her. Often, he had to *wait* to have his wicked way with his wife.

Times such as this evening as he stood on the periphery of the ball they had planned together in her honor, watching her dance with another man.

A man whose thorough drubbing he was imagining with vivid detail. Was the bastard looking at her breasts as they spun about in time to the Scotch reel? Torrie was alarmingly close to stalking onto the dance floor and demanding the Earl of Rearden name his second.

"If you glare any harder, you'll incinerate poor Rearden on the spot," drawled a familiar voice at his side.

Torrie turned to find Monty, glass of lemonade in hand, wearing a vexing grin he wouldn't mind punching off his old friend's face.

"My mood is rather a dark one at the moment," he warned grimly.

"I never could have guessed," Monty returned with an irritating amount of cheer. "You appear so calm and unruffled. A veritable ray of sunshine."

He ground his molars. "I don't suppose you could take your lemonade and your jokes elsewhere?"

"I could," Monty said agreeably. "But watching you drown in jealousy is a damned fine sport, old chap."

"Jealousy?" He laughed, the sound bitter even to his own ears. "I'm hardly jealous of a sad clod like Rearden. Look at him, his hair is beginning to thin."

Monty made an elaborate show of squinting toward the sea of dancers. "His hair looks thick as ever to me."

"It's thinning," he insisted, though he wasn't sure why. It was petty of him, and he didn't like to think he was susceptible to such an unworthy sense of spite.

"Admit it," Monty said quietly, his countenance sobering. "You're falling in love with your wife."

Falling in love?

Hardly.

That couldn't happen with such haste. They had been married for mere weeks. Glorious weeks, it was true, but that was hardly sufficient time for such a vast development.

In lust? Yes, and decidedly so. And he was incredibly fond of her; their lovemaking and the tender moments they had shared were unlike anything he'd experienced before. Like the greedy bastard he was, he wanted more of them. Wanted more of her smiles, her kisses, her laughter, her touch.

But in love? It wasn't as if he spent his every waking hour either with Bess or thinking about when he could return to her side...

Oh damn it, very well. He *did* do that.

"His nose is far too long," he grumbled, still insulting Rearden, this time to deflect from Monty's alarmingly valid assertion.

It wasn't that he didn't want to fall in love, or that he believed himself incapable of that finer emotion. It was merely that love felt heavy. It felt as large as the sky above them. It felt like something he was wholly unprepared for. Christ, he could scarcely recall most of the years of his life. What did he know about love?

"His nose looks reasonably proportional to me," Monty said.

Unhelpfully.

Torrie scowled at his supposed friend. "You aren't helping matters."

"By refusing to agree with you, or by pointing out you're falling in love?" Monty asked, undeterred.

He sighed, trying and failing to look away from Bess moving gracefully over the polished floor, her breasts bouncing temptingly in her daring gown. "I'm not falling in love. I am merely fiercely protective. Bess has been mistreated all her life. First by her greedy relatives, and then by the *ton* during her Seasons."

Including himself, but Torrie was doing everything in his power to make amends for his past self's mistakes in every way he could.

"And if I find the sight of the Earl of Rearden mooning

over my wife irksome, I can hardly be faulted," he added for good measure. "It hasn't a thing to do with love or jealousy."

"Hmm," Monty hummed at his side, as if he didn't believe a word Torrie had just spoken.

Which only succeeded in nettling him further.

Torrie tore his gaze from Bess—thank Christ the reel was soon coming to an end—and pinned Monty with a glare. "What does that mean?"

Monty flashed his devil-may-care grin. "It means that I know what it's like to realize you've fallen in love. It's rather akin to a fist to the jaw, so stunning is the blow."

Realizing he was rubbing his jaw in a reflexive action, Torrie dropped his hand and straightened his shoulders. "What nonsense."

It wasn't love he felt for Bess. Was it?

Dear God, how would he know? Had he been in love before? He didn't think he had. He didn't have the first inkling of what being in love entailed.

"Is it nonsense?" his friend asked quietly.

He sighed. The reel had ended and Bess was coming his way. Rearden had melted into the crush of revelers.

Tenderness washed over him when she smiled in his direction, catching and holding his stare. Another feeling rose, swelling like the banks of an overflowing river. He felt, undeniably, connected to her in a way that transcended all else. He felt as if she knew him, saw him, cared for him as no one did. And he didn't know quite when it had happened, or how she'd done it. But she was the half of himself he'd been missing, and she was the only half that was worth a proper goddamn.

"I don't know any longer," he admitted grimly. "I married her out of a sense of obligation. It was to be a marriage of convenience. I intended to send her to my country seat and carry on as I wished. And yet…"

"And yet?" prompted Monty, his tone knowing.

"And yet I knew, from the moment I kissed her, that I would never want to send her from my side," he said with a rush of searing emotion. "I knew that I wanted her with me, that she was rare and good and kind."

"Is she all you can think about?"

"Bloody hell, yes."

"And you're secretly imagining planting facers on every poor chap who dares to partner her in a dance?"

Another sigh left him as he watched Bess nearing them. She radiated happiness. And she was so damned beautiful in her new ball gown, this one trimmed with pink roses and blond lace, the fabric swirling about her curves with diaphanous elegance.

"If you must know, yes," he conceded. "But let this be enough of your foolish talk of love, Monty. My wife is approaching."

Not a moment too soon, either. Bess stopped before them, a strand of pearls clasped at her creamy neck that he had given her earlier that evening when they had finished preparing for the night's festivities.

"My lord," she greeted, breathless from her exertions on the dance floor. "Your Grace. I hope I haven't interrupted the two of you. It looked as if you were engaged in a rather serious debate as I arrived."

Torrie sent a meaningful look in Monty's direction. One that clearly said *stubble it, old chap.*

"We were merely speaking about a subject on which I am a tremendous authority," Monty said unrepentantly.

He gritted his teeth.

"A tremendous *something*," he muttered.

"Oh?" Bess asked brightly, looking from Torrie to Monty, blithely oblivious. "What subject is that?"

"Falling in—" Monty began.

"Inventing oaths," Torrie finished loudly.

So loudly that several curious heads turned in their direction. And damn it, that hadn't been his intention either, to draw more attention to them. He'd already caused Bess enough headaches by beginning their union in such a scandalous way. It seemed as if every tongue in London was still wagging about how he had kidnapped his own bride. He had seen caricatures of himself spiriting Bess away, hauling her over his shoulder as if he were a villain absconding with the family silver.

Villainous Viscount kidnaps innocent had been one illustration's description. *Lord T- takes a wife (in literal fashion)* had read another.

Bess's brow furrowed. "Inventing oaths?"

Thank Christ. Apparently, he had shouted over his friend sufficiently.

"Monty's favorite is Beelzebub's earbobs," he added stupidly.

Bess laughed, and he found himself suddenly, ridiculously irritated that she found Monty's dreadful curse amusing.

"And God's fichu," Monty added. "My dear Lady Torrington, it sounds as if another dance is striking up. Perhaps a waltz. Would you care to—"

"She's dancing with me," he interrupted.

Because he refused to stew like a wallflower whilst watching Bess dance with anyone else. It was *his* bloody turn, by God.

Bess smiled in his direction. "I do believe I was meant to dance with Lord Carlton."

He was all too aware of Monty grinning at him. The fool had likely been trying to connive just such a response from him. And he'd fallen neatly into the trap.

"Carlton can go to the devil," he said, keeping his stare trained on his beautiful viscountess instead of on his friend, who was now softly chortling in glee. "You're my wife, and if anyone is going to waltz with you, it's going to be me."

Before she could offer further protest or Monty said anything else that made him long to throttle him, Torrie guided Bess to the dance floor as the familiar strains of a waltz began.

He didn't love her.

Did he?

Bloody hell. What if Monty was right?

What if he *had* fallen in love with his Bess?

SOMETHING WAS different about Torrie tonight. Elizabeth couldn't quite determine what it was. There was an intensity in his green gaze that was more than the customary desire she saw reflected there. They danced well together, finding a rhythm with ease, whirling about amongst their fellow dancers with light, sure steps. She felt as if she were floating, giddy with the pleasure of being in his arms.

The ball thus far—despite his mother's grudging attendance and the cold receptions she had faced from some of their guests—had been a resounding success. And she was grateful to Torrie for his steadfast support. More content than she had ever hoped to be in this new life which had suddenly and furiously transformed her world as she had known it.

But there was something, she thought, eating at her husband. Something causing the rigidity in his bearing and his jaw. She had to know what.

"Is something amiss?" she asked him when they executed another flawless turn.

"Of course not," he said smoothly, guiding them through the next steps. "Why do you ask?"

"You're quiet. And it seemed as if you and Montrose were having a fierce debate when I arrived." She studied his handsome face, drinking in the slashing cheekbones, the strong jaw, his sensual lips that called for kissing. "I merely wondered at the reason. I cannot believe it was merely curses you were discussing."

And hoped *she* wasn't the reason. That she hadn't somehow displeased him.

Being married was still quite new to her. She often felt as if she hadn't an inkling of how to be a wife. After accepting the fact that she would never have a husband or family of her own, to suddenly be married to the man who had once been the source of all her girlish dreams was still something of a shock.

"It was also how irritating Monty is," her husband offered.

"But he is your friend, is he not?"

Torrie's lips twitched. "With the greatest of reluctance."

Now she knew that he was teasing her. "You care for him."

"Against my better judgment."

Torrie spun them about again, the waltz nearly at an end now. "He has been kind to me, as has Hattie. I'm thankful to the both of them for making me feel as if I'm truly a part of the family."

"You *are* a part of the family, Bess." His looked down at her, the same intensity she had been noticing all night burning bright in his eyes. "Have I told you how beautiful you are this evening, Lady Torrington?"

"You have."

He had when he had come to her chamber to gift her the pearl necklace she wore. And at least half a dozen other occasions during the ball. In her new gowns, with her husband's appreciation to bolster her courage, Elizabeth truly felt lovely. The painfully shy wallflower in ill-fitting castoffs was a far cry from the elegant viscountess she had become.

"It bears saying again," he told her. "I've been thinking all evening long of how I might manage to whisk you away into a private corner without anyone else taking note so that I can ravish you."

His words made an answering tug of desire pull low in her belly. "How scandalous of you, my lord."

He grinned. "Never say I've shocked you."

He had certainly shocked her in many ways during the weeks of their marriage thus far. And every one of those ways had been quite good.

She found herself smiling back at him, unable to resist his teasing charm. "Of course you haven't. Quite the opposite, in fact. When I was a debutante, I dreamt of a gentleman asking me for an assignation. How desperately I longed to be noticed." She frowned, feeling foolish anew for the revelation. "I was a dreadfully awkward wallflower, and it goes without saying that no one noticed me at all, unless it was to remark upon just how unremarkable I was."

The old, bitter memory returned at the least opportune moment. A plain, plump little partridge.

He frowned down at her, growing pensive. "Every person who ever remarked on you unkindly deserves a cuff to the head. Myself included. I'm so sorry, Bess. I wish I could undo the damage I did back then."

It was silly of her to have mentioned past hurts, and particularly now, when everything between them was so lovely and smooth, when she was dancing in his arms as his viscountess whilst the crush of guests they had invited to their ball swirled around them.

"Forget I mentioned it, if you please," she entreated. "The past is where it belongs."

"Meet me on the terrace," he said suddenly, urgently.

Her eyebrows rose. "On the terrace? Whatever for?"

"For a tryst," he murmured, guiding her through another turn. "I may not be able to change what happened in the past, but I can do my best to make amends for it. If my lady wishes for an assignation, then she'll have one."

Elizabeth blinked at the sudden rush of tears burning the backs of her eyes. She mustn't weep now, not whilst they danced together, an audience surrounding them.

"You needn't," she said thickly, past the emotion clogging her throat.

"I want to."

The waltz came to an end then, and she released her hold on him with great reluctance, having greatly enjoyed the opportunity to dance with him for the second time tonight.

"Take some air on the terrace," he added, keeping his voice low and discreet. "I'll join you in a few minutes so no one will be the wiser."

"Surely you can't mean what I fear you mean," she whispered, thinking of all the ways he had so deliciously seduced her since they had wed.

The smoldering look he gave her was pure sin. "Oh yes I can, love. Meet me there."

With an elegant bow that had her dipping into an answering curtsy, her husband walked calmly away, as if he hadn't just turned her knees to pudding.

And that was when Elizabeth realized that her *tendre* for Viscount Torrington had never truly faded with the intervening years. No, indeed. She had never stopped loving him.

CHAPTER 15

*I*n love.

He was in love.

Torrie had fallen in love with Bess.

It was astounding. Absurd. It was bloody terrifying.

But as he swept through the guests in his teeming ballroom beneath a host of glittering chandeliers, he was willing to admit the truth of it to himself. Monty hadn't been wrong, curse him. He loved his wife.

He *loved* his wife.

The notion was dizzying, and it occurred to him that he was grinning like a fool. But he couldn't seem to stop. Edging closer to the doors leading to the small terrace that overlooked the gardens, he wondered if everyone would think him a Bedlamite if he simply shouted the declaration above the din of the orchestra.

What a bloody lunatic he was. Yes, he had to admit that tongues would wag furiously over such a pronouncement. Likely, it was not what Bess needed or would wish to hear. He could save it for their assignation on the terrace.

How many minutes had passed since he had spied her

sneaking stealthily into the night? He extracted his pocket watch from his waistcoat and discovered that, despite it feeling as if a lifetime had passed, it had only in truth been two and a half minutes. Long enough, he decided. He would make his way to her now.

So single-minded was Torrie in his determination that he crashed into a familiar feminine form, unable to avoid the collision. She fell into his chest breasts first, rubbing them against him as if she were a cat in heat.

"Eugenia," he bit out, taking her arms in as polite a grip as he could manage and setting her away from him. "What the devil are you doing here?"

He most definitely had not issued her an invitation. She had caused him enough scandal and had hurt Bess enough. That she would dare to somehow infiltrate the ball he had thrown in his wife's honor set his teeth on edge.

"I needed to see you," Eugenia said, fluttering her lashes at him. "I've missed you desperately, Torrie."

"You cannot think you are welcome here," he ground out, taking care to keep his voice quiet enough that it didn't carry, for he had no wish to cause a scene.

Not on Bess's day, damn it all.

Already, eyes were drawn to them, the curious stares of gossipmongers eager to scent blood.

"Don't tell me you haven't missed me," Eugenia purred, leaning into him again, her breasts grazing his waistcoat.

By God, the cut of her gown was so low that he could see the dusky shadows of her nipples cresting the decolletage. The sight had no effect on him save pity. Undoubtedly, she was hard at work in search of the next unlucky chap who would help her make a cuckold of Worthing again.

"You are making a spectacle of yourself," he warned tightly.

"Please, my darling." She reached for his arm, the touch decidedly unwelcome.

Discreetly, he disentangled himself. "Lady Worthing, go home to your husband."

She laughed, the sound bitter and sharp, the mirth not reaching her eyes. "Do you think he would welcome me with another man's babe in my womb? Surely you cannot be that obtuse."

Another man's babe in her womb?

Ice began to seep through him where not even a minute ago there had been such prodigious warmth.

"Eugenia," he gritted, needing to know and yet desperately dreading the answer. "What is the meaning of this?"

"I'm *enceinte*, Torrie," she said, a small, triumphant smile turning up the corners of her lips. "Lord Worthing isn't the father of the babe, and he knows it."

The contents of his stomach roiled, shock passing through him with such sudden violence that he feared he would retch on her slippers here and now as half the *ton* eagerly watched their tragedy unfold. The heat of the chandeliers blazing overhead felt suddenly oppressive. The lords and ladies around them blurred and swirled into one indistinct mass of humanity.

"Who is?" he forced out.

"You are, of course, my love," she told him. "There has been no one but you. I was heartbroken after what happened, and now there can be no question of who the father is."

Good God.

He was going to be a father.

But it wasn't Bess who was the babe's mother. Instead, it was the woman who had thrown her from her home in the darkest depths of the night without a care for what would become of her.

His stomach gave a violent lurch. He had to escape the

ballroom, to handle this hideous matter with as much care as he could manage to blunt the damage it would do to his wife.

Torrie nodded jerkily in the direction of one of the doors at the opposite end of the ballroom. "Come with me."

ELIZABETH HAD BEEN WAITING for far too long.

Torrie wasn't going to come to her.

Disappointment and hurt curdled her stomach as she slipped back inside the ballroom from the terrace door, trying not to feel as if she were the same unwanted wall-flower of her failed Seasons.

He cares for me, she reminded herself firmly. *Surely there is a reason he failed to meet me on the terrace as he promised.*

Inside, the throng of revelers made the ballroom feel even more sweltering than it had when she had left, thanks to the time she had spent in the cool breeze of the night. The air was stifling, and grew only more so when she became aware of all the curious and pitying glances being directed toward her.

A lady whispered to another behind her fan, one of them tittering as she looked at Elizabeth. Perhaps it was her imagination, or her old fears, she told herself. Not everyone in the ballroom was staring at her, and they certainly must be speaking of something else.

Her ears heated with embarrassment as she made her way through the crush, small bits of conversation reaching her as she went.

Everyone knew it was a matter of time...
The poor lamb likely has no notion...
Rakes never reform...
Quite scandalous indeed...
And with Lady Worthing...

The mention of Torrie's former mistress caught her attention, the sick feeling inside her only growing more pronounced as she found herself, inevitably, by the potted palms at the periphery of the gathering. Perhaps she could only outrun the past so far, she thought miserably.

For here she was, taking up her post on the edges of the gathering. This time, she was dressed in a stunning gown, she was married, and she had the pearls her husband had given her at her throat. But somehow, those facts gave her none of the confidence she would have hoped as she searched the crowd for Torrie.

And the more she searched for him, the greater the gnawing sense of dread clawing at her intensified.

At length, she spied the dowager nearby in an animated discussion with Lady Althorp. Where was Hattie? Another glance around the crush proved futile. Her only friend amongst this sea of disdainful faces was as impossible to find as Torrie was. But surely there was a reason he had not joined her on the terrace as planned.

Yes, there must be a good reason to keep him from her side. He had been a distinctly attentive husband through the weeks of their marriage, never far from her side. He wouldn't abandon her on this night, when they were hosting a ball, the first of its kind for her as his viscountess. Not when they had determined to put on a united front together and blunt all the gossip surrounding them.

Her mouth was growing dry.

The room was beginning to swirl at the edges, and perspiration trickled down her upper lip, tickled an uneasy path down her spine beneath her stays and chemise. Perhaps she should have stayed in the fresh night air instead of returning to this madness.

Indecision froze her to the spot, misery miring her. Suddenly, it was as if no time had passed. She was Miss Elizabeth Brooke, wearing the castoffs of Lady Andromeda, watching the world from its periphery.

No, she would not surrender to her fears. She would hold her head high. Perhaps her mother-in-law knew where Torrie was. Despite her strained relationship with the dowager, she did not doubt the other woman would be perfectly polite to her with Lady Althorp as an audience.

Her decision made, she moved without thought, reaching the dowager's side as if she were an automaton.

The dowager's lips pinched together at her arrival, but to the other woman's credit, she didn't make any other obvious sign of dislike.

"My lady," Elizabeth greeted. "Lady Althorp." She dipped into a formal curtsy. "Good evening."

Lady Althorp passed a dismissive look over her. "Lady Torrington."

The bitterness in her voice was, no doubt, down to her own disappointment over the nuptials that had never been between her eldest daughter and Torrie. Elizabeth ignored it and turned her attention to her mother-in-law, feeling by now as if she were dripping with the combined effect of her worries and the heat in the room.

"Have you seen Lord Torrington, my lady?" she asked the dowager. "I cannot seem to find him in the crush."

"I'm not certain where he has gone," her mother-in-law answered with an odd, high-pitched quality to her voice that was not ordinarily present.

Almost as if she were lying.

But why?

Elizabeth had her answer in the next moment, for Lady Althorp gave her a triumphant smile and pronounced, "The last I saw of his lordship, he was escorting the Countess of Worthing from the ballroom."

And with that simple statement, all the fears that had

been chasing her throughout these last few, happy weeks with Torrie finally caught her in their relentless, crushing grip.

TORRIE'S THROAT burned from the whisky he had poured down his gullet the moment he had brought Eugenia to his study for a dreaded conversation. One that would be best conducted privately instead of before the watching eyes of hundreds of others.

Don't say a word, he had warned her grimly before rushing to the stores he scarcely touched these days and taking a hearty swig.

Then another. And another. And another.

But when he finally wiped his dripping lips with the back of his gloved hand and turned around, Eugenia was still standing there with a victorious smile on her face, as if she had won a great battle. And he began to fear that she had, and that everything he had built with Bess these past few glorious weeks was about to come crashing down, like a priceless vase teetering on the edge of a table.

"Say it again," he ground out harshly. "Tell me the truth, here where no one else shall overhear."

"I'm carrying your babe," Eugenia repeated, cradling her belly through her diaphanous gown.

Was that a slight rounded curve on her ordinarily willowy frame? He couldn't tell, and he hated himself for looking, for hoping there would be none and that he had somehow misheard her in the cacophony of the ballroom. That this was all some twisted joke she was playing upon him. That it was anything other than the truth. Because every second of being alone with her felt like the greatest of betrayals to Bess.

But the worst of it—and the part his numbed mind could not seem to grapple with—was that Eugenia was pregnant with his child. His own flesh and blood. He tamped down the urge to retch, for it was undeniably a betrayal of the most egregious sort, even if it had happened before his marriage to Bess.

He would lose her for this, he feared.

"How?" he demanded hoarsely. He had taken care to prevent such a possibility, using a sheath every time they had been together.

Eugenia gave a chuckle, moving nearer, bringing the cloying scent of her perfume with her. This evening, thanks to the heat in the ballroom, it was mixed with the sharp staleness of sweat.

He gagged and then brought the whisky bottle directly to his lips, taking another long pull from it.

But oblivion wouldn't claim him that easily. Apparently, this night, he was meant to suffer.

"How do you suppose it happened, my love?" Eugenia asked, trailing a nail down his chest. "In the ordinary way. You bedded me, often and passionately. Need I remind you of all the ways in which it happened? The details? The many, many times you fucked me with that big, hard cock of yours?"

What had he ever seen in this woman?

He shrugged away from her touch, his stomach giving another violent lurch. "No details. You know what I am saying, madam. How can you be certain that I am the father of this presumed child? I made every effort to prevent such an unwanted event from occurring."

A triumphant smile curved her lips. "I can only imagine that your efforts failed in some fashion. For only you have been in my bed, my darling. Heaven knows Worthing hasn't.

He couldn't even find his cock if he tried these days. He's far too fat."

Her unkind assessment of her significantly older husband wasn't far from the mark, but Torrie took no joy in it.

"You haven't taken another lover in all the weeks since we parted?" he demanded, hoping she would tell him otherwise.

That she'd taken a string of men into her bed. Because she was Eugenia, and her appetite was insatiable. It had been one of the qualities about her which had drawn him, fool that he'd been, aimlessly seeking something that had forever been out of reach.

Happiness.

That was what he had been searching for, what he had been missing. And he had found it with Bess. But now, he was going to lose it. He was going to lose *her*, and it was all his bloody fault for thinking with his cock when Eugenia had first propositioned him instead of seeing her for the viper she was.

"Of course, I haven't taken another lover," Eugenia said, reaching for him again, her hand on his sleeve. "You are the only man I want. I realized it too late, after we had that dreadful argument, and then you refused to see me or return any of my notes. My heart was broken. But then when I learned that I was carrying your babe, I realized it was fate bringing us back together again."

It was true that she had sent him countless notes. He had cast each one into the grate and watched it turn to ash without bothering to read it. He had vowed faithfulness to his wife, and he had begun a new chapter. Eugenia belonged to the past.

Except, here she was, haunting him. Looking at him with pleading eyes and telling him she was carrying his child. A child he did not want, but one he would nonetheless love and provide for as was his duty.

But how? He could not openly acknowledge the babe. Eugenia was married to Worthing, and Torrie was married to Bess. What a hopeless, tangled mess they had made.

"Lady Worthing," he said, careful to revert to formality with her, lest she have expectations of resuming their affair, "I am married now. We cannot be together, not in any fashion."

Her lips twisted in a cruel sneer. "You are married to that plump, plain cow of a governess. Pray do not pretend as if you harbor tender feelings for her. You married her out of necessity, and we both know it."

"Never speak of her that way again," he ground out, furious on Bess's behalf. "I'll not allow you to utter another unkind word about her in my presence. She is neither plump, nor plain, and by God, if I ever hear you refer to her as a cow again, I will make certain you are banished from every ballroom of note in London. I won't stop until you are turned away from every door. Do you understand me?"

That she would dare to speak of his wife in such a manner before him was as infuriating as it was insulting. It was jealousy which forked her tongue, he knew. But he would not allow Bess to be disparaged by anyone, and most assuredly not by the woman who had so callously turned her away in the darkest depths of the night, without a care for what might become of her.

Eugenia's mouth had fallen open, and she drew her shoulders back in a defensive pose. "You dare to defend her to me?"

"Of course I defend her," he snarled, feeling ugly. "She is my wife, and I love her."

The first time he made the acknowledgment aloud.

He hadn't intended for it to be spoken to Eugenia. And most certainly not like this. But he had lost control of his wits the moment she had told him she was carrying his babe in the ballroom. It was still far too much for him to comprehend. The happiness which had forever been out of his reach was finally within his grasp, and yet he knew without a doubt that it was about to slip from his fingers.

He was angry.

Angry at Eugenia.

Furious with himself for landing himself in this untenable position.

"You cannot love her," Eugenia said with a bitter little laugh. "You've only just married her."

She was echoing the words he had been thinking not long ago in the ballroom. But she was just as wrong as he had been.

"The amount of time which has passed is immaterial to my feelings," he countered coolly. "None of this is any concern of yours. Tell me what you want from me, and it shall be done. I take care of that which is mine."

Eugenia sidled closer, her hand traveling up his bicep to his shoulder, coasting down his chest as she pressed her breasts against him. "What I want is you, Torrie. I want you in my bed again."

He caught her hand before it could travel any farther. "That will never happen, Eugenia. I meant as it pertains to the child. Do you require funds? Is Worthing demanding you be sent away? Tell me what you need for the babe. That is all I can offer you."

"You cannot mean that." Eugenia wrapped her other arm around his neck and clung to him like an ivy vine. "She can't possibly give you what I can, my darling."

He shrugged her off him, no easy feat given her tenacity.

"I do mean that, madam," he snapped. "I will do my duty to the child upon its birth, but I have no wish to be involved with you or any woman other than my wife."

"No," Eugenia cried out, desperation in her eyes, in her

voice. "Please, darling. Remember what it was like between us, how good it was. We can go away to be together. We don't need to stay here. We'll leave London behind, go to the Continent, forget all about Worthing and that dreadful governess. I know you don't truly love her any more than I love my husband."

Her determination to hear only what she wished was suffocating. Torrie spun away from her, stalking across the chamber. But Eugenia followed, dropping to her knees before him and reaching for the fall of his trousers.

"Let me suck you," she said, fumbling with the buttons. "I'll remind you of how good it was for us. How good it will be again."

He caught her hand in an iron grip, attempting to keep her from mauling his person without hurting her. In that same terrible moment, as his former mistress was begging him to let her suck his cock, the door to Torrie's study flew open.

There, on the threshold, face stricken and pale, stood Bess.

She gasped, the sound so laden with pain that it was like a blade slicing into him.

"Bess," he said, disentangling himself from Eugenia, who was still on her knees on the Aubusson. "Please, I can explain."

But for the first time in their marriage, his wife's forgiving nature and sunny disposition had disappeared. Tears shone in her eyes as she shook her head.

"You needn't bother," she said, and then she whirled away in a swirl of pink roses and blond lace.

CHAPTER 16

*E*lizabeth woke to puffy, red-rimmed eyes and utter misery in the same guest chamber at Hamilton House that she had previously inhabited on her stays with the Duke and Duchess of Montrose. Angel was curled up against her side, a warm and comforting presence. Loyal and loving.

Unlike her husband.

She closed her eyes in anguish and let her head fall back against the pillow as she remembered the devastating sight of Torrie in his study at the ball the night before, Lady Worthing on her knees before him, half the buttons on his falls undone. Another wave of agony washed over her at the memory, the bitter humiliation.

The realization that her greatest fears had come to fruition and that the husband she had fallen in love with didn't love her in return. Worse, he had no intention of being faithful to her. He hadn't even been able to wait until the ball was at an end to allow his mistress to service him.

Tears came, salty and hot, rolling down her cheeks. Violent, body-wracking sobs that made Angel move from her position at Elizabeth's side and curl up at her head instead, as if to offer comfort.

But there was none for her. Her heart was shattered in a thousand tiny, irreparable shards. When she had run from the study in shock, she had been fortunate to find Hattie, who had taken one look at her and led her to a private chamber. Through tears and hiccups, she had relayed the tale of what she had seen in Torrie's study. Although Torrie was her brother, Hattie had been grim and protective, deciding that Elizabeth should spend the night at Hamilton House.

Torrie had come to the door, his tone pleading, begging to offer an explanation as Hattie's carriage had been brought around. But it had been far too much for her. She had refused, not wanting him to see how distraught she was. How humiliated. How devastated.

A light knock sounded at her bedchamber door, interrupting the latest round of sobs.

She sniffed. "Who is it?"

"It's Hattie," came the familiar voice of her sister-in-law.

Elizabeth knew that she ought to rise from the bed and at least slip into a dressing gown. To attempt to wash her face and dry her tears. But she was too miserable to move, so she called for Hattie to enter between sniffs and sobs.

The duchess entered, already dressed in a white morning gown of jaconet muslin trimmed with a double flounce at the hem, her raven hair perfectly coifed. Her countenance was pinched with concern as she crossed the chamber toward Elizabeth.

"How are you this morning, my dear?" she asked, her tone soft and low and steeped in sympathy.

"Broken," she admitted, somehow leveraging herself into a sitting position, wishing she had a handkerchief to dry her cheeks.

"Of course, you are, after that dreadful scene yesterday."

As if reading Elizabeth's mind, Hattie offered her a handkerchief she'd been carrying, apparently for just such an occasion. "I could box Torrie's ears for what has happened."

Elizabeth accepted it and scrubbed at her cheeks, mopping up the evidence of her devastation as best as she could. "Th-thank you for your kindness and your hospitality and your h-handkerchief."

"We are sisters now." Hattie perched on the edge of Elizabeth's bed, smiling sadly. "I am here for you always, dearest."

Torrie had spoken similar words to her, but those had been a lie.

Had everything he had said to her been nothing more than one ceaseless prevarication? She wondered now. Had he no loyalty, no concern for her at all? Had he merely been carrying out a duty, biding his time until he could return to his mistress's bed? She didn't want to entertain such thoughts. Couldn't bear it.

"I wish the ball had never happened," she said. "I wish that I never went to his study or opened that door."

Most of all, she wished she could erase the memory of Torrie in a moment of intimacy with someone else. And not just anyone, but the beautiful Countess of Worthing. His former mistress, and perhaps, if last evening was any indication, his mistress once again.

"I understand." Hattie patted her hand and then reached for Angel, who had once more settled at Elizabeth's side. "There was a time in my own marriage when I witnessed something similarly devastating."

But the duke and duchess were such a perfect couple. Their happiness and love for each other was palpable.

She frowned. "There was?"

"Yes." Hattie gave her a sad, small smile. "You see, my husband was trying to push me away. He believed—and quite wrongly—that he wasn't good enough for me, so he arranged for me to see him…well, I needn't go into detail. Suffice it to say that the scene was just as distressing as what you witnessed last night in Torrie's study."

Elizabeth swallowed hard against another stinging rush of tears. "What happened?"

"I proved to him how thoroughly wrong he was," Hattie said gently. "I told him how much I love him, how much I would always love him."

It was plain to see how blissful the duke and duchess were now, and Elizabeth was happy for them, truly she was. But her marriage with Torrie was an entirely different matter.

"Forgive me," she said, sniffing again when her nose began to drip as a result of all her tears, "but I don't understand what that has to do with what I witnessed last night with Torrie. I have no doubt he was not intending to push me away. He was quite obviously shocked to see me standing there at the threshold of his study. He and Lady Worthing hadn't intended for a witness to their tryst."

So many questions churned through her. Had he sent her to the terrace so that he could steal away with the countess? Had he become distracted and forgotten his invitation to Elizabeth? Had his wedding vow to remain faithful to her meant nothing to him?

She closed her eyes, wishing for darkness to blot out the morning light, but nothing could chase the image of the countess on her knees before Torrie from Elizabeth's mind. Nor the damning evidence of what they had been about—the buttons undone on the fall of his trousers. And nothing would banish the triumphant expression on Lady Worthing's beautiful face from her memory either, regardless of how desperately she longed for it to be decimated.

"What I'm trying to tell you, my dear, is that sometimes, there is more to the story than what you see," Hattie said, giving Elizabeth's shoulder a consoling squeeze. "If I had walked away from my husband that day, believing everything that was before me, I never would have found the happiness that I have with him now. We wouldn't have our beloved son, and Titus has brought us such great, everlasting joy. If I had walked away from my husband in anger that day and never forgiven him or attempted to understand what I had seen, I would have simply believed the worst, and our marriage would have been at an impasse."

Elizabeth inhaled deeply and forced her eyes open, ashamed to find they were once more filled with scalding tears. "He lied to me, Hattie, and he betrayed me with Lady Worthing. I don't think I can ever trust him again. I most certainly cannot tell him that I love him, for it would grant him far too much power over me."

Belatedly, it occurred to her that she had just revealed her feelings to Torrie's own sister. She had grown so close to Hattie over the last few weeks that sometimes, it was difficult to recall where her true allegiance must lie—with her brother.

"You do love him, then," Hattie said quietly.

She thought of the man who had kissed her with such passion, who had made her feel beautiful and wanted for the first time in her life, who had sworn he would always champion her. The lover who had shown her such tender passion, who had brought her Angel and remembered the name of her girlhood cat.

And she couldn't deny it. Even after what he had done, the shock of finding him not just alone with the Countess of Worthing, but with the woman on her knees before him, just as Elizabeth had been not long ago.

Because he had asked her to.

Had he asked Lady Worthing to do so as well?

Her stomach roiled at the thought of it.

"I do," she managed. "God help me, but I do."

"I can see how badly you're hurting, dearest Bess, and I understand why," Hattie said quietly. "My brother is here, waiting downstairs, asking to speak with you. If you want me to send him away, I will. Although it may be of no consolation to you, he looks every bit as miserable as you are, and I doubt he slept at all last night."

Torrie was here.

The knowledge sent alarm washing over her. She scrambled from the bed, emotions overwhelming her. "I have no wish to be the cause of strife between brother and sister. I'll go."

Angel made an alarmed mewl and followed her to the edge of the bed as she wrestled with her night rail in an effort to maintain her modesty. She had brought almost nothing with her in her haste to escape the ball and Torrington House both. Now, she wished she had at least packed one of her serviceable gowns from Lady Andromeda. Heaven knew she had no wish to wear anything Torrie had bought for her.

Her new wardrobe could be sent to the ashes where her heart already was, a burning, smoldering ruin.

"Please, Bess, don't go," Hattie urged, hastening to her side. "You are welcome here at Hamilton House for as long as you wish to stay with us. And you are not the cause of strife in any way. I love you and Torrie, and all I want is to see you both have the happiness you deserve."

"I'll not find it with him," Elizabeth said, adamant. "He fooled me into believing that I could, that it was possible for a beautiful rake like him to care for a plain, plump wallflower. But I've learned my lesson now. How I wish he had simply let me go that night, to whatever fate awaited me. I cannot help but to feel I wouldn't be as miserable as I am now."

"You are neither plain, nor plump, and the woman I saw

last night at the ball was no wallflower. You had gentlemen fawning over the chance to win your hand for a dance."

"Only because I am Viscountess Torrington," she said bitterly. "And only because they were curious. They wanted to know just how scandalous I was, a governess who had failed on the marriage mart and managed to secure a handsome lord as my husband." She paused, shaking her head. "None of those men desired me. They desired the idea of the tempting *on dits* they might learn from me. Or perhaps they were bored. But I don't fool myself. How can I, after what I happened upon last night?"

The ball had been much like the misery of her Seasons, only worse. Far, far worse. Her Seasons had ended in disappointment, but at least they had not ended in a broken heart. She did not think it would be possible to recover from her devastation.

"I think you are far too unkind to yourself," the duchess told her, frowning. "You were glorious last night. Everyone I spoke to was saying so. They were all impressed by your grace and your composure, your elegance and your beauty. I overheard ladies saying they wished to have a gown made in the fashion of yours."

She loved Hattie for trying to bolster her shattered confidence, but all the praises in the world couldn't change the rest of what had happened last night.

"Nothing matters," she said, trying to explain herself. "Not the gowns, not the acceptance of everyone who once ignored me. I could have every gentleman in London wishing to dance with me, falling at my feet for the next waltz, and it wouldn't matter. All I ever wanted was to be a wife. To be Torrie's wife. And for a few precious weeks, I had that. But now it's gone. Your mother was right. I reached too high, and now I must pay the price."

"Oh, Bess." Hattie swept her into a comforting embrace,

and Elizabeth allowed it, finding solace in the sisterhood Torrie's sister had shown her. "My brother cares for you. I know that may be difficult to believe, given everything that has happened. But I've never seen him with anyone else the way he is with you. Not before his accident, and most assuredly not after. I want to believe that this was all some sort of dreadful misunderstanding."

"I want to believe that as well," she whispered. "You have no idea how much I wish for that, but I cannot believe there is any sufficient explanation for what I witnessed in his study."

"Shall I tell him that he must go?" Hattie asked, drawing back to search Elizabeth's face, her own countenance drawn.

Yes.

No.

God in heaven, she didn't know. If there was a correct answer to offer, it eluded her. Because part of her wanted to give him the opportunity to explain himself, and yet another part of her couldn't bear to allow herself to be so vulnerable to Torrie ever again. Everything was too raw, too new. Her hands were trembling. Her stomach was on the verge of casting up what remained of the little she had eaten the day before. She was weary and broken.

Elizabeth shook her head. "I'm not certain just yet."

Hattie nodded, giving her shoulders another firm pat. "I'll see that some breakfast is sent up to you. Torrie has brought a valise containing some of your gowns. I'll send my lady's maid to you with that as well, so that you may dress. Take all the time you need to find your answer."

"Thank you," she said with feeling, taking her sister-in-law's hand in hers. "But if you please, Hattie, I don't wish to wear one of his gowns just now. I'd prefer something else. Anything else will do."

Even a sack.

Or her night rail.

The bedclothes.

She didn't care. All that seemed to matter was that whatever she wore must not be anything from that cursed wardrobe he had provided for her. Every gown signaled the futility of her dreams. A reminder that regardless of how fashionable the gown was, beneath it she was still the same unwanted wallflower she had always been.

"Of course," the duchess said without hesitation. "I'll send you one of my gowns instead."

Elizabeth strongly doubted one of Hattie's gowns would fit her, but she thanked her anyway, fearing she had already caused far too much trouble for her hostess as it was. When Hattie had taken her leave of the chamber, she slid back beneath the coverlets and curled up with Angel, soaking the cat's thick fur with her tears.

"You've spoken with her, then?" Torrie asked Hattie as she arrived in the drawing room where he had been cooling his heels with an alarmingly somber Monty.

His sister's expression was laced with pity. "I have."

"Thank you." He began striding across the chamber, intent on finding his wife and explaining at last. Allowing her to leave him last night had been the most difficult decision he'd ever faced. In the end, he had done so out of deference to her, and because he had feared that anything he would say or do in that moment would only make the troubling circumstances facing them even worse. He had required his own time to comprehend what Eugenia had told him as well. Time in which to ponder what he would do, what he must do.

"Torrie, wait." Hattie stopped him, snagging his sleeve. "She doesn't wish to see you just now, I'm afraid."

Fuck.

He turned to his sister, not too proud to allow her to see his desperation. "I need to see her."

"She's distraught," Hattie said quietly, "and understandably so. She hasn't told me what she saw in your study last night at the ball, but given her reaction, it cannot have been good."

Christ.

"It wasn't," Monty confirmed from somewhere behind him.

He glanced back at his friend, who had remained with him at Torrington House when Hattie had rushed Bess from the ball. He had told Monty everything. Every despicable detail of what he had learned and what had happened in his study.

What Bess had seen.

Dear God, what she had seen. But he wouldn't think of that now.

"You haven't told her?" he asked Monty, surprised.

For he knew the strength of the bond Hattie and Monty shared. He had supposed his friend would tell his sister everything so that he wouldn't have to do so.

"She said she didn't wish to know," Monty said with a shrug. "Christ knows I would have told her had she asked. But then, I didn't truly find the notion of telling my wife about her brother's mistress undoing the buttons on his trousers."

Hattie gasped. "Torrie!"

His attention snapped back to his outraged sister. "*Former* mistress, Hattie, and she damned well wasn't doing anything with my permission."

Not that it mattered either way, for the damage had been

done. Bess had been hurt, and he hated himself for that. Hated himself even more for the rest of what he had to reveal to her. For the further pain it would cause her, when she had already endured far too much.

Hattie shook her head, lips pinched. "As I said to Ewan, I don't wish to know. What you choose to do with your paramours is your concern. But what you do to your wonderful wife, my friend and sister, *is* my concern. And you've hurt her badly, Torrie."

"Damn it, Lady Worthing isn't my paramour," he snapped. "And I would never betray Bess as she thinks I've done. The truth of it is…worse, I fear."

Hattie's brow furrowed. "Worse?"

Monty strode to his wife's side, sliding a protective arm around her back. "Perhaps not worse, but dreadful, nonetheless."

"I don't understand." Hattie looked from her husband to Torrie, her countenance equal parts worried and confused. "What are the two of you speaking of?"

Dear God, this was not a conversation he wished to have with his sister. It wasn't a conversation he wanted to have with anyone. Indeed, he wished it had never bloody well happened, his disastrous affair with Eugenia and what it had unintentionally led to. But it had, and here he was, with a wife he loved who refused to speak to him, the woman he had been bedding before his marriage carrying his child, and his sister and best friend looking at him as if he were Beelzebub himself.

"Lady Worthing wasn't invited to the ball," he forced himself to say. "She made her way inside and sought me out because she wished to tell me that she is *enceinte*."

"Well, how lovely for her. I'm sure Worthing will be pleased to have another spare…" Hattie's words trailed off as she searched his face, her own expression changing. Falling. "Oh, Torrie. Please don't say that you're the father."

He nodded grimly. "The lady informs me that I am. When I tried to take her to a private chamber so that I might quell the wagging tongues and avoid anyone overhearing, she took it as an invitation for more. And she wouldn't accept that I didn't want her. Bess walked in on a disastrous scene, and although the fault was not entirely mine, and I most definitely was not a willing participant, I can understand how it must have looked to her. I can understand the hurt she must be feeling."

He had hated it, knowing that she had been so wounded, so devastated, that she had left their home. His sole comfort had been that she had taken Angel with her, and that she had come here to his sister's care at Hamilton House.

"Dear God." Hattie pressed a hand to her mouth, apparently at a loss for words.

"Satan's breeches," Monty added—for good measure, Torrie supposed. "I told you last night, and I'll tell you again, old chap. You're going to have to grovel if you truly want to win your wife back."

"And as I told you," he reminded Monty grimly, "I'm more than prepared to do so, if she will but allow me. That, however, requires my ability to speak with her. And also, my ability to deliver the news of Lady Worthing's impending child."

He couldn't bring himself to say *my child*. Not yet. The notion was too new. Not even a day had passed. He needed time. After everything that had unfolded, he was queasy, exhausted following a sleepless night, and terrified he was going to lose Bess.

"You can't force your way into her chamber and make her listen," Hattie advised him gently.

Did part of him want to race up the staircase, set his

SCARLETT SCOTT

shoulder to her chamber door, and ram his way inside as if
he were a marauder attacking the castle portcullis? Yes. But
he was also willing to wait. He would wait forever for her if
he had to.

"I know, Hattie." With another heavy sigh, he raked his
fingers through his hair. "I may feel beastly, but I'm hardly a
beast. I'll give her all the time she needs. Until then, I'll
simply wait."

His sister's brows rose. "Here in our drawing room?"

"Wherever you would have me." He scrubbed a hand over
his jaw, glancing at Monty. "You are the one who befriended
me first. You ought to have known better. Now, here I stand,
your bugbear."

"Hardly that, old friend," Monty reassured him, giving
him a considering look. "Do you remember Eton?"

He blinked, scouring his mind, and realized it was
happening again. More memories were returning to him,
and it was like the sun parting the clouds after a furious rain-
storm. Light after darkness.

But this time, so much more than the other occasions.

He remembered.

He remembered *everything*.

His father, his mother, their contentious marriage, Father
always in his cups and yelling so loudly the servants
cowered. Mama weeping in her chamber, Hattie hiding away
wherever she should, always with a book in her lap to escape
from the unhappiness surrounding them. He recalled his
years at Eton, his friendship with Monty, their endless
scrapes. He remembered Hattie as a girl.

He remembered Bess, too. Bess falling at his feet, wearing
some dreadful gown that was far too large for her, looking
horrified and too embarrassed to speak before she had scur-
ried away.

Like a mouse, he had thought, being chased from the

kitchen by a tabby cat. He had noticed her eyes even then, the deep brown with golden flecks, ringed by long lashes. And her mouth, far too large for fashion, yet made for kissing.

He recalled being intrigued by her, but then telling himself that she was an innocent, and that he didn't dally with women on the marriage mart. Particularly when he had no intention of finding himself caught in the parson's mousetrap.

And he remembered what had happened just before she had tripped over her too-long hems and fallen at the Althorp ball.

He had been speaking with an old acquaintance, the Marquess of Brisbin. He had asked Brisbin if he had been introduced to Miss Brooke. Torrie had seen her at a number of balls, their gazes clashing several times, always an answering spark lighting in his belly. He had wanted an introduction.

"Miss Elizabeth Brooke?" Brisbin had repeated, laughing. "Why should you want to be introduced to that dreadful nobody? She's a plain, plump little partridge, isn't she? And not a dowry to speak of."

It all came rushing back.

He had never called Bess those hideous words. It had been someone else. And she had overheard and mistaken Brisbin's voice for his own. Relief washed over him, along with outrage at Brisbin's cruel remarks.

It hadn't been him.

He had been drawn to Bess, even years ago. Because she had bloody well always been meant for him.

Always.

"Torrie?" Monty was standing before him, his countenance lined with concern. "You're deuced pale. Beelzebub's banyan, you aren't going to swoon, are you?"

237

"That's a new one," he muttered, thinking he had never heard his friend use that oath before and then wondering why he gave a damn.

But for some reason, his friend's odd oaths from over the years were raining in his mind. He remembered them all.

Monty grinned. "It's a recent invention. It has delightful alliteration, don't you think?"

"Christ," he mumbled. "You're a Bedlamite."

"So you've been telling me for years," Monty said. "I happily ignore all the aspersions you cast upon my character. Since I love you like a brother, I'm willing to forgive you."

His mind was whirling. He felt...dizzied and over-whelmed and relieved and terrified and overjoyed, all at once.

And confused.

So very confused. Because suddenly, the old Torrie was merging with the new Torrie, and he didn't know which of them he was. Didn't know where his old self ended and his new self began.

"I think I need to sit," he managed.

Monty directed him toward a Grecian couch. "Here you are."

He lowered himself to the cushions in a daze.

Hattie was at his elbow, looking at him as if she feared he might shatter into pieces like a broken glass. "Shall I fetch you something, Torrie?"

He looked at his sister and felt his world shift. She was no longer a stranger tied to him by the fragmented shards of what he could recall. She was the sister he had known since he was in leading strings. She was a mischief maker with a generous heart and a love of cats, and she had followed him and Monty everywhere in the careless days of their youth.

"I remember," he told her with feeling. "It has all returned to me, Hattie. Suddenly and just now."

"Oh," she breathed, staring at him solemnly for a moment before her expression gave way to a tremulous smile. "Oh, thank heavens. Does this mean that I finally have my brother back?"

Torrie swallowed down a lump of emotion. "You do."

She threw her arms around him impulsively, her exuberance taking him by surprise and knocking him into the cushions at his back. But he held his sister tightly, relief and elation and another strange, indefinable sensation sweeping over him.

She didn't just have her brother back.

He had himself back, too.

Now, all that remained was to win back his wife.

Because one thing hadn't changed when his memory had flooded his mind. Torrie still loved Bess more than he had ever thought it possible to love another. And he would do whatever it took to earn her forgiveness.

CHAPTER 17

A day passed.

And then another.

On the third day following the disastrous ball, Elizabeth woke from a fitful slumber in her guest chamber at Hamilton House and performed her morning ablutions before dressing in yet another ill-fitting borrowed gown from Hattie. Angel rolled onto her back and stretched, her mouth opening in a kittenish yawn.

She had spent every hour hidden inside her guest chamber, visited solely by Hattie and the maid who brought her tea and meals she left mostly untouched on their trays.

Each time Hattie appeared, Elizabeth asked her the same question.

"Is he still waiting?"

And on every occasion, the answer remained the same.

"He's still waiting."

Like her, Torrie hadn't left Hamilton House either. He was here, beneath the same roof, waiting for her to agree to see him. His persistence was steadily chipping away at her resolve to keep him at bay. But it wasn't just his refusal to leave without her.

It was also the small gifts he had delivered to her chamber at regular intervals. Books of poetry. Chicken livers for Angel. A plate of her favorite apple pudding, which she hadn't even supposed he had noticed she favored. A small wooden half heart he must have carved himself. A sketch of Angel he had neatly inscribed with *Lady Razor Claws*.

Elizabeth wasn't sure which was worse, his quiet acceptance of her refusal to see him, or the gifts. The thoughtfulness inherent in them, each a reminder of what she had come to love about him: his caring, his charm, his sense of humor, the way he noticed and remembered everything about her.

"Oh Angel," she murmured, returning to the bed where Angel remained comfortably curled and giving the cat's belly a fond rub. "I'm afraid that I miss him."

And that she still loved him.

That she would never stop loving him, regardless of what he had done with Lady Worthing. Her emotions were not like a water pump, turned off with ease.

"What shall I do?" she asked Angel miserably.

She could not carry on as she was, a guest in Hattie and Montrose's town house, avoiding her husband indefinitely as she hid away in a chamber with no companion save her cat. And she was strong enough now, she thought, to at least face Torrie again without humiliating herself.

"I suppose you are right," she told the cat. "I must see him."

But oh, how difficult it would be to guard her heart as she knew she must. She would have to cling to her resolve and to the bitter memory of him alone in his study with Lady Worthing. Those undone buttons on his falls.

A knock sounded at the door, and she gave Angel another pet before straightening and marching across the chamber.

No doubt, it was a servant bearing a breakfast tray, or perhaps even Hattie paying her routine morning call.

But when she opened the door to her chamber, it wasn't a servant standing before her, holding a plate of chicken in his large, capable hands. Nor was it her hostess.

It was him.

And everything inside her reacted to his familiar, beloved form. His dark hair rakishly falling over his brow, his sensual lips unsmiling, his bold, green eyes even more vibrant than she had somehow recalled. They burned into her now, searching. Searing.

"Bess," he said.

One word—her name. But there was such reverence in it, as if he spoke a prayer instead of a greeting. Her knees trembled.

"Why have you come?" she asked coolly, knowing she must not allow even a hint of her vulnerability where he was concerned to show.

He held out the plate of chicken. "Breakfast for Lady Razor Claws."

She accepted the plate, their fingers brushing, and the same awareness she always felt whenever they touched washed over her like warm honey. It would seem that her body was a traitor.

"Thank you," she said past numb lips, reaching for the door, intending to close it again and blot out the sight of him, so handsome, so forlorn, plum half circles beneath his eyes in a sign that sleep had proven as elusive for him as it had for her.

He flattened his palm on the door before she could pull it shut. "Wait. Please."

She clutched the plate tightly. "What do you want?"

"To beg your forgiveness," he said earnestly. "To explain."

Elizabeth swallowed hard. "I should think that what I saw explained itself well enough."

"It doesn't." His tone was pleading. "Bess, I need to speak with you. If you wish for me to beg, I will."

"You are the one who has been leaving gifts for me these past few days, are you not?" she asked instead of answering him, still thinking about that half heart and wondering at its significance.

He didn't hesitate. "Yes. I know you didn't want to see me, but I needed you to know I've been thinking of nothing and no one but you. I understand you are angry with me."

"Furious with you," she corrected.

And hurt. So desperately, badly hurt. But she kept that to herself.

"Furious," he echoed, nodding. "Hate me if you must, but please at least grant me a few moments of your time. The chance to explain myself."

Part of her was afraid that if she did allow him the opportunity to explain, he would charm her again. And inevitably hurt her again.

She couldn't trust him.

Couldn't trust herself around him.

"I think it would be best if you go," she said hesitantly, with far less conviction than she would have preferred.

Torrie sank to his knees, holding her stare. "I'm begging you, Bess. I'll stay here on my knees all bloody day if I must."

She did not doubt him.

Elizabeth sighed, feeling weary and weak. "A few moments," she relented. "No more, however."

He nodded. "This is a conversation best had in privacy, Bess. May I come in?"

She should tell him *no*. She should ask him to go and never return. She already knew that her ability to resist her husband was woefully inept. What good could come of a private dialogue between them *in a bedchamber*?

She had caught him alone with another woman, and her heart was still pounding as fast as it ever had in his presence. But then, she had no wish to prolong this uncomfortable discussion. The sooner he said what he wanted, the sooner he would be on his way, and she would be alone again.

Why did that notion leave her feeling nothing but hollow bitterness inside?

Elizabeth took a step backward in retreat, still clutching the plate of chicken in one hand, allowing the door to open wider in reluctant welcome. "Come inside then if you must."

He crossed the threshold in two long-limbed strides, crowding her with his presence, his nearness. Tempting her, too. She couldn't lie. Every part of her still longed for this man. Likely, she would always yearn for him, even if her rational mind knew all the reasons why she must not.

She busied herself by hastening across the Aubusson to where Angel yet lounged on the bed, blissfully unaware of the turmoil surrounding her. Elizabeth held the plate of chicken to the cat for her to sniff, and when Angel decided she was indeed hungry for her feast, she slowly placed the saucer on the floor.

The feline leapt from her perch instantly, her tail curling around her as she turned her attention to decimating the chicken Torrie had brought.

"Lady Razor Claws was hungry," he observed. "She said you ought to have realized she needed a chicken breakfast."

He was being charming. Lighthearted. Picking up where they had left off.

She couldn't bear it.

With a deep breath, she turned toward him. "Don't. Please."

He nodded, his expression darkening, growing serious.

"Forgive me. It wasn't my intention to cause you further upset."

She wrapped her arms around her waist in a defensive gesture, hugging herself. "Then why do you persist in sending me gifts and remaining here at Hamilton House if you don't want to bring me further pain? Why come to my door this morning with chicken for Angel? Why send half a dozen gifts to my room?"

"Because I'm desperate for you to let me explain what you saw in my study." He had followed her across the chamber, and he was standing alarmingly near to her now, close enough to touch. Close enough that his scent wrapped around her. Leather and bay and citrus and Torrie.

The man she loved.

The man she would never stop loving.

She released a shaky breath she hadn't realized she'd been holding. "Explain yourself then, if you think it will make a difference."

"I don't know if it will," he said, his voice tinged with sadness. "Not when you hear the entire tale. But I owe you the truth. The whole truth. And I mean to give it."

Some foolish part of Elizabeth had hoped Torrie would reassure her. That he would tell her she hadn't seen at all what she supposed she had seen. That he would profess his undying love for her, and they could pretend she had never seen him alone and in a state of alarming dishabille with the Countess of Worthing.

But his countenance looked as if it had been chiseled in marble, and his tone was grim. Any remaining hope inside her shriveled and turned to dust.

She swallowed hard, willing herself not to weep. Not to allow him to see her inner devastation. "Go on. Do it. I cannot bear the waiting."

"Will you not sit with me?" he asked.

The question nettled. She resented it, resented him.

Elizabeth shook her head. "Standing shall suffice."

He gave another nod. "As you wish."

And then he said nothing else. Simply stood there staring at her, looking as if he hadn't slept in days and he was the one with the broken heart instead of her.

"Do you love her?" she blurted, and then cursed herself a hundred times for allowing her weakness and fears to so thoroughly rule her.

"No." He reached for her, finding her hands although they had been hidden in the skirt of her borrowed gown, gently plucking them from her waist. "There is only one woman I love. Only one woman I'll ever love, and she isn't the Countess of Worthing."

Her breath caught. Was he saying…? *Her*?

No, this Elizabeth could not believe. It was more of his tricks. More attempts at persuading her to believe whatever he wanted her to believe. Manipulation, just like the plate of chicken for Angel.

Wasn't it?

"I wish you would speak plainly, my lord," she managed, still afraid to look at him.

Torrie was her Gorgon, and if she stared at him directly, he would cause every modicum of common sense she possessed to flee, along with any ability to resist him.

"Bess, look at me. Please."

The pleading in his voice affected her. How could it not? He sounded a hundred times more vulnerable than she had ever heard him, and so she turned.

Looked at him as he had asked.

And saw it there, written plainly on his handsome face. Saw the emotion, the tenderness, the caring. Saw what she had seen so many times before, only magnified a thousandfold.

Saw it and wasn't certain she dared to believe it.

"I'm in love with you," he said quietly. "You're the woman I love, Bess. Not Lady Worthing, not anyone else. You, only you."

There was such earnestness in his countenance, blazing in his beautiful green eyes. She couldn't look away. It seemed vastly impossible, yet another weapon in his arsenal of seduction and manipulation against her, and yet she *wanted* to believe him.

"You...love me," she repeated weakly, confused.

Desperately hoping he was telling her the truth. Terrified he was using her own emotions against her. Afraid that she was too deeply in love with him herself to tell the difference between Torrie attempting to save himself and Torrie being brutally honest.

"I love you." He didn't look away, the intensity of his stare burning into her like twin flames. "This isn't how I intended to tell you, but neither will I stand before you and lie. You're the woman I love, Bess. Now and forever."

"How?" she bit out. "And why? Why would you do what you did with Lady Worthing if you loved me?"

His jaw hardened, and he raked a hand through his hair, thoroughly mussing the dark strands. "She attended the ball uninvited."

Elizabeth had worked diligently on the invitations for the ball with Hattie at her side as guide, and she knew well enough that the countess had not been on the list of lords and ladies meant to be in attendance that evening.

"You didn't invite her?" she asked.

"Christ, no."

Once again, he seemed to be telling her the truth. There was no sign of prevarication. He held her gaze without flinching or glancing away. Her inner desperation to believe

247

everything he had said was overwhelming her. Confusing her, too. She didn't know what to think.

Elizabeth inhaled slowly, forcing her roiling mind to think. To demand answers.

"And yet, you left the ball with her to go alone to your study," she countered. "That hardly seems the action of a man who didn't wish for the countess to be present at his ball."

"I took her to my study to speak with her," he said. "Nothing else. Everything that happened after we crossed the threshold was my fault, and I beg your forgiveness. But I didn't want any of it to happen."

She closed her eyes and sucked in another breath, before expelling it, trying and failing to make sense of her turbulent thoughts. He told her that he loved her, and yet he admitted to taking Lady Worthing to his study. He said he hadn't wanted anything to happen between them, and yet he acknowledged everything that had transpired was his fault. He begged her forgiveness, and yet he had not said anything thus far to prove to her that he deserved it.

"Explain," she demanded. "Your trousers were unbuttoned. She was touching you. I saw it, Torrie. You cannot tell me that it didn't happen, for I was there."

Words failed her, for fury and outrage were once more clawing up her throat, making it tight, hampering speech.

"I'm not telling you it didn't happen. God, Bess. Please. Open your eyes and look at me."

There was such pleading in his voice, and her rational mind knew she should ignore him, but she couldn't seem to keep herself from obeying. She opened her eyes. Drank in the sight of him as if it were the first time she had looked upon Viscount Torrington, the sinfully handsome, unequivocally charming rake she had loved for far too long. Initially from afar, and later, from too near.

"Lady Worthing came to the ball to impart some…news,"

Torrie said, as if the words were acidic on his tongue, difficult to form. "I was coming to find you on the terrace when she found me first, and she told me that she is carrying a child."

A child. Of course, she was. How like a woman as lovely as the Countess of Worthing, who already had three young children, to have another. Elizabeth stifled the surge of envy inside her, knowing it was unworthy. The remnants of a woman who had been forced to become a governess and surrender her dream of having a family of her own.

"I fail to see why Lady Worthing carrying Lord Worthing's babe would be of such significant import that she would attend our ball uninvited," she said, before a strange, unwanted thought occurred to her.

"Because..." Torrie's eyes closed, his expression anguished. When they opened again, his brilliant gaze was bleak. "Because I am the babe's father."

The father.

Torrie.

He was having a child with Lady Worthing?

Elizabeth reeled, nearly losing her footing and grasping the back of a nearby chair for support to keep her upright. Suddenly, she understood all too clearly the reason for his suggestion that they carry on with this conversation whilst seated.

"She is carrying your child?" she managed.

Torrie inclined his head, looking grimmer than she had ever seen him. "Although I took great pains during my association with Lady Worthing to avoid an unwanted issue, apparently, she is *enceinte*. She was announcing so, and with great pleasure, to everyone within our vicinity. I took her to my study to spare you the gossip. It was wrong of me to take her there, and I realize that now, believe me, Bess, I do. But I was shocked, and all I could think was that I was going to lose you and cause you shame, and I couldn't bear either of those outcomes, so I took her away to my study. Only, that made everything worse."

"Yes," she agreed numbly. "It did."

"I told her that I'm a happily married man, but she was insistent. I didn't welcome her advances, Bess. Her touch repulsed me."

Elizabeth stared at her husband in the early-morning sunlight, the cheer at his back casting him in an ethereal glow that made her wish this was nothing more than a dream from which she would wake, thankful none of it had been real. His jaw was so strong and rigid, held at such a firm angle, and the fanciful, ridiculous thought occurred to her that if she touched it, that jaw might cut her open and make her bleed.

She felt as if she were bleeding now. As if she were losing a part of herself she hadn't known existed until it was gone.

Torrie was having a child with the Countess of Worthing.

He was waiting for her to speak. It was her turn. She had to say something. But what? None of this made sense and her mind was a hopeless, helpless jumble.

"You say that her touch repulsed you, but the buttons on your trousers were open," she reminded him tightly, those words nearly choking her in their bitterness. "She was on her knees before you when I opened the door."

A muscle in his jaw worked, those startling eyes remaining pinned on her, not allowing her to look away. "Of her own volition. Certainly not from any invitation from me. I don't want her. The only woman I want, now and forever, is you."

Her heart yearned to believe those words, but her mind was all too familiar with the landscape of disappointment and betrayal.

"The half heart," she said, thinking again of the smallest

offering he had left outside her chamber door, the smooth wood he must have spent hours carving away at, his nimble fingers shaping and cutting. "Why did you give it to me?"

He ventured even closer to her. A dangerous proximity. She knew she should move away, but she couldn't force herself to do it.

"Because you are the other half of my heart, Bess," he said softly, tenderly.

So tenderly that tears sprang to her eyes. She swallowed hard against a surge of emotion she didn't want to feel.

"Please, Torrie," she whispered, only she didn't know what she was pleading for.

She was afraid to hope. Seeing him with Lady Worthing had devastated her.

"I was broken when you came back into my life," he continued, reaching out and brushing a stray tendril of hair behind her ear, "but you fixed me and made me whole. And when you did that, you claimed me as yours. That is why I made you the half heart. I had forgotten just how much I enjoyed whittling, but I remember now."

"You remember more?" she asked, sensing the importance in what he'd just said, concentrating on that instead of the rest of his confession.

Because she wasn't sure what to do with Torrie telling her he loved her. That she had made him whole. That she was the other half of his heart. She didn't know what to do with the way he was looking at her now, with such intensity and open admiration and—dare she think it—love.

"I remember everything."

His quiet admission shook her as much as his revelation that Lady Worthing was carrying his child had.

Her fingers tightened on the back of the chair, every muscle in her body tensing. "*Everything?*" she repeated.

"I remember the Althorp ball," he said, his countenance

serious. "I remember what happened before you tripped over your hems and fell at my feet. I was speaking with an old acquaintance, the Marquess of Brisbin. I had asked him if he had been introduced to you, and that is when he said the words you overheard. It was Brisbin, Bess, not me."

Could it be possible? Her thoughts whirled back to that day which now seemed as if it belonged to a different lifetime. Torrie had been standing with a group of friends, and the Marquess of Brisbin had indeed been amongst them. From her place behind the potted palm, she hadn't been able to see who had spoken.

Had she leapt to the wrong conclusion?

And was she leaping to the wrong conclusion now?

The words from that night echoed in her mind.

She's a plain, plump little partridge, isn't she?

She had been so certain the voice had been Torrie's. But she had never spoken to him directly. The extent of their interaction had been being in the same ballroom at the same time. Their eyes had met and held. They'd never been introduced.

"Why would you ask him if he'd been introduced to me?" she asked.

"Because I wanted an introduction myself," Torrie said. "I was drawn to you even then."

It couldn't be true. Could it? Had Torrie been somehow interested in her when she had been nothing more than a dowdy wallflower in Lady Andromeda's castoffs? When no one else had noticed her?

Her heart leapt.

"I was always meant to be yours, Bess, and you were always meant to be mine. I think I knew it then, but I wasn't ready for you yet," he continued, voice steeped in affection. "I'm ready for you now, even if I don't deserve you. And Christ, believe me, I know I don't deserve you. I've done everything wrong. I've made mistakes. I've hurt you when hurting you is the last thing I would ever want to do. All I want to do is love you, if you'll let me."

Dear God.

Her knees threatened to give out in truth.

Elizabeth circled the chair and sat in it heavily, with a complete lack of grace. But she didn't care at the moment. She was far too busy sorting through all the revelations Torrie had just made.

He loved her.

He hadn't been welcoming Lady Worthing's advances.

He was having a child.

He remembered.

He remembered, and it didn't change the way he felt about her.

Torrie followed her and sank to his knees on the carpets for a second time, taking her hands in his. She didn't pull away, because she needed his touch. Needed the connection.

Needed *him*.

"I'm sorry," he said again. "This isn't the way I wanted to tell you. I'll give you all the time that you need. And if you can never return my love, I understand. I'll love you enough for the both of us."

He was breaking her heart. Breaking it all over again, but in a different way. Because she could see now that she had allowed her own fears to overtake her. She hadn't trusted in him, in the man he had shown her he was—compassionate, tender, loving, charming, loyal. Instead, she had rushed to believe the worst of him and had closed herself off from him in the process. How deeply she had wronged him.

"I should have trusted you. I'm so sorry that I didn't." Tears pricked her eyes, fell down her cheeks. "I love you too, Torrie. I think that I always have."

His fingers tightened on hers. "You love me?"

253

She nodded, sniffling. "You are the other half of my heart as well."

He brought her hands to his lips for a reverent kiss. "Thank God, Bess. I was afraid I'd lost you forever."

"You could never lose me."

She knew that now. Their bond was unbreakable. She had merely been too afraid to believe in it. Her confidence far too easily shaken.

More kisses rained over her knuckles. "Say it again. Please."

"I love you," she repeated. "But Lady Worthing and the child…what do you intend to do?"

"I will do my duty by the child," Torrie said. "I would never ask you to acknowledge the child publicly or to see the child. But I intend to make certain the child has everything he needs."

He wouldn't be the first lord with a child born on the wrong side of the blanket, and nor would he be the last. And Elizabeth was no hypocrite. Her own father had been illegitimate, even if she had only made the discovery recently through Torrie. She would love the child, would support Torrie in any decision he made.

"I will love the child because he is partially yours," she told him. "Whatever must be done, we will do it. We'll do it together."

Angel had finished her plate of cooked chicken and wound herself sinuously against Torrie's side.

"Will you come home with me where you belong, my love?" he asked her. "You and Lady Razor Claws?"

She smiled through her tears, love for him banishing all the doubts and worries, all the pain of the last few days. "Yes, we will."

CHAPTER 18

"You are certain, my love?" Torrie asked Bess for what was likely the tenth time in as many minutes as their carriage ambled through Mayfair on its way to the Earl of Worthing's town house.

"I'm certain," she said firmly, giving him a reassuring pat on his thigh.

Under ordinary circumstances, his wife's gloved hand in such delightful proximity to his cock would have stirred him. However, this was decidedly not ordinary circumstances, and the call they were about to pay was one he had been dreading every day since Bess's return to Torrington House. Still, he knew that it had to be done.

"I deeply regret having to involve you in this tawdry affair," he said grimly.

For it was the devil's own coil in which he found himself, and thanks to his own aimless stupidity. Thank Christ for Bess, who had forgiven him for the debacle at the ball, and who loved him in spite of himself.

How he appreciated the woman at his side. Gloried in

her. Loved her desperately, more with each passing day. He was so damned proud to have her on his arm, at his side.

"I would far prefer to be at your side than anywhere else," she said, cutting through his heavy musings. "I promised to be your wife for better or for worse, for richer for poorer, in sickness and in health, to love and to cherish you. And I meant those vows."

To think that their marriage had initially been caused by a carriage ride not too dissimilar to this one. The same carriage, the same man and woman and yet also so very different now. They had changed and grown together. Bess had shown him what love was, and he was doing his utmost every day to show her the same.

"I'm so damned grateful you did," he told her, taking her hand and bringing it to his lips for a kiss, thwarted by kidskin leather. How he wished for her bare skin, but there was time aplenty for that later, after this cursed meeting was at an end. "Heaven knows I've caused more than my share of strain on them already."

"As have I," she said softly, smiling up at him, the gold flecks in her eyes catching in the sunlight and coming to vibrant life. "I ran from you that night when I should have stayed and listened. I should have trusted in you and the man I know you to be instead of clinging to my hurts and fears and doubts instead."

He didn't blame her for fleeing that night. He had handled everything poorly, and he regretted ever taking Eugenia to his study. Regretted ever touching her to begin with, before he had been with Bess. But that was in the past now, and the past could not be rewritten, merely learned from.

"All that matters is that you came back to me, my love," he told her, so grateful that she had.

Those three days of uncertainty had been the worst of his life. Nothing less than sheer agony as he had waited at

Hamilton House, praying she would forgive him. Hoping she would see him. Making small pilgrimages to her chamber door to leave her offerings.

"I'll always come back to you," she reassured him softly now, giving his hands a gentle squeeze. "You're mine, and I am yours."

And he couldn't be more grateful for that distinction, knowing that despite all the mayhem surrounding them, he had Bess to come home to. Bess in his bed, in his heart, in his arms. He was a most fortunate man.

"I've said it before, but I'll say it again. I don't deserve you." He couldn't resist claiming her lips with his in a quick, possessive kiss. "But I'm greedy when it comes to you, so I'll keep you just the same."

"Keep me forever," she murmured, giving him a smile that made him want to demand the coachman turn around and take them directly back to Torrington House.

But they couldn't do that. Not until they had this matter settled, and he knew it.

So Torrie appeased himself by giving Bess another kiss as the carriage drew to a halt outside their destination. He inhaled her familiar scent, floral and sweet, trying to keep the crushing sense of dread dwelling in his stomach at bay. They had spent the past few days following her return to Torrington House in an idyll.

Most of which had been spent in either his or Bess's bedchamber.

But now, the ugliness of reality was about to intrude.

As if sensing his disquiet, Bess laid a calming hand on his forearm. "The sooner this is all settled, the better you will feel."

She was right, of course. She always was. But he didn't want to have to drag her into such a tangled mess. And he had no notion of how Eugenia would react to their call. The note she had sent in response to his request for a meeting had been terse. He couldn't blame her; when they had last parted, he had been cold and furious, his words sharp.

He hadn't been thinking of needing to strike a conciliatory tone with her then. He had been terrified of the prospect of losing Bess.

"I do believe you are more accepting of all this than I am," he said wryly, for he was still reconciling himself to the knowledge that his firstborn child would not be with Bess. It would be a child he could not publicly claim as his own, and one with whom he may have precious little involvement, depending on Eugenia and Worthing.

"I believe in doing what is best," she said simply, her calm demeanor imbuing him with a sense of purpose.

Once again, she was right.

Together, they descended from the carriage and made their way up the walk, where they were met by the frowning butler Torrie had often avoided on his previous calls during his association with Eugenia. He and Bess stood together in awkward silence in the front entry, fingers entwined, while their call was announced to Lady Worthing. After a several-minute wait, the butler returned and escorted them to the drawing room where their hostess awaited them with a look of ill-concealed disgust as she rose to her feet. Her willowy figure was swathed in a gown that was nearly transparent, and her pale loveliness was no comparison to Bess's dark-haired beauty and kindhearted compassion.

Eugenia had the grace to wait until the butler had left them in privacy to make her displeasure known.

"You wrote that you wished to speak with me," she said, raising an icy, blonde brow. "However, you never mentioned an audience. If I had known you were bringing my grasping former governess along with you, I most assuredly would have denied your request."

"Lady Torrington is not an audience," he countered, trying to keep his ire in check. "And I will thank you to keep from insulting her."

Eugenia's lips twisted in a bitterly mocking smile. "I do wish you would have come alone, Torrie."

"Torrington," he corrected her, for their time of informality had long since passed.

She stiffened at his light reprimand, nostrils flaring. "Forgive me, my lord, if I was too familiar. It is an old habit drawn from experience, you see."

Her words were meant as an affront to Bess, who had stiffened at his side but still maintained her remarkable sangfroid.

"Leave the past where it belongs," he snapped, not liking the implications of what Eugenia had said.

"Hmm." Eugenia cast a narrow-eyed look at Bess. "And look at you. Daring to enter my drawing room. You must be quite pleased with yourself. Playing the whore for Torrington has suited you well."

His fury was as sudden as it was murderous. Bess laid a staying hand on his arm, reminding him wordlessly that he needed to maintain the peace with the viper before them.

"Never dare to speak of my wife with such disrespect again," he bit out.

"Are you threatening me in my own home, my lord?" the countess demanded.

"It isn't a threat, it's a promise that you won't like the consequences if you fail to heed my warning."

Bess squeezed his arm. "I thank you for your hospitality, Lady Worthing," she said calmly, refusing to be ruffled by the other woman's antagonism.

"As you may have guessed, we've come to discuss provisions for the child," he said tightly, just barely keeping control over his emotions.

The countess's abominable behavior toward Bess continued to rankle. But if Bess could rise above it for the greater good, then so too could he.

He had no other choice.

"The child?" Eugenia paled. "Why should you wish to speak of that?"

"Because I want to make certain the child is well provided for," he said, trying and failing to maintain his own calm.

Her hostility toward Bess was infuriating. He didn't want to be here. Most especially, he didn't want to be in this drawing room with the Countess of Worthing as she insulted the woman he loved. But he had an obligation to the child. A duty he had every intention of upholding, regardless of how unpleasant Eugenia made the task.

"You needn't concern yourself on that account," she said breezily.

Tension knotted his gut. Damn it, perhaps he should have held more tightly to the reins of his temper. He had angered her, and now she would want him to pay the price.

"If you intend to keep the child from me, I will fight you, Lady Worthing," he warned grimly. "I can assure you of that."

"There is no child," she said quietly.

Bess's grip on his arm tightened.

He stared at Eugenia, thinking he must have misheard her. "What did you just say, madam?"

Surely, she had not just said that there wasn't a child. How could there not be one? Had she lost the babe in the days since the ball?

Her gaze dropped from his. "There isn't a babe. I'm not with child."

His knees almost buckled, his hands clenching into fists at his sides. "You're not carrying my child any longer?"

Eugenia huffed an irritated little sigh, looking much aggrieved. "Apparently, I was mistaken, and I never was."

Mistaken?

She had never been carrying his child?

Torrie felt winded, as if he had just run a great distance, his mind too sluggish to comprehend. Slowly, the truth settled in, damning and undeniable.

"You lied to me?" he snarled, wondering if it was all just a ploy on her part, if she had used her announcement as a means to attempt to seduce him back into her bed.

If she had, by God.

The pain she had caused…

So severe was his anger that the hand reaching for Bess trembled. Their fingers tangled again, the comfort he needed, the reminder that she was his and he was hers.

"I didn't lie," Eugenia said coolly. "I told you the truth as I imagined it to be, and I thought at the time that it was fate bringing us back together. Clearly, I was wrong."

He shook his head slowly. "I don't understand."

A flush stained her cheeks, quite unlike her—he didn't think he had ever seen her put to the blush during their entire acquaintance.

"My courses were unusually late," she murmured, "but they have since arrived. There is no child. Now, if you please, go. Leave my drawing room, the both of you."

"With pleasure, madam," he managed past the shock and roiling emotions within.

And then, he escorted his wife from the Earl of Worthing's town house for the second and last time. On this occasion, however, he took her home with him.

Which was precisely where his Bess belonged.

"ARE YOU DISAPPOINTED?"

"About spending the afternoon in bed with my beautiful

wife?" Torrie's voice was a decadent rumble beneath Elizabeth's ear. "Not for a moment, my love."

After abruptly ending their call on Lady Worthing, she and Torrie returned to Torrington House, where they had slipped into her chamber and out of their respective garments. Now, she was lying on her belly, sated and happy, her head on her husband's chest, listening to the steady beat of his heart as he idly sifted through the strands of her hair.

"Not about the manner in which we've spent our afternoon," she said softly, exploring the bands of muscle on his abdomen with a slow, tender caress. "About the babe, I mean. Learning that the child never was."

"If anything, I'm relieved not to be tied to Lady Worthing any longer in any capacity." He lifted her long hair and dropped it steadily, piece by piece, to her bare back. "I would have cared for the child, loved the child. But I want to become a father when you become a mother. I want our children to be raised in a happy home with parents who love each other."

Our children.

Hers and Torrie's.

Oh, how she liked the sound of that. How she liked this unexpected second chance she had been given, the opportunity to find love and a deeper contentedness than she had ever known possible. To become a wife and one day, she hoped, a mother as well.

"You will make a wonderful father," she told him, unable to resist pressing a kiss to his chest.

Torrie's hand swept beneath her hair, his touch igniting a trail of fire over her bare skin as he followed the length of her spine. "I cannot say I'll be a wonderful father. Christ knows my own sire fell far short of the mark, and my mother was no better. But I will try."

The return of his memory had lessened the strain

between Torrie and his mother. However, the dowager still remained rather frosty with both Elizabeth and Torrie. Their paths infrequently crossed, and by design. Elizabeth still hoped that gradually, bit by bit, she might loosen the stones in the wall Lady Torrington had built around herself. Thus far, however, the dowager had been far more willing to accept Angel into her heart than Elizabeth.

But time was a healer, and Elizabeth was eternally optimistic. After all, time had eventually given her the greatest gift of all, and his heart was beating directly beneath her ear in a steady, wonderful rhythm.

"I caught your mother sitting with Angel in her lap this morning," she said. "I was quite shocked when I saw it. She claimed that Angel jumped into her lap without provocation, and she was too fearful of her claws to demand she move, so she allowed it."

Torrie chuckled. "What rot. I've seen her slipping chicken livers about the house on a plate. She is bribing your cat, darling."

Elizabeth smiled, finding the trail of hair on his abdomen that led lower, to another part of her husband's anatomy she also admired. "I think she is lonely. It will be good for her to find some companionship in Angel, and Angel is willing to eat whatever delights are offered her."

"Always kindhearted and compassionate, my beautiful Bess." His hand passed between her shoulder blades, his touch warm and reassuring, but also bringing her desire back to life. "Always willing to give the undeserving another chance. Myself included."

"Oh, but you are most deserving." Her fingers trailed deliberately lower. "I would be happy to show you just how much."

"My sweet, proper wife," he murmured, arching into her touch. "Whatever can you be suggesting?"

Her fingers wrapped around his length. Already, he was rigid and thick, despite their earlier lovemaking, and she felt an answering pulse between her thighs. He had such a beautiful cock. But then, that was hardly surprising. Torrie was beautiful everywhere, inside and out.

"I think you know precisely what I'm suggesting, Lord Torrington," she murmured, feeling naughty.

She flicked her tongue over his nipple.

He made a low sound, deep in his throat. "I'm afraid you'll have to say the words, Lady Torrington."

She glanced up at him, holding his glittering green gaze. "I want you inside me."

He gave her a slow smile. A burning smile. The smile of a reformed rakehell who knew the effect he had on his wife. A viscount of villainy no more.

"Which part of me, Bess?" he asked wickedly. "My tongue?" He caught the hand that was nestled against his shoulder and brought it to his lips, sucking her forefinger into his mouth and swirling his tongue over it before releasing her. "My fingers?" The hand on her back glided down her spine, past her bottom, and his fingers dipped into her folds from behind to tease. "Or my cock?" At the last, he thrust himself into her hand.

She stroked him just the way she knew he liked and smiled back at him, feeling deliriously contented and desperately yearning all at once. "All three."

"That's my girl." Grinning, he took her in his arms and rolled them, so that she was on her back, and he was atop her, his body a warm, welcome weight. "I'm happy to oblige."

His lips found hers, the kiss slow and deep, a promise of more, stoking her need ever higher with each tender brush of his mouth and sinuous glide of his tongue. She reveled in him. He was all hard sinews and planes, smooth, hot skin. Each flex of his body brought them closer, and he kissed her as if his next breath depended on it. Her fingertips traveled over his muscled shoulders, her entire world condensed to this chamber, this man, the love they shared.

Years ago, she had thought herself in love with him. But those old emotions paled compared to the depth of emotion she felt for him now. In his arms, she was loved and protected and cherished. Her fears and doubts had been firmly cast aside since that day at Hamilton House. Together, they were one.

Together, they were formidable.

Torrie broke the kiss to drag his lips along her jaw, down her throat. "Which shall I give my lady first?" he asked against her skin.

At the question, his hand slid between their bodies, lightly cupping her aching sex.

Instinctively, she rocked against that touch, needing more. "Whatever my lord prefers," she answered breathlessly.

"Carte blanche," he growled. "I approve."

He strummed her pearl and kissed down the curve of her breast before taking the peak in his mouth for a hard suck that she felt deep in her core. Still playing with her, he laved attention on both breasts, licking and nipping and suckling until she was writhing beneath him.

Just when she was sure she could endure no more, he kissed down her belly, where she had always thought she had been far too rounded.

"My beautiful Bess," he said, the veneration in his voice melting her as his wicked mouth continued dropping worshipful kisses along her bare body. "I think I'll give you my tongue first. My tongue in your gorgeous, dripping cunny."

Wetness sluiced from her at his words, her sex pulsing with new need. His clever fingers left her as he shifted himself so that he was more fully between her legs, his palms caressing her inner thighs to guide them apart.

"Would you like that?" he asked, his thumbs gently dipping into her folds to reveal her swollen clitoris to his avid gaze.

He blew a hot stream of air over her.

She whimpered, unable to keep the desperate noise from fleeing her throat. "Yes."

"Do you know how perfect you look like this?" His dark head lowered, and he rewarded her with one stroke of his tongue.

She wanted him to tell her. Wanted him to say wicked things to her.

And he knew what she wanted without her needing to ask.

"All pink and wet and pretty, ready to come for me again." Another slow lick. "I love the way you taste. So sweet." His tongue flicked her pearl. "You like to come for me, don't you? You want it so badly."

"Yes," she hissed, on the edge already from their earlier lovemaking and now nearly out of her mind from his sinful words and teasing play.

"Tell me what to do." He sipped at her tenderly, as if she were a delicacy.

"Make me come," she said, part plea, part command.

"My sweet Bess, I thought you'd never ask."

He latched on to her aching bud, sucking just as she wanted, and plunged his fingers inside her, where she was dripping and needy. Her wetness mingled with his seed from their earlier lovemaking, the wet sounds of him sliding in and out of her sinful and filthy.

"So wet," he whispered approvingly against her sex, fingers probing deep. "Your cunt is dripping."

It was. She could feel it sliding from her, coating his

fingers as he filled her, pressing on that same place of excru-ciating pleasure only he could find. And she didn't care that she was making a mess of him, a mess of the bed. All she cared about was the sensation he was coaxing from her body. His tongue flicked over her faster, and she tipped back her head on the pillow, eyes closing, losing herself.

Her orgasm hit her so suddenly and unexpectedly that she cried out, body shuddering as wave after wave of uncon-trollable bliss washed over her. He withdrew his fingers and replaced them with his tongue, licking inside her as the ripples of her release continued to roll through her.

She moaned his name, thoroughly boneless and mindless. He moved again with lightning quickness, dragging his body along hers so that they were hip to hip and breast to chest, his hard cock aligned with her sex.

"My love," he said.

And then he filled her. Filled her so deep and so full that she thought she might burst with the exquisite wonder of it. She wrapped her legs around him, clinging to him, loving him and wanting him, her body and mind and heart solely his. How right it felt, this joining. How right he was for her, this man.

He moved, slowly at first, his cock gliding easily through her slickness. His expression was intent, his jaw locked, his eyes burning green fire into hers as he held her gaze and made love to her until they both lost all control. His measured thrusts became faster and harder, and her nails scraped down his back. He kissed her, and she tasted both of them together. It was wicked and it was wonderful, and when he reached between their joined bodies to press on her aching clitoris again, she came undone.

Her inner muscles clenched on him, and Elizabeth moaned into his mouth, holding on to him as he continued to fuck her deeply, deliciously. He made an answering sound deep in his chest, a rumble so primal that it vibrated against her breasts. Another few pumps, and he came apart as well, spilling inside her, filling her with the hot release of his seed, their lips never parting.

When the last drop had been wrung from him, he ended their kiss, his breathing as ragged as hers, looking down at her with the tender expression she adored.

"Sweet God," he said, reverence in his voice, in his eyes. "That was incredible, my love."

He was still pulsing inside her, and she wasn't ready for him to withdraw just yet. She kept her legs locked around him, her arms twined around his neck.

"*You're* incredible," she told him.

"Hardly." He kissed the tip of her nose. "I'm just a sinner and a scoundrel."

"You're far more than that," she countered softly. "You're my husband." She kissed his jaw, his cheek, his lips, any part of him she could. "And you're the other half of my heart."

EPILOGUE

"*A*ngel," Torrie called in a singsong voice, feeling ridiculous as he swept through the town house in search of one tortoise shell cat. "Angel. Here puss, puss, puss. Where have you gone, you sly little bit of fur?"

He was seeking the cat for good reason, of course. Bess wanted to feed the minx her breakfast, and Bess was decidedly not in a state to be chasing about an errant feline. She was doing precisely what she ought to be doing at the moment: resting in bed, propped up with an array of pillows.

Torrie passed the breakfast room and caught a flurry of motion from the corner of his eye. Had it been the cat?

He stopped and doubled back, entering the room to find his mother sitting at the table with Angel at her side. The cat was atop the table, eating delicately from whatever feast his mother must have procured on her behalf from the laden sideboard.

"Mama," he said, for now that time had passed and he had regained his memory, the endearment no longer felt foreign and unfamiliar.

And at his wife's urging, he was attempting to mend his relationship with his mother.

"I would give anything to speak to my mother one more time," she had told him. *"Yours is still here."*

And as always, Bess with her compassionate heart had persuaded him that he must give his mother another chance. He had been willing, provided that his mother continued to treat Bess kindly. And in recent months, her ice had gradually thawed.

"Torrie," his mother greeted him, looking a bit ruffled at his unexpected arrival.

No doubt because she was allowing the cat to dine atop the table.

He cleared his throat. "Good morning. Bess was searching for Angel, but I see that she is already enjoying her breakfast."

Color tinged his mother's cheekbones. "The vexing creature was hungry. What else was I to do?"

The cat's frequent presence on tables now made perfect sense.

"You've been spoiling her," he said without heat.

For in truth, he found his mother's grudging adoration for Angel amusing. She insisted that she disliked the cat and yet, at every opportunity, she was feeding her or holding her in her lap.

"Why would I spoil her?" His mother asked dismissively. "I don't even like her."

"Of course, you don't," he agreed wryly.

Mama gave an imperious sniff. "She is a little beggar."

"Who knows where to beg," he pointed out.

"How is Lady Torrington this morning?" his mother asked, surprising him with her concern for Bess's welfare.

"She is doing well. Perhaps you would like to visit with her?"

He continued to hope his mother would extend an olive branch to Bess. And he continued to be disappointed by her refusal.

"Yes," she agreed suddenly, shocking him. "I do think I shall. Will you see that the cat eats the rest of her breakfast? I don't want her to follow me about complaining all day."

He tried to stifle his grin and failed. "Of course, Mama."

She inclined her head, every bit the regal viscountess she had always been. "Thank you, Torrington. Her meow is quite vexing, you know. It makes me bilious."

Angel's meows weren't the only thing that made his mother bilious, but Torrie refrained from saying so as she took her august leave of the breakfast room, leaving him alone with the cat.

"Just you and I, Lady Razor Claws," he said to Angel, who was watching him with a keen emerald stare. "What shall we have for breakfast?"

"COME," Elizabeth called at the tap on her chamber door, supposing it was her lady's maid returning with a tray of tea.

She was desperately ungainly these days with her lying in fast approaching, and resting in the morning instead of making her way downstairs helped her aching feet and back immensely.

When the door opened, however, it revealed not Culpepper, but the dowager.

Elizabeth instantly shifted in the mound of pillows Torrie had thoughtfully arranged for her before leaving to find Angel. Good heavens, what was his mother doing at her chamber door? She had no doubt she looked a fright, wearing nothing but a dressing gown, her hair unbound and falling in a wild tangle down her back.

"Good morning," the dowager offered quietly, along with a tentative smile as she hesitated at the threshold. "May I come in?"

"Of course." She struggled to pull her body into a more upright position. "Good morning."

Although the dowager had gradually become less frosty with her over the course of the last few months, Elizabeth still didn't know where she stood with her husband's mother. Her presence in her chamber this morning was unexpected. Almost troubling.

"I hope that nothing is amiss," she added, thinking of her missing companion and fretting. "Have you seen Angel? Torrie went to look for her, but he hasn't returned."

The dowager crossed the chamber, looking elegant as always, her dark hair beneath her customary cap. "The feline is making herself at home in the breakfast room. You needn't worry on that scamp's account."

Elizabeth detected the note of fondness in the other woman's voice, despite the manner in which she spoke about Angel, and couldn't suppress her smile. "That is a great relief to me. I feared she had made her way into the kitchens and escaped again."

Angel had indeed been intrepid enough on several occasions to find her way into the mews. But fortunately, some clever groomsmen had always been about to catch her and return her to safety.

"May I sit?" the dowager asked, gesturing toward a chair near the bed.

"Of course. Would you care for me to join you?" Although hauling herself from bed was no easy feat, she would happily do so if the dowager wished it.

After all, she would have to find her way to her feet eventually, even if the prospect alone made her weary.

"Remain where you are, my dear," the dowager said,

seating herself primly. "I remember what it is like to be in your slippers. Torrington was a dreadfully large babe, and I spent weeks of my confinement in bed, too tired and ill to move."

Elizabeth had been plagued with only a small bout of sickness early in her pregnancy, and the rest—aside from her tremendous belly—had been blessedly smooth. She was grateful for that, and grateful too for the child who would soon arrive.

"I'm fortunate that I haven't been ill," she said, still wondering at the reason for her mother-in-law's unexpected visit.

"Your disposition is too sunny for it, I suspect," the dowager said, and Elizabeth couldn't tell if she was paying her a compliment or an insult.

"I suppose that perhaps it is," she agreed politely.

"You're wondering why I've come."

The dowager's pronouncement took her by surprise.

"Yes, I reckon that I am," she allowed.

"You are about to give me a grandchild," the dowager said. "And I wish for you to know that...I regret my treatment of you earlier in your marriage to my son. I was unkind, and I am sorry for it."

An apology?

Elizabeth blinked, wondering if she were dreaming. But no, her mother-in-law remained in her chair, regarding her seriously.

"Thank you," she said at last, finding her tongue through her shock.

"It is I who must thank you. I have watched my son these last few months, and he is the most happy I've ever seen him. For so long, I feared that he was in the mold of his father, but I can see now that my fears were unfounded. He is a good man, and you are a good wife to him."

Better than Lady Althorp's eldest daughter? Elizabeth wanted to ask, but didn't dare push the dowager any further than she had already been willing to come.

"I am happy you think so," she told her. "I love your son very much."

"As do I," the dowager said.

Elizabeth would have responded, but in the next moment, a great rush of fluid came from her, and the persistent aching in her back all morning made perfect sense. "Oh dear."

The dowager was on her feet, looking concerned. "What is it, my dear?"

Elizabeth cradled her belly, wonder filling her. "I believe it is time."

"WHAT THE BLOODY hell is taking so long?" Torrie demanded as he paced the Aubusson for what must have been the hundredth time.

It was a miracle he hadn't yet worn a hole in it.

"God's fichu, sit down before you fall," Monty said. "You've been stalking across the room without cease for the better part of three hours."

He spun on his heel and pinned his friend with a glare. "How can you be so calm?"

"Because I have two beautiful, healthy children with my incredibly lovely wife," Monty said, grinning. "I've ridden down this particular road twice before, and I know it well. It's bumpy and terrifying, and it's the worst ride of your life. But then, your bairn is born and you hold your child in your arms, and everything is suddenly right in your world again."

His friend's Scottish roots were showing, a sure sign that he wasn't quite as unaffected as he pretended. Likely, he was putting on a calm façade for Torrie's sake.

"I'm worried about her," he explained, feeling like a fool and terrified nonetheless. "I'm worried about the babe, too. It feels as if an eternity has passed."

"The doctor is with her and so is Hattie," Monty reminded him, offering a consoling pat on his shoulder. "All will be well, old friend."

Hattie, whose second child with Monty had been born mere months before, was attending Bess. He was damned glad that his sister was here. That Monty was here. But he was still out of his mind with worry.

Bess's labor had begun this morning, and it was now nearly half past nine in the evening.

"I pray you're right," he said hoarsely, trying not to think of what would happen if Monty was wrong.

If everything was not well.

He resumed pacing, running his hands through his hair. Wishing he had whisky, even if he knew better than to drink in the presence of his friend, who no longer touched spirits.

"Hattie, my love," Monty greeted at his back.

Torrie whipped around to find his sister, smiling at the threshold, looking exhausted but happy. Surely a good sign?

"How is she?" he blurted.

"Bess is well," his sister told him. "You have a daughter."

A daughter.

He had a daughter.

Joy burst open inside him, and then he was moving, his feet and legs having a mind entirely of their own, separate from the rest of him.

"You may go to her," Hattie called after him, laughing at his eagerness.

"Name her after me," Monty added.

He might have laughed; he wasn't certain. He also might have cried. Tears were burning his eyes and blurring his vision as he took the stairs two at a time, desperate to be by his wife's side again. To see his daughter.

His daughter whom he would decidedly *not* name after Monty.

He burst into Bess's chamber, ignoring the flurry of activity still taking place within. Soiled linens being discreetly carried off, the doctor packing away the tools of his trade. He had eyes only for his beloved wife and the small bundle she held in her arms. She looked weary but well, and his gratitude was so sudden and thunderous that it nearly sent him tumbling to his arse.

"Bess," he said, going to her side on the shaky legs of a newborn foal, astounded and elated and relieved all at once.

He perched on the bed with great care, trying not to jar mother and babe too much. Needing to sit before he fell, just as Monty had said not long ago.

"My love," Bess said. "Meet your daughter."

Torrie took the swaddled infant in his arms and stared down at the red, wrinkled face. His daughter began to cry. And he was crying too. Weeping tears of happiness, so filled with love that he couldn't speak.

"She is perfect," he managed at last. "Just like her mama."

"What shall we name her?" Bess asked softly.

He glanced up at his wife. "Let's name her Cassandra, after your mother."

His wife's eyes welled with tears.

"Cassandra," she repeated. "She would have been honored."

Torrie glanced back down at his daughter, filled with gratitude and awe and above all else, love.

So much love.

~

HUGE THANK you to the readers of this series who have so patiently waited for Torrie's story to be told. I appreciate you all so very much. I hope that you loved his happily ever after with Bess, Angel, and Cassandra, and that you enjoyed spending a little more time with Monty and Hattie (from *Duke of Debauchery*) along the way. You may also recognize Winters soap and Winter's Boxing Academy, nods to my The Wicked Winters series.

Please join my reader group for early excerpts, cover reveals, and more here. Stay in touch! The only way to be sure you'll know what's next from me is to sign up for my newsletter here: http://eepurl.com/dyJSar. And if you're in the mood to chat all things steamy historical romance and read a different book each month, join my book club, Dukes Do It Hotter right here: https://www.facebook.com/groups/hotdukes because we're having a whole lot of fun!

WANT MORE DELICIOUSLY WICKED Regency romance reads from me? Read on for an excerpt from *Her Ruthless Duke*, Rogue's Guild Book One, a guardian/ward forbidden romance with age gap and all the steam…

Chapter One

TREVOR WILLIAM HUNT, sixth Duke of Ridgely, Marquess of Northrop, Baron Grantworth, glared at the menace who had invaded his home, doing his utmost not to take note of the tempting ankles peeping from beneath the hems of her gown and petticoats. A damned difficult task indeed when the menace in question loomed above him from the top rung of the ladder in his library. There was nowhere to look but up her skirts.

In his time as a spy working for the Guild, reporting directly to Whitehall, he'd faced fearsome enemies and would-be assassins. He'd been shot at, stabbed, and nearly trampled by a carriage. But all that rather paled in comparison to the full force of Lady Virtue Walcot, daughter of his late friend the Marquess of Pemberton, Trevor's unexpected and unwanted ward, and minion of Beelzebub sent fresh from Hades to destroy him.

"Come down before you break your neck, infant," he ordered her.

He hadn't a conscience, but he had no intention of beginning his day by witnessing the chit tumbling to her doom. He had yet to take his breakfast, after all.

"I am not an infant," she announced, defiance making her tone sharp as a whip from her lofty perch.

The minx hadn't even bothered to cast a glance in his direction for her response.

No, indeed. Instead, she continued thumbing through the dusty tomes lining the shelves overhead, relics from the fifth Duke of Ridgely. Likely, the duke had wanted to impress his mistress of the moment. Trevor strongly doubted his sire had ever read a word on their pages. *Hmm.* When he had an opportunity, he'd do away with the lot of them. He'd quite forgotten they were there.

"Child, then," he allowed, crossing his arms over his chest and keeping his gaze studiously trained on the shelves instead of the tempting curve of her rump overhead. "For a woman fully grown would never go climbing about in her guardian's library, putting her welfare in peril."

"She would if she were looking for something to occupy her mind, aside from the tedium her guardian has arranged for her."

Lady Virtue was, no doubt, referring to the social whirlwind he had arranged with the help of his sister, all in the name of seeing the vexing chit wedded, etcetera, and blessedly out of his life.

"Ladies love balls," he countered, uncrossing his arms and settling his hands on his hips instead.

Lady Virtue made him itchy. Whenever she was within arm's reach, he found himself wanting to touch her, which made absolutely no sense, given that she was an innocent, and he didn't bloody well *like* the chit.

"Not this lady," she called from above.

Trevor was certain she was disagreeing with him merely for the sport of quarreling. "Ladies adore those terribly boring affairs with musicians."

"Musicales, you mean?" She sniffed. "I despise them."

"A tragedy, that," he quipped. "In order for you to find yourself happily married, you need to attend society events."

Another disdainful sniff floated down from above. "I have no wish to be married, happily or otherwise."

So she had claimed on numerous occasions. Lady Virtue Walcot was as outspoken as she was maddening. But she remained his burden for the year until she reached her majority and was no longer his ward. Those twelve months loomed before him like a bloody eternity. The only respite would be in finding her a husband, which he intended for his sister to do. Clearly, Pamela was going to have to work harder at her task.

When Lady Virtue married, she would still remain his ward, but her unsuspecting spouse could at least be burdened with keeping her out of trouble, and Trevor could carry on with life as he wished.

He caught another glimpse of Lady Virtue's ankles and then cursed himself as his cock leapt to attention. He'd always had a weakness for a woman's legs. Too damned bad these delicious limbs belonged to *her*.

He cleared his throat. "You'll change your mind."

"I won't." She pulled a book from the shelf. "*The Tale of Love.*"

Oh, Christ. He knew the title. Knew the contents within. Despicably bawdy, that book. Decidedly not the sort of tome she ought to be reading. If anyone corrupted her, it wasn't going to be Trevor.

Unfortunately.

"That's not for the eyes of innocent lambs," he said. "Put it back on the shelf."

"I never claimed to be an innocent lamb." The unmistakable sound of her turning the pages reached him. "Why, it's an epistolary. There can hardly be any harm in that, can there?"

He ground his molars and glared at the spines of books before him, surrendering to the need to touch something and settling on the ladder. At least it wouldn't go tumbling over with him acting as anchor.

"Don't read it, infant," he called curtly. "That is a command."

"I'm not that much younger than you are, you know." More page turning sounded above. "*Oh!* Good heavens…"

"Saint's teeth, I told you not to read the book." He gripped the ladder so tightly, he feared it would snap in two. "If you don't get down here this moment, I'll have no choice but to come after you and bring you down myself."

"Don't be silly. The two of us will never fit on this ladder, and your head would be nearly up my skirts."

Yes, precisely.

And he wouldn't hate it, either.

Want more? Get *Her Ruthless Duke* now here!

DON'T MISS SCARLETT'S OTHER ROMANCES!

Complete Book List
HISTORICAL ROMANCE

Heart's Temptation
A Mad Passion (Book One)
Rebel Love (Book Two)
Reckless Need (Book Three)
Sweet Scandal (Book Four)
Restless Rake (Book Five)
Darling Duke (Book Six)
The Night Before Scandal (Book Seven)

Wicked Husbands
Her Errant Earl (Book One)
Her Lovestruck Lord (Book Two)
Her Reformed Rake (Book Three)
Her Deceptive Duke (Book Four)
Her Missing Marquess (Book Five)
Her Virtuous Viscount (Book Six)

League of Dukes
Nobody's Duke (Book One)
Heartless Duke (Book Two)
Dangerous Duke (Book Three)
Shameless Duke (Book Four)
Scandalous Duke (Book Five)
Fearless Duke (Book Six)

Notorious Ladies of London
Lady Ruthless (Book One)
Lady Wallflower (Book Two)
Lady Reckless (Book Three)
Lady Wicked (Book Four)
Lady Lawless (Book Five)
Lady Brazen (Book 6)

Unexpected Lords
The Detective Duke (Book One)
The Playboy Peer (Book Two)
The Millionaire Marquess (Book Three)
The Goodbye Governess (Book Four)

The Wicked Winters
Wicked in Winter (Book One)
Wedded in Winter (Book Two)
Wanton in Winter (Book Three)
Wishes in Winter (Book 3.5)
Willful in Winter (Book Four)
Wagered in Winter (Book Five)
Wild in Winter (Book Six)
Wooed in Winter (Book Seven)
Winter's Wallflower (Book Eight)
Winter's Woman (Book Nine)
Winter's Whispers (Book Ten)

DON'T MISS SCARLETT'S OTHER ROMANCES!

Winter's Waltz (Book Eleven)
Winter's Widow (Book Twelve)
Winter's Warrior (Book Thirteen)
A Merry Wicked Winter (Book Fourteen)

The Sinful Suttons
Sutton's Spinster (Book One)
Sutton's Sins (Book Two)
Sutton's Surrender (Book Three)
Sutton's Seduction (Book Four)
Sutton's Scoundrel (Book Five)
Sutton's Scandal (Book Six)
Sutton's Secrets (Book Seven)

Rogue's Guild
Her Ruthless Duke (Book One)
Her Dangerous Beast (Book Two)
Her Wicked Rogue (Book 3)

Sins and Scoundrels
Duke of Depravity
Prince of Persuasion
Marquess of Mayhem
Sarah
Earl of Every Sin
Duke of Debauchery
Viscount of Villainy

Sins and Scoundrels Box Set Collections
Volume 1
Volume 2

The Wicked Winters Box Set Collections
Collection 1

ABOUT THE AUTHOR

USA Today and Amazon bestselling author Scarlett Scott writes steamy Victorian and Regency romance with strong, intelligent heroines and sexy alpha heroes. She lives in Pennsylvania and Maryland with her Canadian husband, adorable identical twins, and two dogs.

A self-professed literary junkie and nerd, she loves reading anything, but especially romance novels, poetry, and Middle English verse. Catch up with her on her website https://scarlettscottauthor.com. Hearing from readers never fails to make her day.

Scarlett's complete book list and information about upcoming releases can be found at https://scarlettscottauthor.com.

Connect with Scarlett! You can find her here:
    Join Scarlett Scott's reader group on Facebook for early excerpts, giveaways, and a whole lot of fun!
    Sign up for her newsletter here
    https://www.tiktok.com/@authorscarlettscott

facebook.com/AuthorScarlettScott

twitter.com/scarscoromance

instagram.com/scarlettscottauthor

bookbub.com/authors/scarlett-scott

amazon.com/Scarlett-Scott/e/B004NW8N2I

pinterest.com/scarlettscott

Printed in Poland
by Amazon Fulfillment
Poland Sp. z o.o., Wrocław

25886645R00165